WHAT PEOPLE ARE SAY[...

SUSAN MAY WARREN

"I'm proud of Susie; my friend gets better with every book."
DEE HENDERSON, author of *The Marriage Wish*

"Susan May Warren is an extremely gifted storyteller, always keeping her readers in suspense to the end. . . . [Her] books are guaranteed to entertain, thrill, and inspire. Without question, they fall in the can't-put-down category!"
D.M., Amazon.com reader

"This author needs to write more books! I love her style."
C.T., Amazon.com reader

"Susan Warren is a writer to watch! . . . Susan's characters are so real you can almost hear them breathe."
Amazon.com reader

Expect
the
Sunrise

TEAM
+
HOPE

Susan May Warren

Tyndale House Publishers, Inc.
CAROL STREAM, ILLINOIS

Visit Tyndale's exciting Web site at www.tyndale.com

TYNDALE and Tyndale's quill logo are registered trademarks of Tyndale House Publishers, Inc.

Expect the Sunrise

Designed by Catherine Bergstrom

Edited by Lorie Popp

Scripture quotations are taken from the *Holy Bible,* New Living Translation, copyright © 1996, 2004. Used by permission of Tyndale House Publishers, Inc., Carol Stream, Illinois 60188. All rights reserved.

This novel is a work of fiction. Names, characters, places, and incidents are either the product of the author's imagination or are used fictitiously. Any resemblance to actual events, locales, organizations, or persons, living or dead, is entirely coincidental and beyond the intent of either the author or publisher.

Library of Congress Cataloging-in-Publication Data

Warren, Susan, date.
  Expect the sunrise / Susan May Warren.
    p. cm. — (Team hope ; 3)
  ISBN-13: 978-1-4143-0088-7 (sc)
  ISBN-10: 1-4143-0088-3 (sc)
  1. Search and rescue operations—Fiction. 2. Government investigations—Fiction. 3. Terrorism—Fiction I. Title.
  PS3623.A865E97 2006
  813'.6—dc22   2005031403

Printed in the United States of America

11 10 09 08 07
 7   6   5   4   3   2

Acknowledgments

God's provision always amazes and delights me. I'd like to thank the following co-laborers on this project with me. Thank you for not laughing at my questions. As usual, any errors are mine alone.

Dwayne and Carolyn King, Alaskan and Russian missionaries extraordinaire. Your insights into the life of an Alaskan bush pilot and your attention to flying details made this story come to life. More than that, your example and influence in our lives have been treasures to us. Thank you for your willing hearts to serve in so many ways.

Olaf Growald, hero on His shift. Thank you for helping me injure Sarah and then get her off the mountain. Thank you for your wisdom and patience. I'm so grateful for you.

Michele Nickolay, my kindred adventure author. Thank you for enjoying this story, for your critiques, and for enjoying the same Scottish things that I do. Your friendship is such a blessing to me.

Sharron McCann, my Titus woman. Thank you for the recipes and the insights into Scottish life. More than that, thank you for sharing your life with me. You're an inspiration to me.

Jane Howard, the woman who makes me ponder. Your writing makes me want to go deeper. Thank you for setting the bar for me and for your constant encouragement. I so appreciate you.

Anne Goldsmith, my friend and editor. Thank you for your wisdom and your dedication to take this story deeper, to make it resonate. I've learned so much from you. May the Lord bless you richly.

Lorie Popp, the woman who wades through the jungle with me. Thank you for pushing me, for helping me grow, and for your patience! What would I do without you?

My sweet children—David, Sarah, Peter, Noah—for holding down the fort as I traveled, wrote long hours, or even asked you to make dinner for me. I am so blessed by you, and I know God is going to do great things in all your lives as you trust Him. Y'all rock!

Andrew, my fairy-tale knight in a flannel shirt. With you, baby, there are no regrets.

FOR YOUR GLORY, LORD.

Joyful are those who have the God of Israel as their helper,
whose hope is in the Lord their God.

PSALM 146:5

Prologue

Stirling McRae should have known he couldn't escape his duty, even deep inside the forests of northeastern Alaska, a hundred miles from civilization.

No, it found him in the form of a grimy terrorist in an orange hunting vest and cap. Only, said terrorist hadn't a prayer of escaping the McRae brothers. At least that's what Mac told himself as another branch slapped him across the face and he plowed through a bramble of thistle.

So much for having some hang time with his brother. Brody would probably deck him the next time Mac suggested they go fishing together.

He heard Brody behind him, thundering like a bulldozer through the forest, occasionally yelling his name.

Mac didn't stop. Couldn't. He'd been hunting Ari Al-Hasid and members of his cell for nearly three years. It seemed sheer dumb luck that he happened upon Al-Hasid now at the height of the summer pumping season and near one of the weakest points in the pipeline that was scheduled for replacement.

The river of black gold inside a forty-eight-inch-wide, double-steel-walled pipe, referred to as the Trans-Alaska Pipeline System (TAPS), stretched eight hundred miles from the northern slope of Alaska to Valdez. Difficult to monitor, even harder to protect, it was one of the most vulnerable terrorist targets in all of America.

A target that Al-Hasid and his group had been plotting to attack for years, according to the maps and sketchy intel that littered Mac's office at the FBI.

Perhaps this wasn't dumb luck but good hunting. For months Mac had suspected that Al-Hasid and his cell would launch their attack this summer. He just never expected it during his annual fishing trip with Brody.

Okay, maybe a little, which was why he had guided Brody near a salmon stream that ran parallel to the pipeline. Just to follow his gut and keep an eye out, despite his boss's skepticism. After all, Bureau Chief Tanner Buchanan had ordered him out of the office . . . not out of his skin.

And bingo. Just as he and Brody were motoring south toward a promising run of chinook salmon or arctic grayling, they had startled Al-Hasid checking his weapon only thirty feet from the pipeline. He'd looked up, guilt on his face, and bolted.

Now Mac could barely make out Al-Hasid's form, a sickly orange blur between a stand of bushy black spruce. If Mac caught him, he might be able to breathe a little deeper, sleep more than two or three hours at a stretch, and rip down one of the many mug shots and wanted posters clipped on the office bulletin board.

He needed to get out into the open and close the distance between them. But he knew Al-Hasid carried a .338 Winchester, a weapon that could blow a nice hole through a bear and lay waste to a man. Mac needed the trees for protection, even if he was picked off like a Lakers forward.

"I'll cut him off!" Brody yelled.

Mac glanced behind him, saw Brody heading for the clearing. His brother didn't know the first rule about suspect appre-

hension: don't announce your intentions to the enemy. For the
second time in ten minutes, he wondered if he should stop, call
the sighting in, and let the on-duty heroes handle Al-Hasid.

No, not if it meant Al-Hasid escaped.

Mac parted the brush with his gloved hands.

A gunshot.

Mac froze. *Not around the pipeline!*

A scream rent the air.

He whirled and felt his pulse in his throat when crows
scattered into the sky.

Mac dived after Al-Hasid, blood pounding in his ears. More
than fifty hunters had accidentally hit the pipeline over the years
without puncturing it, but a shot from a .338 just might—

Another shot. It pinged against metal.

Mac ducked, plowing nearly headfirst into a tree. "Stop
shooting!"

He crouched behind the larch and peered out, feeling sweat
bead under his woolen cap. His feet felt clunky and chapped in
his hiking boots; his body trembled under the layers of wool.

"Get away from me!" Al-Hasid shouted into the trees.
"I ain't done nothin'!" He sounded drunk, his accent slurred.
No doubt Al-Hasid had perfected redneck lingo after living in
the country for the past ten years under an assumed name.

"Throw down your weapon! I'm a federal agent."

Nothing.

Mac peeked out, saw Al-Hasid searching the forest.
Peeling off his vest, Mac crept along a fallen log, then angled
toward the terrorist. He schooled his breath and heard Al-
Hasid's labored breathing just ahead.

Al-Hasid scanned the forest where Mac had been, then
beyond toward the pipeline clearing. The sun glinted off the
metal, rays of heat rippling the air surrounding it.

A branch cracked.

Mac stiffened. He glanced toward the sound, and his stomach dropped when he spotted Brody hunkered down, sneaking along the pipeline, peering into the forest.

Al-Hasid raised his gun.

"No!" Mac launched himself at Al-Hasid just as the gun reported. The recoil knocked him in the face even as he tackled Al-Hasid.

The terrorist elbowed him, thrashing.

Mac hung on, fighting to clear his head. He tasted blood running from his mouth or maybe his nose. Al-Hasid took out Mac's breath with a jab to the ribs.

The gun went off again.

Gulping for air, Mac grabbed the barrel and ripped it from Al-Hasid's grip.

Al-Hasid rolled to his knees and swung at Mac's face.

Mac dodged and muscled Al-Hasid into a guillotine hold, one arm locked around his neck, squeezing off the blood supply to his brain. If Mac could hold him, in a moment Al-Hasid would pass out. Mac wasn't a fan of UFC wrestling for nothing.

Al-Hasid slapped at Mac's head, wringing his ears.

Mac gritted his teeth and held on.

Al-Hasid started wheezing. Still the man kicked, wasting the last of his energy on flimsy punches. He finally slumped atop Mac, his body heavy.

Mac let him go, checked his breathing, then whipped off his bootlace and tied the terrorist's hands. He heard rain begin to fall softly, wetting the leaves, the ground.

The sound filled Mac's ears even as he propped Al-Hasid up, slapped at his face. He stood, dread pooling in his stomach as realization rushed him.

No, not rain.

He held out his hand, and the blood of the earth fell from the sky. One drop, two—black, thick, and sticky.

The pungent smell turned Mac's stomach as he tasted his worst fears. Running toward the clearing, he saw that the ground had already turned black and soggy. A geyser of oil plumed into the sky from a gash in the side of the pipeline.

He needed his radio.

He needed his four-wheeler.

He needed to get to the nearest pumping station and tell them to close the valves.

"Brody!" Mac turned as he yelled his brother's name. The fact that Brody hadn't appeared to jump Al-Hasid suddenly felt odd. . . . "Brody?" *Oh, Lord, please—*

His gaze caught a shadow on the ground just inside the rim of forest.

Brody.

"No!" Mac nearly fell as he scrambled toward his brother. He hit his knees as he knelt and turned him over.

Brody groaned, blood-drenched hands pressed against his gut.

Oh no. Mac's breaths thundered in his chest, panic shutting out every scrap of training. He pulled off his hat and pressed it against Brody's wound. "Why did you follow me?"

Brody closed his eyes, leaned back onto the ground. "I'm in a bit of a barney here, Mac." His voice sounded strangely weak, and it took another swipe at Mac's calm.

"I gotta get you some help." Mac reached out awkwardly, not sure how he'd carry his younger brother now that the man had surpassed him in size. Like true Scots, they weren't small men, but Brody had taken from the McRae side, warriors down the line. His girth and muscle had made him the grappling champ of Deadhorse High.

Mac pulled Brody's arms over his shoulder. Oil rained down around them, and he fell trying to get Brody into his embrace.

Brody cried out in a burst of agony. "I can't. Go . . . go get the four-wheeler." His face had turned chalky white. "Go." He nearly pushed Mac.

Mac stumbled back, blinking at Brody. "Brody, I'm so—"

"Go!"

Aye. Mac raced back to their encampment. His breath felt like razors inside, but fear pressed him through the pain. He slipped once, then twice, and fell face-first in the oil. He spit out a mouthful of filth as he scrambled to his feet.

Mac found the four-wheeler right where he'd sprung off it. In seconds he had it turned around and gunned it back toward Brody. He dug out his high-frequency, two-way radio while he drove, now thankful he'd packed it, despite Brody's ribbing.

"Hello, anyone!" He couldn't remember the EMS channel or even pipeline security. He scanned the channels. "Hello? Please!"

"Pipeline Security here. Identify please. Over."

"Agent Stirling McRae, FBI. I have an injured camper just north of the Kanuti River. Need assistance. Out."

Crackle came over the line.

Mac slowed as he reached the oil-slicked area but plowed through, shielding his eyes as the oil continued to rain from the sky. "Hello?"

"Roger that. We'll send assistance. Over."

"No! I'm coming to you." He braked and leaped off the ATV, stumbling toward Brody.

Thank the Lord, he was still breathing.

"Be advised that the nearest ranger station is at Cross Creek, seventeen clicks northwest of the line. Over."

Seventeen miles. Mac crouched beside Brody. Oil slicked his face, and his breathing seemed labored. Blood mingled with oil, and Mac hadn't the first clue how much blood Brody had lost. He'd never make seventeen miles.

"Negative. He'll never make it. We need an emergency extraction." He glanced at the plume of oil. "And be advised that there is a leak in the pipeline at my position."

Silence.

Mac could imagine the security agents spilling their coffee on their jumpsuits.

"Say again? Over."

"A leak. Terrorist shot the pipeline. But I need medical assistance."

"Give us your exact position. We'll find you. Out."

Mac glared at the two-way, wishing he could somehow reach through it to throttle the dobbers on the other end of the line. "Need medical—"

Overhead, he heard a buzz, a low hum that anyone who'd lived in the bush for longer than a week would know immediately.

A plane. A beautiful white-hulled bird with red stripes floating in the sky like a gift from heaven. Such a bird could land on the Dalton Highway, just a skip away.

If God was on his side, that beautiful little bird would already be turned to the Fairbanks Airport frequency, the same one he'd used during his flight-training days.

"Hello? I'm talking to the plane flying over Cross Creek. Come in, please."

Static.

"Please! Come in."

"Sir, this channel is authorized by the FAA for air-traffic control—"

"My brother's been shot!" Mac felt himself unraveling. "Please, will the plane overhead come in—?"

"This is November-two-three-seven-one-Lima; how can I help you?"

Yes, yes! "I have an injured man here. He's in bad shape. I need a life flight to Fairbanks. Please, can you land on the Dalton? I'll meet you." Mac held the two-way against his forehead, trembling.

Static. Then, "That's a negative. November-two-three-seven-one-Lima is en route with another life flight. I'm sorry but I—"

"Please!"

The line went static. The plane came into view. He stared at it as it flew over, a long moment when his heart stopped beating and turned to a singular gripping pain in the center of his chest.

Then it vanished.

No. He felt sick, hollow. His knees buckled.

"Mac?" His brother opened his grease-covered eyes, reached out, and curled his fist weakly into Mac's jacket. "Get me outta here."

Mac nodded, grabbed Brody by the collar, and dragged him over the slick ground to the four-wheeler. He could still hear the sound of hope dying in the distance.

As he draped Brody over the back of the ATV, wincing as he groaned, Mac made a promise.

If his brother died, he would never forgive that pilot.

✦ ✦ ✦

"Brother of FBI Agent Killed in Freak Accident."
Andee MacLeod read the headline slowly. And again.

Then closed her eyes, feeling a wave of guilt. Choices. Her life felt defined by them, by regret and confusion.

She scanned the article, wincing at the mention of an aborted possible rescue. She folded the newspaper, picked up her cold coffee, and dumped them into the trash as she exited the hospital cafeteria. What that reporter didn't know was that she'd been responsible for two deaths that day . . . indirectly at least.

The woman she'd been life flighting had bled out while Andee circled the airport for a third time, waiting for the weather to clear.

She hadn't had a choice to answer the panicked call for help, not really. But there were times when her decisions seemed to rise up and strangle her.

Andee stopped in at emergency services, waving to the night nurse. "I'm going home. I've got my pager."

The nurse nodded.

Andee stepped into the cool night air. June's eternal sun and energy would eventually mellow into normal days of sunrise and sunset. By late September the sun would turn reluctant to crest over the terra firma of Alaska, and night would steal into every nook and cranny of life. Before the deep freeze of winter, Andee would head south toward sunshine and her mother. And her *real* family—Micah, Dannette, Sarah and Hank, Conner, Lacey, and maybe someday, Will. The memory of her friend Dannette—who now referred to herself as Dani—and Will at Lacey and Micah's wedding last week filled her with a sweet warmth.

Team Hope. Her search-and-rescue pals *were* family— the kind who loved her despite her weaknesses or failures.

Brother of FBI agent . . . the memory of the man's panicked voice over the radio hovered in her thoughts, slicing through quiet moments to bring her back to that moment when she'd had to choose. She'd landed on the Dalton Highway a number of times before. But the life of the dying mother of four had been ticking away—and she'd kept altitude.

But what if it had been Sarah or Conner down there . . . hurt and dying? What if it had been her on the other end of the squawk begging for help? Would she ever forgive the pilot who'd turned his back?

Andee felt hollow as she walked to her Jeep in the parking lot, the midnight sun pooling on the hood.

According to the newspaper, the agent thought he'd been chasing a terrorist. Instead, he'd captured a drunk hunter with a Magnum rifle who managed to spill over two hundred thousand gallons of oil on the ground. She had to cringe at that as she opened her door and slid into her vehicle. Doomsdayers said the sabotage of TAPS could happen. In the new age of Homeland Security, it felt far-fetched. Not now.

She, as well as every other citizen of Alaska, knew the importance of the pipeline to the way of life in the Lower 48, even the war on terror. During 9/11, panic had flowed from one end of Alaska to the other, putting every security agent, cop, and pipeline affiliate on high alert. In Valdez, they'd stopped loaded tankers and simply sent them out of port. It was a well-known fact that even a small disruption in the flow of oil would cause it to cool, slow, and stop, costing millions of dollars in repairs, not to mention a shortage of oil across the nation and the return of the long gas lines of the early eighties. What was worse, her life flights north would grind to a standstill. Lives—at least in her neck of the woods—would be lost.

Andee had to wonder at the real story behind the so-called accident. She didn't put it beyond the FBI to concoct a cover story to stave off public panic. Still, the agent's brother had died, even if it hadn't been part of a terrorist plot. She guessed that was something that might haunt the man on the other end of her radio into eternity.

Just like it haunted her.

She started the engine, pulled out, and headed to her efficiency apartment in Earthquake Park.

The entire story didn't make sense. It had probably been a hunter, just as the news had reported. If some terrorist was going to sabotage the pipeline, it wouldn't be a lonely hunter with a Magnum rifle.

And it would take a lot more than a desperate FBI agent to stop him.

Chapter 1

Three Months Later

NO MATTER WHICH route she took, Andee MacLeod always found herself headed straight for Disaster. She didn't have to circle her destination on her aerial chart to know what awaited her in the hamlet with a population of thirty that was tucked under the shadow of the North Slope of the Brooks Range.

Heartache. Regret. To be precise, her father, Gerard MacLeod. A fifty-five-year-old bush pilot who refused to budge from his life in the wild, who'd survived so many Alaskan winters that she'd started to wonder if the cold had begun to reach his heart also.

Not that he didn't love her. But the very fact that he refused to move south, even to Fairbanks, seemed a metaphor for their relationship. As if when he stepped outside the woods that he'd hidden in for nearly two decades, he might find himself stripped and defenseless. Dependent on someone other than himself.

Not the way of the MacLeods.

"Emma, do you copy?" Doug's raspy voice from dispatch filtered through the static on Andee's radio.

She set the map on the opposite cockpit seat and reached for the handset. "Emma here. What's up, Doug?" She could see the control tower from her plane's position on the tarmac and nearly waved at him.

"Are you heading to Disaster after your stop at Prudhoe Bay?"

"That's affirmative." When *didn't* she stop at Disaster on her trips north? Her airplane practically flew itself.

"Please check on Maricel Fee. She's due any day now."

"Roger that." Andee replaced the radio mike and climbed out of her Cessna. *Please don't let Maricel go into labor on my watch, Lord.* She still had nightmares from the last pregnant woman she'd flown into Fairbanks. She'd taken off from Anaktuvuk Pass with one passenger and landed with two.

The need for decent medical services in Alaska never stopped, even when the temperature dipped into the minus-thirty range—and lower—during the coldest months of winter. Thankfully, for the past few years Andee had escaped the clench of Alaskan cold that could about-face a cheechako and send him hustling back to the Lower 48. She could hardly be called a tenderfoot after being raised in the bush, twenty miles from Disaster on the Disaster Creek, but sometimes she wondered just what brought her back here every summer.

Maybe it was the sunrise climbing over Doonerak Peak, the aurora borealis over the North Slope, or the purple moss campion that carpeted the taiga. Maybe she returned to see the caribou migrate or an occasional moose rubbing his back on the bracings of the Alaska pipeline as she flew her Cessna 185 supplied with medicines and foodstuff to remote villages north of the Arctic Circle.

No, it was probably the chance to see Gerard MacLeod again. Her daughterly responsibilities pushing her past the hurt. This year she hoped to convince him to move to Disaster township, which would mean she wouldn't have to trek into the backwoods, armed with supplies and extra gas for his four-wheeler. Andee barely kept away the nightmare that someday she'd knock on the door to his two-room cabin, not receive an answer, and find him frozen stiff, too injured from some hunting accident to carry in the wood.

Then again Gerard would probably prefer it that way. MacLeods didn't ask for help.

If only her mother had stuck around, maybe Andee wouldn't have to live like a nomad, babysitting a stubborn Scotsman every summer and her driven doctor-mother every winter.

Andee finished her preflight cabin check on the new Cessna Stationair, then got out and did her preflight walk around, checking the flaps and ailerons, the tires, prop, cowling, nose wheel, and fuel drains.

Glancing at her watch, she marched back to the North Rim Outfitters hangar at the Fairbanks International Airport, where the five passengers for this excursion to the north waited inside for her all okay. Most of them were tourists, although she'd read that one was a missionary heading to serve in the Inupiaq community of Resurrection, Alaska. She wondered if a missionary in her own little town might have prevented the heartache of watching her parents fight over her, separate, and tear their only daughter in half.

"*Choose.*" Her mother's stiff voice still stung her ears, especially on days like today when the fall air felt heavy and had a snap to the breeze that lifted her jacket collar. That moment so many years ago on this very tarmac haunted her still.

She stopped, looking northward, and she didn't like what she saw. Oppressive, gray clouds, although high, had the potential to ground her if she didn't get airborne soon. The last thing she needed was another delay in Fairbanks. One more trip and

she'd have enough to jump-start her mutual fund. Then she'd
pack her Jeep and head south to her mother's home in Iowa or
farther to the Galloway ranch in Kentucky. She wondered how
Lacey and Jim Micah were handling being newlyweds.

"I *really* do," Micah had said on their wedding day. Andee
had all but burst into tears at her friend's happy ending after
rescuing Lacey's daughter from a kidnapper/murderer/traitor
nearly a year ago. Seeing Micah holding little Emily in his arms
at the wedding had tugged at all Andee's private longings. A
family. A home. A man who might give her a reason to stop
chasing her dreams around the Northern Hemisphere. Or
rather a man who might drop his own dreams and follow *hers*.
Wouldn't that be a miracle?

But heroes didn't magically materialize, especially here in
the frozen north. Besides, she didn't need a knight in shining
armor. She had different dreams. An airplane. A medical operation to the northern villages. Lives saved. She didn't usually
bother to think about someone to share it with. Because, really,
who would she find who might want to eke out a life in this
barren wilderness with her? He'd have to be hardy, stubborn,
romantic, and loyal . . . and she wouldn't mind if he also had
strong arms that could protect her just a little.

Oh, brother. Maybe she'd read one too many fairy tales.

She went inside and picked up the passenger manifest.
The austere vinyl chairs and cement walls of the lobby gave
adequate warning of the travel ahead.

Andee hoped the passengers had packed well—warm
clothes and sleeping bags. Weather in the Brooks Range
changed hourly, especially this late in September. More than a
few times she'd landed on a lonely strip of meadow to wait out
the moods of the ceiling. And with the new restrictions on flying
over Dalton Highway and the nearby pipeline, she'd have to veer

west over the peaks and smack-dab into the dark weather. Hopefully she'd make it to Disaster by nightfall, reading to her father while he fried up a griddle of sourdough flapjacks.

She skimmed the passenger list, then glanced at the group assembled. Five total. Two sat in the chairs. One leaned against the reception counter, looking at brochures. A tall, broad-shouldered man stood by the window, his duffel bag between his feet, as if someone might run by and grab it. She shook her head. Tourists—they suspected trouble everywhere. Or maybe the restlessness came from all the flights and security checks and cautions they had to endure to get to Alaska from the continental U.S.

"Nina Smith?" Andee read the name and saw a large-boned woman rise, her long black hair in a braid down her back. She wore a red fleece-lined jacket and cap, well dressed for her excursion to the North Slope. Her overstuffed, external-frame backpack leaned against the chairs. Probably headed out for some late-season hiking. Her dark brown eyes pinned Andee's, and she smiled. "That's me."

Andee nodded. "Floyd Dekker?"

"Hey, y'all." Mr. Bo Duke with a goatee and about ten years of padding waved two fingers at her. He wore a brown, flannel-lined, canvas coat and tugged on a Take Back America baseball cap. "Call me Flint," he said with a Southern drawl.

Andee guessed his itinerary included hunting. While the moose and bear season had just started, the weather hadn't cooperated and a number of game hunters had trudged home without their kill. Usually Andee made a practice of refusing to fly in hunters to the northern regions after September 20, right after moose season. The temperamental weather could leave them stranded, unable to be flown out before their supplies were exhausted. But winter seemed to be taking her time this year, and when North Rim Outfitters offered her a bonus, she felt her dreams of purchasing her own plane nearly attainable.

"Okay, Flint." She hid a smile at his nickname. What was it about coming to Alaska that made people adopt new personas? Then again, up here when she was flying she went by Emma, her call name and the only pet name her father had ever given her. A term from the old country, it meant "lady," according to Gerard. The name gave her purpose, identity, and inclinations toward strength.

But probably like Flint, Emma was an illusion, a poor cover for a woman who never seemed settled in her own skin.

"Martin Ishbane?" She scanned the room.

No answer.

"Maybe he's the one outside," Nina said, nodding toward a man standing with his back to the windows.

Andee opened the door, leaned out. "Mr. Ishbane?"

The man turned and blew out a stream of smoke.

Andee recoiled slightly, not trying to offend. At least he'd chosen to smoke outside. She found a smile for him. "I'm the pilot, just trying to track down my passengers."

"I'm Ishbane," he said quietly as he glanced at her with gray, expressionless eyes. He held a briefcase in his gloved hand. Under his thin leather jacket, he wore a black turtleneck, and the wind tangled his long hair, held back into a ponytail. She hoped he owned a hat—he definitely wasn't outfitted for a jaunt into the north woods. After dropping the cigarette, he crushed it under his hiking boot.

Andee stifled her comments and returned inside, followed by Ishbane. "Jake Phillips?"

The man who was leaning against the counter nodded at her, a smile on his chiseled, square face. He had dark eyes and dark, tightly curled hair, and he wore a down parka and a wool cap. With his barrel chest and muscular arms, he looked like he played defensive end for some pro football team or maybe squared off on center ice for the Stanley Cup. He reminded her of an oversized Jim Micah in a way.

She smiled at him in return. Then the other man, standing arms akimbo, one shoulder holding up the wall, and a pair of sunglasses hooked low on his nose must be— "Stirling McRae?"

The man glanced at her, a hardness in his eyes that rattled her for a moment. He stood about six feet three. With broad shoulders, slightly long, curly brown hair tucked behind his ears, and reddish stubble, he seemed unexpected, rumpled, yet with a quiet power about him that sizzled just below his unassuming stance. He wore faded jeans and an open fleece-lined canvas jacket. He looked as if he needed a good meal and a few hours of shut-eye. And warmer clothes, where they were heading.

She sighed. Why did tourists assume they could dress like they might on a January day in Tennessee instead of September on the north side of the planet? The higher areas already had snow, even if Fairbanks had yet to be dusted. Still, winter could swoop down without warning, and even now her airplane hardly kept the interior temperature above forty.

"Aye," the man answered finally.

Oh, terrific. A Scot. He probably had arrogance to match that slightly accented deep voice and warrior build. Good thing they had only a five-hour flight ahead of them. She knew this type—bullheaded, cantankerous, with way too much confidence for anyone's good. And she should know—having been accused of the same by her Scottish father on more than one occasion.

"Okay, we're all here." Andee grabbed her sunglasses and added her flight plan and weather update to the clipboard. "Call me Emma. I'll be your pilot. We're flying in a six-seater,

nearly new Cessna Turbo Stationair, courtesy of North Rim
Outfitters." She nodded at Flint, the outfitter's client. The
other passengers paid a higher price for the charter-flight
service, but it made up for the cost of flying one client nearly
four hundred miles.

"We have a scenic flight for you today over the Gates of
the Arctic National Park and the Brooks Range. Hopefully, out
of the west passenger windows you'll catch a glimpse of
Doonerak Peak."

She checked her watch. "We have a storm front moving in,
and I'd like to get into the air and out of reach of those winds.
Let's load your gear." She held open the door as the passengers
filed out.

Nina's backpack caught on the door. Andee winced when
she heard a tearing.

Nina made a face. "Guess I'm about due for a new rig." She
forced the pack through, and Andee wondered how she would
manage on whatever backpacking trip she had scheduled.

Flint followed her, his duffel bag slung over one shoulder,
his gun packed in a padded and locked leather case, regulation
for airplanes these days. He'd had to fill out a form and have an
extra security check from here to Fairbanks, and Andee had a
special locked compartment in the back of the plane to store it.
The only gun allowed aboard was the one she kept hidden and
secured under her seat—a .40-caliber Glock she used for
protection from bears.

When Ishbane passed, she swung into step with him. "I'm
assuming you know this, but there's no smoking on the plane."

"Yeah. Sure." Andee detected an East Coast accent.

"Thanks," she said and jogged toward the plane.
Unlatching the belly pod between the landing gear, she squat-
ted beside it to stow the passengers' luggage. Nina's pack nearly

sent her to her knees. "How much does this weigh?" she asked Nina as she shoved it deep inside.

"Oh, nearly a hundred pounds. I'm bringing home gifts for my children."

"Where are you from?"

"Prudhoe Bay. My husband and two children are there. I've been overseas on an assignment." She tapped a lumpy bag slung crosswise over her shoulder. "I'm a photographer." She climbed into the plane.

Andee tossed Flint's duffel into the pod, then reached for his hunting rifle. "I have to ask you to stow that, sir. Regulations."

"You worried I'm going to hijack the plane, sweetheart?" Flint asked.

Andee gave him a mock glower. "Should I be?"

Flint winked at her. "Depends on whether I can throw off the other passengers, maybe fly away with you to Hawaii."

She'd encountered a few of these types over the summer. She smiled. "We'll run outta gas before then, land in the ocean. Sharks will have us for dinner."

"Then maybe I'll need it." He grinned at her.

"Listen." Andee lowered her voice. "I know you're kidding, but we had an attack on our pipeline a few months back, and they're just a little gun-shy around here, if you'll pardon the pun. Surrender the gun or there's no ride."

His smile dimmed, and he handed her the weapon, climbing aboard the plane without another word.

Ishbane had only a small carry-on—a backpack on wheels—besides his briefcase. He handed Andee the carry-on and climbed in behind Flint.

Uh-oh. She recognized a man with a slipping grip on his control of aerophobia when she saw it. And flying over the Brooks Range translated to turbulence—lots of it.

Phillips tried to load his army duffel and balked when Andee reached for it. "It's too heavy, ma'am."

Ma'am? But his courtesy made her smile. "Sorry, Mr. Phillips. Rules say I have to load the bags."

He shook his head as he handed it to her.

Yes, it seemed painfully heavy.

McRae approached her last, scrutinizing her as if gauging her ability to fly the plane. He handed her his bag with a dubious look. She half expected him to ask if she was serving cocktails in first class and when the pilot would arrive.

After McRae boarded, Andee secured the passenger door, then crawled out from under the plane. The wind had picked up, and she smelled rain. Or maybe snow. Behind her, she heard a Piper Cub firing up. It would be first in line for takeoff. If she didn't move quickly, she'd be grounded.

Andee jogged around to her cockpit door, giving one last visual check before climbing inside. She adjusted her radio headset and began her pre-engine start checklist.

Preflight—complete.

Passenger briefing. Andee keyed her mike and explained the seat and belt adjustments and emergency-exit procedures and asked them to remain silent during radio calls.

Briefing—complete.

Fuel selector—on.

Avionic and electrical switches—off.

Brakes test—Andee held the brakes.

This would be her last commercial flight of the season. Besides her emergency gear and the extras she'd packed for her passengers in her own gear, she'd added a fresh supply of amoxicillin—just in case Gerard got injured or an infection— as well as a couple new best sellers, some canned meat in the event Gerard's bear supply dwindled, and a laptop computer, with the errant hope that her father might want to figure out how to enter the twenty-first century and send her an e-mail. Last time she was in Disaster she'd discovered a satellite hookup at the township hall. If Gerard had the desire, he could take his laptop to town and keep in touch with his only daughter.

She hoped she wasn't courting heartache.

Brakes—check.

Circuit breakers—check.

"Okay, folks, we'll be in the air in a few minutes." Andee turned the master switch on, pushed the mixture to rich, and primed the engine. Checking to see that the prop area was clear, she cracked the throttle and hit the starter.

The Cessna spit, then popped to life, its prop whirring and cutting out cabin chatter.

Making sure the magnetos were on, she pulled the throttle back to 1,000 rpm and checked the oil pressure. How she loved the sound of a well-tuned engine.

Something hit her shoulder. She jerked and turned. Phillips was leaning forward, his mouth moving. She moved her headset off her ear.

"—someone out there waving at you."

Andee looked out the window toward the terminal. A smile gathered on her face, and for the first time in three months she felt the cloud of loneliness lift. Sarah Nation, her best friend, stood on the tarmac in a black parka, waving wildly.

Andee cut the engine and unbuckled her belt. "Hang on, everybody. I'll be right back." She nearly leaped out the door, raced around the plane, and flew into Sarah's embrace. "What are you doing here?"

"Happy birthday!" Sarah grinned, her blue eyes lighting up. She'd shoved her blonde hair into a stocking cap, and Andee noticed fatigue around her eyes.

"Are you kidding? You came all the way from New York for my birthday?" But Andee couldn't hide her elation.

"Your last e-mail sounded a bit blue." Sarah shrugged, but Andee saw the faintest edging of worry. "Besides, I haven't been to Disaster since we were in college. How's your dad?"

"Stubborn and as friendly as a badger. Are you sure you want to trek all the way up there? It's liable to be a cold flight." Andee eyed the sky. "And the ceiling is dropping so we need to leave ASAP, and you look beat."

"I'll sleep on the flight. Is there a movie?" Sarah had always been one to seek out her friends. Only four months ago she'd helped their search-and-rescue cohort Dani search the Boundary Waters Canoe Area in northern Minnesota for a lost teenager.

"I can't think of a better place to spend your birthday than in Disaster," Sarah said, turning toward the plane.

Andee caught up to her, thankful that her friend never left room for doubt about her loyalties. "Gerard will be thrilled to see you," Andee said. "Want to ride copilot?"

"He still makes you call him by his first name?" Sarah handed Andee her bag. Andee stowed it in the belly pod as Sarah slung her backpack over her shoulder.

"I don't get it. Like he doesn't want anyone to know I'm his daughter or something. My mother was the same way. A free spirit, hoping to change the world. I'll never understand what they saw in each other."

"True love conquers all," Sarah said before climbing into the copilot seat.

Andee grinned. No, true love had never been their problem. *She* had been their problem.

How fun was it to be her?

Andee went through the engine check again and restarted

the plane. She finished her takeoff checklist, then radioed the tower and asked permission to take off.

Andee prayed for safety as she studied the darkening ceiling, hoping this trip would be the best one of the season.

✦ ✦ ✦

Sometimes Stirling McRae couldn't believe the stupidity of his own decisions. Like after vowing never to set foot in a plane three months ago, here he sat, wedged into a flying tin can manned by a wisp of a woman who looked like she should be serving meals rather than pushing a Cessna up to four thousand feet.

Or maybe his stupidity began the moment he saw Ari Al-Hasid and lit out after him like a fox on a rabbit, without a thought to the future. The terrorist had blasted a hole through the Trans-Alaska Pipeline System and another through his brother's gut. Mac could still see Brody's blood etched into the pores of his hands.

What was worse, however, was that Mac's impulsiveness had blown three years of surveillance, careful scrutiny, and an FBI master plan. They still hadn't discovered the whos and wheres of Al-Hasid's terrorist cell, despite three months of interrogation. To add to the horror, the FBI's only other lead—a former drug-running-murderer-turned-mercenary-terrorist named Constantine Rubinov—had vanished, and not even a 24/7 eye on his family connections in Valdez had uncovered him. At best, the cell knew they were under surveillance. At worst, Mac's knee-jerk reaction had accelerated their agenda. He wouldn't be so lucky that they'd simply pack up and leave town.

No, Al-Hasid's cohorts were still out there. Plotting. Waiting.

Mac closed his eyes slightly, bracing himself as the Cessna hurtled over the runway and slipped gracefully into the air. He never did like flying, even when he did it in an agency-procured plane. It wasn't just being crammed in with six strangers; it was the fact that he had no control, and that made him jumpy. One wrong move by the pilot and they'd crash into the jagged line of mountains in the far-off horizon.

And said pilot didn't exactly inspire confidence. He'd bit back a remark about his bag being larger than she was, but the truth lingered. He'd met his share of pilots, and the majority were levelheaded, commonsense, salt-of-the-earth types who knew how to tie down their airplanes in the middle of an ice field, make camp in fifty-below weather, and take down a bear with one shot.

How could this petite woman keep herself alive, let alone her passengers, if they crashed? Emma? He thought pilots were supposed to have names like Lucky Joe or One-Eared Butch. Not . . . Emma. He barely stopped himself from unbuckling his seat belt and diving from the plane as they began to taxi.

If he had his druthers, he'd be in the copilot's seat. Just in case they went into a steep dive and he needed to resurrect his flight training.

Mac massaged his temples. There he went again, conjuring up worst-case scenarios. *"You should write conspiracy theories on the Web the way you see diabolical plots in every situation."* His boss's voice rang in his ears. Tanner Buchanan had followed that statement with the suggestion that Mac would be better off taking a vacation from his theories—somewhere very, very remote—and while he was there take a long, hard look at his future. And if he wanted the same one he'd had three months ago before Brody's death.

Mac wasn't sure what his answer might be.

Perhaps Buchanan had a point. Mac had lived this job so long he was starting to lose it . . . maybe. For example, take the man sitting next to him—Phillips, Emma had called him. He looked like Sly Stallone with a smile. Yet all Mac saw in his clenched hands and the bulge in the upper right-hand side of his jacket was Rambo hiding a weapon, ready to hijack the plane.

When Mac looked at the smoker in a leather coat behind him, he saw a decoy, someone who had a bomb in the briefcase he held on his lap.

What a dunderhead Mac had turned into. He even saw terrorism in the eyes of the dark-haired woman heading home to her children. What was that she held on her lap in the camera-shaped bag? Certainly not a . . . camera?

Clearly, he needed time off to clear his head.

After Mac had returned from Brody's funeral, his thoughts of Hasid had tangled with his personal need for revenge. He'd called the hangar and found out the pilot's name, the one who'd flown over as his brother died in his arms. How Mac longed to go toe-to-toe with Andy MacLeod, grab the man by the shirt, and ask, "Why did you let my brother die?"

An answer. That's all he wanted. Just an answer. And the opportunity to tell MacLeod all he'd cost the McRae family.

But three months of grief had worn Mac out, and his da's most recent telephone call—the one tempting him with family and a place to heal—had pushed Mac into buying a ticket north to Deadhorse, the tundra town south of Prudhoe Bay. There he could enjoy some of his mother's home-cooked haggis and oat bread, hold his sisters' babies, and captain one of his brother-in-laws' fishing boats while he figured out what to do about his future.

Maybe he'd also finally be able to shake free of the scenarios that had plagued his sleep and knotted his brain for nearly the last three years. Scenarios that included Hasid's cell or other terrorists sneaking into Alaska and destroying America's homeland source of oil, the Trans-Alaska Pipeline System. The destruction of the pipeline would cause America to seek new alliances with Arab nations and Russia and even tuck tail in its relationships with dictator governments that supported terror, like Venezuela's Hugo Chavez. The cost of the war on terror would skyrocket and bring the troops home in defeat. Villages like the one he'd grown up in would have to return to dog-sledding to receive supplies. If they received them at all.

Keeping the pipeline safe meant keeping the American way of life and soldiers safe. Families fed.

Yet he had to concede that maybe his bureau chief was right. Security in America had tightened since 9/11, especially around the pipeline. Hadn't they caught two attempts just the past year?

He should be focusing on the word *caught* and not *attempts*.

Paranoia only sharpened his regret when he had returned from burying his little brother in the family plot. And it fortified his inclinations to resign from the bureau. Perhaps it was time to exorcise this . . . patriotism—or whatever drove him—from his system.

The plane's engine droned in his ears, a hum that pushed into his brain, turning it numb. Below, he saw the pipeline, a metal snake winding through the lush forest. Fifty feet to the west of the pipeline, the gravel Dalton Highway furrowed the forest north, some four hundred plus miles. To the west, through the cockpit window, he saw the jagged spires of the Brooks Range, a gateway to the Arctic looming closer. Hovering like smoke, wispy gray clouds bulging with rain shrouded the peaks to the north. Taiga swathed the valleys, a boggy, half-frozen carpet that never fully thawed.

"We're climbing to four thousand feet," came the voice over the loudspeaker. "I want to get over these clouds, so we'll have to go through them. It might get a little bumpy, so prepare for turbulence."

Mac held on to his seat, wishing he'd driven his half-ton Chevy. Still, air travel, even in a small plane, made better sense than driving in the iffy weather of northern Alaska in late September without a town for two hundred miles.

He cut his gaze to the pilot. Dressed in a leather jacket, jeans, a scarf, and gloves, she wore her curly dark hair behind her ears. He'd been taken for a moment by her dark eyes. Emma. Interesting. Scottish vernacular for "lady." He'd heard his father use the name occasionally when referring to his mother. *"Aye, she's a real Emma, that one."* He smiled as his father's brogue laced through his mind. Although Mac considered himself an American first, having become a citizen when he was in his teens, his father made sure Mac knew and appreciated his heritage.

Emma seemed confident enough. He noticed she hadn't had a problem telling Ishbane to not smoke during the trip or lifting the bags into the belly pod. She probably had to be in shape to run flights all summer long, loading and unloading cargo. But she seemed so small, even breakable. Maybe it was the way she had hugged her friend. Mac had watched out the round Plexiglas window, and as they embraced, he'd felt a pain so intense slice through him that he had to clench his jaw. He even pushed against his chest as if to massage it away.

He'd had a friendship like that with Brody. And his death left a hole inside that still took Mac's breath away sometimes.

"You need to come home, Stirling. Get a wife, start a family." Brody had sat by the fire, his legs crossed at the ankles, drinking Cragganmore.

Mac looked out the window, remembering his answer. "I don't have time for a wife. A woman would have to crash-land at my feet to get my attention."

Brody had stared into his glass, swirling the liquid, his voice dropping. "Maybe you just haven't found one worth paying attention to yet."

"No," Mac had wanted to say. "I've seen the destruction of too many marriages, the debris from trying to balance a family with a dangerous and demanding career." Besides, he just wasn't the roses, birthday-remembering, poetry-quoting, romance-hero type that a woman dreamed about.

Sleet pelleted the wings, and a flash of lightning crackled through the sky. Mac grabbed his armrest as the plane jittered in the air.

"Turbulence?" Ishbane snapped from behind him. "*This* is turbulence?"

Mac hadn't liked the skinny man from the start, and now his tone only made Mac bristle. Like they needed reminders? Mac watched the pilot. Her posture betrayed no emotion as she held the plane's yoke.

Mac had flown using his instruments only a few times, but here in Alaska, approaching the Brooks Range, it couldn't be more dangerous to fly in zero visibility. More than that, he saw a film starting to form on the wings.

Ice.

Turn around. The feeling clutched his gut as the plane's engine began to labor. The high-pitched whine sounded like a scream.

Next to Mac, Phillips closed his eyes.

The plane jerked and dropped altitude. Mac's stomach hit his ribs, and he sucked a breath.

The woman behind him screamed.

Emma didn't flinch, just levered the plane into a steeper climb.

Mac gripped his armrests, eyes on the wings. *Climb. Climb.* If they could get above the clouds, find the sunshine and better weather . . .

The plane slowed, time turning to syrup as Mac watched the ice layer the wings. Then through the whine of the engine Mac heard it. The sound that cut through his soul and stole his breath.

Stall warning.

The plane stopped climbing, and for a white-hot second of silence, simply gave up life as Mac and everyone else in the cabin sucked in a horrified gasp.

And then they were falling.

Chapter 2

THE SUNLIGHT FOUND Gerard MacLeod's neck, heating the layers of flannel and wool as he loaded his arms full of the last of his firewood and turned toward the cabin. The smell of autumn hung in the air—pine and dying deciduous leaves, the breath of winter just above the darkening clouds to the south. He stood for a moment, reading the sky. Days like today that hinted at trouble despite the seeming calm made him anxious when he knew that Andee was up there.

Please let me have taught her well. He let the thought calm him. Of course Andee would be fine. She had turned out to be a better pilot than he—he should have expected that since she'd lived most of her life with her overachieving mother. Mary MacLeod knew how to instill determination into her daughter, and he'd done his part by making Andee face those moments of crisis and helping her breathe through them to think clearly.

At least he *hoped* that's what he'd given her. Something to temper the legacy of abandonment in Andee's mind. He could still see lingering fragments of hurt in her eyes, especially during this time of the year when her upcoming departure to her mother's in Iowa loomed like a death sentence over them, turning his past decisions into blinding moments of pain, reminding him anew of all he'd sacrificed.

Then again it had only been in the last few years that he'd let himself feel anything. After Andee and her mother had left, he'd made himself go numb. It seemed like the only way to get through each day.

But today he felt the warmth of renewed relationship with his only child as he thumped into his tiny cabin, let the wood fall into the bin, and bent to stoke his stove. Andee would be here by tonight, and he had dinner planned—a tall stack of buttermilk pancakes with chocolate chips. He wished her mother would join them. Mary hadn't been to see him in years—a fact that still felt like a hole inside him, even though they corresponded regularly. But maybe time would heal that wound also.

Time and forgiveness.

He still remembered the first time Andee had shown up in Disaster—right after her sophomore year in college, toting a blonde-haired friend with a New York accent. Those were the days when he still looked over his shoulder, spooked at every creak in the forest, and didn't leave the cabin without his gun. Andee had appeared on the four-wheeler, stacked with supplies, clearly intent on spending time with him.

It had felt like living water to his parched soul. He drank in her company, her smile, and her laughter and ignored the waves of regret that threatened to pull him under.

A stronger and wiser man might have made her leave. Instead, he hoped and prayed that the danger had passed. After twenty years, certainly the Rubinov family had forgotten or at least moved on to bigger acts of vengeance. Certainly his daughter and wife were no longer targets. He'd started to hope that they might be a family again. Despite Mary's fears, Gerard had broken his own rules and let Andee stay. Not only that, he looked forward to her visits. Now he prayed for Mary to join her. And from her recent letters . . . well, a man had reason to hope.

He closed the door to the stove and rose, walking to the cold storage to retrieve his breakfast. Usually he lived like a lonely hermit, evident in the scarce canned goods, the absence of curtains and pictures. But since Andee's appearance, the place had lost its grease and fish odors. She'd cleaned, added the purple blossoms of Jacob's ladder to the vase on the table, embedded the smells of oat bread and porridge into the pine walls, and displayed new photos of her and Sarah and her other Team Hope pals.

Pictures that he'd hidden with nearly rabid paranoia years before.

But those days had passed. *Certainly*, they'd passed. He'd even begun to consider Andee's pleas to move to Disaster proper. He knew she'd feel better with him closer to town.

He opened the cool-storage door, grabbed a slab of bacon, and turned. He froze, staring at the man in the doorway, the one holding a gun.

He didn't see the one behind him until a split second before the man's blow sent him to the floor in an explosion of pain.

✦ ✦ ✦

Andee blocked out the screams that could be heard through her headset and above the noise of wind as the Cessna plummeted. Her entire body felt weighted, as if it too had gathered the ice that was forcing the aircraft to the ground. The plane fell like deadweight, the stall warning still sounding, scraping her nerves. If she could get the plane below this cloud with enough air left, she could level it out and land . . . maybe.

Andee tried to pull back on the yoke. Judging from the way her controls responded, sluggish at best, the ice had the final say on their rate of descent. Currently, they were plunging at 100 knots per second, banking west toward the mountains.

And she couldn't seem to pull them out of the dive. In a moment, they'd start to spin.

Exhaling hard, she pulled back on the controls, struggling to even the artificial horizon. Her ailerons must be frozen into place, along with the rudder. Her foot pedals didn't respond.

Why had she climbed into the clouds? She'd collected ice over Murphy's Dome on more than one occasion, but she'd always been able to fly through and cut out into the warming, lifesaving sunshine.

Why hadn't she listened to her instincts and simply stayed on the ground?

Not now. She wouldn't listen to the voices of guilt until later. When they were on the ground. Alive.

"Mayday, Mayday. This is November-one-three-seven-four-Lima. We've been hit by lightning and are going down. Over."

Nothing but static. Had her radio been iced over too? The weight on the antenna may have broken it off. She turned on the Emergency Locator Transmitter and the responder to 7700 MHz. *Please, please let the ELT be working.* Had she remembered to check the batteries? If they crashed, any plane flying overhead would hear their distress call.

Andee glanced at Sarah. Her friend stared straight ahead, clasping the door grip.

They cleared the buffer of clouds, and the rugged landscape below threatened to cut off her air. *Calm down.*

The plane began to spin. Andee ordered herself to slow her breathing and mentally catalog her responses.

Center the rudders. She fought the controls; her hands

whitened as she forced her head to stay clear. The plane spun once, then leveled out. *Thank You, God.*

What was her checklist for a forced landing? *Turn fuel selector off. Throttle, closed. Mixture—idle cutoff. Mags, off. Land . . . ASAP.*

She pulled back on the yoke. The elevator responded and pulled the nose up slightly. She nudged her flaps down, slowing the plane.

Land.

The plummet and spin had driven her course northwest over the foothills and rising horizon of the Brooks Range, glistening peaks of doom. Crippled, she would descend until they splotched nose first onto some jagged spire. She glanced at her falling altimeter. With this much ice, even the engine running at full power couldn't keep the plane in the air. They'd never keep the height—even over Foggytop Mountain. She had to find a place to land, one that wouldn't rip them apart piece by piece. She felt sweat bead underneath her cap, but inside her leather coat a shiver ran up her spine.

"Sarah, get on the horn and keep calling Mayday." She handed Sarah the mike.

The stall warning continued to blare.

Andee evened the flaps, praying for response. The plane nosed up slightly, but at this speed, they'd be nothing but bear bait.

The plush carpet of tundra beckoned below, but the Cessna refused to respond in time. They passed a canyon dissected by a stream of glacier flow, and she willed them above a sawtooth ridge and past the furrows of a glacier field at the mouth of a high-altitude basin.

"Mayday, Mayday." Andee heard the reined-in panic in Sarah's voice.

The scenery hurtled by, and the yoke shook in Andee's grip. She adjusted the throttle to get a better mixture for more power, but to her dismay, it didn't cut their descent.

Praise the Lord, the flaps miraculously responded. She barely missed clipping the wing on a snowy boulder outcropping.

The screaming in the passenger area stilled. She tasted their fear.

She needed to find another carpeted basin to set them down in before they crashed so high they'd never be able to hike out, let alone survive the landing.

Ripping off her headset, she glanced at Sarah. "Find me a meadow or a gravel bar to land on."

Sarah's eyes widened.

Andee heard moaning. A furtive glance behind her showed ashen faces. All except for McRae, who wore a grim, dark look, as if he might hold her personally responsible for the storm clouds that drove them from the sky.

Then again she did too.

"Prepare for crash landing." Andee knew she didn't have to yell to get her message across. She throttled back to an airspeed of 100 knots, then released the lock on the door.

Nothing more than the roar of the motor filled the cabin.

"There!" Sarah pointed to a swath of reddened tundra surrounded by cut granite spears and falls of gray scree splotched with white snow.

Andee nodded and descended hard into the high meadow. *Short approach, here we come.* She cut her speed to 71 knots, thankful she now had flaps, and nosed the Cessna down, barely clearing the greedy claws of a sharpened peak.

The plane hummed as she angled down. Andee was painfully aware that she'd probably lose her left wing at this angle. *Please, Lord, straighten her up!*

The ground rose to meet the plane, and an eerie silence filled her ears as she cut the engine. The plane bumped hard on the tundra, skipped, bumped again, then bounced as the wheels hit a boulder. She heard ripping and guessed they'd lost at least one wheel. Then the wing caught and the world upended.

Rolled.

Sparks littered her knees; heat rushed her body.

Andee held on to the straps and for the first time let herself scream.

✦ ✦ ✦

Darkness and the smell of avgas, hot and pungent, filled his nose and mouth. Mac's head throbbed with the sting of fresh blood, and his arm burned. He opened his eyes and clawed through the layers of confusion.

He hung upside down, his arms over his head. He heard groaning and moved his head. Beside him and slightly higher, Phillips hung unconscious, his thick arms obscuring Mac's view. Behind Mac—or rather above him—Ishbane and the hunter and Nina hung from their seats. Blood dripped off Nina's face.

He did a mental check, touched the gash on his head, moved his arms and legs, and found that right behind the adrenaline rush of relief the only thing that really ached was his stupidity muscle. Why had he stepped inside an airplane? Obviously he needed a good head slap . . . if they got out of here alive. He reached to unlatch his seat belt, then grunted as he landed with a whump on the ceiling of the Cessna.

Phillips was just rousing.

"Hey, wake up," Mac said.

Phillips opened his eyes, frowned, and stared at Mac.

Aye, me too, pal. "We crashed," Mac said. "You okay?"

Phillips stared at him as if he were speaking Swahili.

"You okay? Anything broken?"

Behind Phillips, Ishbane came to with a few choice words.

"I think I'm intact," Phillips mumbled, then reached for his seat belt.

Mac leaned out of the way as the man kerthumped beside him. "How's the pilot?"

They'd landed roof down, leaning on the right wing side, the left side up at an angle. He heard sparks, probably what was left of the instrument panel. Chemistry 101 told him that sparks plus leaking fuel equaled a big bang. They needed to exit this craft—and now. From his two-second evaluation inside the darkened cabin, he surmised the only way out was through the pilot's door.

Mac hustled to the front to check on Emma. Her pulse at the base of her jaw bumped under his two fingers. Relief blew through him in a hot breath. Her eyes were closed, and a nasty bruise swelled in the center of her head, probably where she'd hit the yoke. But at his touch, she roused, moaned.

"Shh. Don't move. You could be hurt." He'd like to snap a C-collar on her, his days in first-responder training kicking in. But for now, getting out of the plane seemed top priority.

He'd let the fact they'd made it alive sink in later.

"Sarah. How's Sarah?" Emma turned her head, searching for her friend.

Mac turned and barely concealed a groan. Sarah's seat had sustained the brunt of the landing. Although still strapped in, Sarah lay crumpled against the crushed aluminum of the plane, her face white, blood trickling from her nose.

He reached around her head and felt for injury. Wetness dampened his fingers, and he felt softness and raw flesh. His hand came back bloody.

He glanced at Emma. Her face was white, her dark eyes laced with horror. "Oh no." She reached for her buckle and landed hard in a crumple, nearly kicking him as she righted herself.

So much for rescuing her.

"We need to get out of here and get Sarah onto a backboard." Emma looked back into the cabin at the other passengers. "Anyone else hurt?"

"No thanks to you," Ishbane snapped. He undid his buckle and filled the cabin with expletives as he untangled himself and crouched on the ceiling.

"Enough. Just be glad we're alive," Mac said quietly. Not that he particularly felt like reserving judgment against Emma—he had his own choice words of frustration brewing in his gut—but blame wouldn't get them to the nearest hospital any faster.

"Help me get her out of here," Emma said, apparently ignoring Ishbane.

"The passenger door is wedged," Phillips said. He gave it another good bang with his shoulder, and Mac made a face.

"We'll have to go out the pilot-side door." Emma unlatched it, then pushed it open with her feet. It groaned on its hinges, then cracked. Emma startled, as if reliving their harrowing descent.

They all startled really. Mac felt his nerves buzz right below his skin, and adrenaline made him light-headed.

"Let's see what we can find to get your friend out," Mac said, trying to keep them focused. He sucked in his breath as he squeezed out between the rock face and the door.

Emma climbed out of the wreckage and stumbled away from the plane, rubbing her shoulder.

They'd wedged against a fall of Volkswagen-sized boulders. It had probably stopped all of them from becoming flapjacks by bracing up the tail section, which lay nearly severed from the plane somewhere on the other side of the boulders. They must have cartwheeled, although Mac didn't remember much—lots of blurring and screaming, heat and fear.

Mac surveyed the debris trail that littered the wake of their crash. The belly pod had ripped off, most likely at the same time as the struts. Baggage had ripped open, strewing socks, shirts, backpacks, papers, books, and shoes in the churned-up tundra. The air smelled of gasoline, and the cloud cover that had taken them down moved in to finish them off. Mac tasted snow in the air, and the wind whipped his jacket against his body. They seemed to have landed in a high bowl. Jagged peaks framed his view from every direction, spires of ice and cold and death that ringed them in and would obstruct any attempt at communication.

"Did anyone hear the Mayday?" he asked Emma.

"I don't know," she said, picking her way through the debris. "We need to evacuate the passengers right now. I don't know how much fuel spilled, and the engine's still hot. Help me find something to put Sarah on."

Emma stepped around the remnant of the left wing, which Mac guessed had been sheared off during the spectacu- lar landing, and as he watched, she lifted it and tugged out a backpack. Pulling it free, Emma took out a knife from her belt—where had she gotten that?—and cut off the straps hold- ing the external metal frame to the canvas.

A backboard.

"Good thinking," he said as she worked.

She didn't respond, her movements tight, nearly robotic. Then again, her friend had a serious head injury. Apparently that drove Emma's thoughts for now. That and the smell of gas and a few sparks still jumping from the instrument panel.

Yes, get the passengers out—fast.

He noticed that the bump in the center of her forehead had swelled and turned purple. "Your head looks bad. Are you feeling dizzy?"

She looked at him. In her dark brown eyes, he saw the inklings of fear, despite her seeming calm. What he didn't want was for the fear to take over and invade everything else. He needed her calm until he figured out where they were.

"It'll be okay. We'll get through this." Only, even to him, his words sounded empty. Especially with the wind swooping down the sides of the bowl, carrying winter in its breath, flattening their clothes to their bodies, stinging their ears.

She nodded. "I know." And just like that, the emotion vanished, her eyes became flat, her mouth set in a grim line.

Phillips emerged from the plane, groaning and holding his chest. A big man, he'd probably have bruises from the seat belt.

Ishbane had already exited and sat not far away, shaking. He held his hand to his bloody nose. Mac guessed it might be broken.

"What about Nina and Flint?" Emma asked as they maneuvered the makeshift backboard close to the plane.

As if on command, Flint emerged. He held his knee, gritting his teeth.

"Are you okay?" Emma pulled his arm over her shoulder and assisted him as he limped out.

He settled with a moan. "I think so. It's an old injury. Probably just twisted it." But by the grimace on his face, Mac had his doubts.

"See if you can find a towel or a piece of foam," Emma said, turning to Mac.

"Foam?"

"For a C-collar."

Aye. He had to admit, she might look rattled, but she thought in a linear, controlled pattern that spoke of experience. How many times had she crashed an airplane? He shook that thought loose and focused on her request while she climbed back inside the plane.

Maybe he could find a sleeping pad in one of the passenger's camping gear. He scanned the litter as he jogged over to the pink backpack. His own duffel had broken open, spilling his clothing and the pictures of him and Brody. He nearly stepped on one of Brody hauling in a chinook salmon out of Prospect Creek. He snatched it and shoved it into his back pocket.

Mac grabbed the remains of Nina's pink pack. A couple of the pockets flapped in the breeze, shredded. Inside the pack he found clothing, a stuffed orca, two wrapped gifts, and a foam pad at the bottom next to her sleeping bag. *Jackpot.* Mac snatched it and ran to the plane.

Nina had pulled herself out of the plane and slumped against the rock, a hand over a gash behind her ear. She looked dazed.

He poked his head inside the wreckage. Emma was leaning over the seat, assessing Sarah's injuries. Somehow she'd dug out the first-aid kit from the rear cargo area. He hoped that she also had a survival kit somewhere in her bag of tricks.

"Did you find foam?" Emma asked.

He nodded and passed it in to her. Producing the knife again, she made quick work of ripping it into a long, wide strip. Then she wrapped the foam around Sarah's neck, securing it with medical tape. "I'd rather have a miniboard, but this will have to do." Emma looked at him, her eyes dark and tense. "We need a sleeping bag or something."

"Phillips!" Mac yelled. "Grab a sleeping bag!" He glanced again at Emma. She touched her friend's cheek, then found her

arm and took a pulse. Her tender movements made him wish
he'd had someone this calm around when Brody had been shot.
Mac had unraveled on the spot. If it hadn't been for his
brother's thinking, Mac would have remained frozen in shock.

In many ways, however, he still felt frozen.

Phillips came running with the sleeping bag.

Mac untied it, then handed it to Emma.

"I'm going to unbuckle her and brace her fall," she said.
"Try and move her onto the bag. We'll ease her out and put her
as gently as we can on the backboard."

She seemed practiced as she braced her back against the
victim and loosed the buckle. Sarah's weight eased onto Emma.
With a grim look she crawled toward Mac. He rolled Sarah
as carefully as he could onto the bag. Her face looked gut-
wrenchingly pale.

Phillips helped Mac as they pulled Sarah out as smoothly
as possible and lowered her onto the bracings of the backpack.

Emma climbed out. Other than her rapid breathing, no
one would suspect her stress. She knelt beside her friend.
"I need a cloth to press against her wound."

Mac looked to Phillips, who scrounged up a couple of
wool socks in less then ten seconds.

Emma pressed them to Sarah's head wound, then wrapped
that with tape. "I need a few towels or something to secure her
head." Exhaling hard, she leaned back and pushed bloody hair
from Sarah's eyes while Phillips went in search of towels. He
returned and handed Emma a pair of pants and a fleece sweat-
shirt. She rolled them into tubes, braced them on each side of
Sarah's head, then rolled out more tape and secured the
woman's forehead to the makeshift stretcher.

Emma closed her eyes. In the silence, the wind lifted her
collar, blew her dark hair from her face. Mac saw her swallow

hard. "She's my best friend. She only came to Alaska to cele-brate my birthday."

Mac didn't know how to respond to that.

Emma looked up abruptly, away from him, moistened her lips, and took a deep breath. "We're going to get out of this."

He wasn't sure her words were meant for him. *Aye, she is a tough one, this lassie.*

"What now, Captain?" Ishbane approached, making no attempt to conceal his anger—or maybe fear. "I have an impor-tant meeting in Prudhoe Bay that I can't miss."

"Let me call you a cab," snapped Flint. "I think we should be thanking her for keeping us alive. We could've been killed!"

Ishbane glared at Emma.

She didn't flinch, simply regarded him with emotionless eyes.

"Or still in the air if she hadn't tried to fly through that storm," Ishbane responded.

"Speaking of storm," Nina spoke from her perch behind them. "I think it's moving in." She looked beyond them.

Mac didn't miss the tremor in her voice. He glanced over-head. Sure enough, the ceiling had darkened, and thunder rolled in. "We need shelter."

"We need to get out of here!" Ishbane said. "How far are we from the highway?"

Emma shook her head. "Twenty, maybe thirty miles. I have a map in my gear. I'll try and chart our path, but once we went into that spin . . ."

They'd all been thinking about hitting the ground. Prefera-bly in one piece.

Thunder growled again. Mac looked to the sky as did Phillips.

"We need to quickly get as much as we can out of the

plane." Emma's voice cut through the gathering panic. "Mr. McRae, will you and Mr. Phillips carry Sarah away from the plane? Keep an eye on her breathing. If she starts to labor at all, get me immediately. I'll dig out my emergency kits."

Mac felt a gust of relief at the words *emergency kits*. Okay, he'd give her points for preparation.

He moved with Phillips to lift the injured woman while Emma moved toward the wreckage. The smell of gas hung heavily in the air, and the sounds of sparks made his stomach clench.

Spark plus leaking fuel . . . the thought clung to him as he watched the pilot wriggle her way back inside.

Chapter 3

THE SMELL OF fuel leaking from the severed wings nearly knocked Andee back as she unlatched the door in the back of the plane. Sparks spit out from the instrument panel. Ignoring them, she focused her attention on retrieving her emergency supplies. Alaska flight rules dictated that she carry enough emergency provisions for each passenger. She had packed that, including her personal bag of provisions. With Sarah's sudden arrival, however, they were one kit short.

Please, Lord, let Sarah be okay. She let that prayer fill her soul as she tugged out the duffel bag of supplies, fighting her shaking hands. Being a pilot demanded that she be prepared to land and spend the night in the bush at any time. She'd overnighted near Koyukuk River twice over the summer after rain had forced her down on mail runs from Bettles. But during those overnights, she'd never had to look after passengers— a job she steered away from. She'd been on too many high-altitude rescues and experienced the whims of Alaskan weather too often to enjoy watching out for passengers.

Please, Lord, don't let anyone die!

She heard a grunt behind her and looked over her shoulder. McRae had wedged himself inside. "Get out! This plane could explode," she ordered.

"Hand me the duffel."

Andee waged a half-second debate with herself, then shoved the bag toward him. She yanked another one out. Prying herself through the door, she gritted her teeth as she tugged. The canvas caught on the sharp edges.

Phillips came up behind her and lent his strength to the handles. She heard the material rip but didn't care as they carried it away.

"Get away from the plane," Andee said as she saw Nina approaching.

"My camera!"

"No, Nina. There are still sparks. It's not safe."

"It's an entire month of work!" Nina started for the cabin, panic in her movements.

Andee dropped the pack and grabbed at Nina. "I said no!" She pulled Nina away from the plane.

Nina clawed at Andee's hand on her arm. "Get away from me!"

A spray of sparks spit from the instrument panel. Andee tackled her, bracing herself for the explosion as she threw an arm over the woman.

Nothing.

Andee's heartbeat filled her ears as she waited.

Nina squirmed beneath her, finally untangling herself from Andee's grip. "You're crazy!" She stood, shaking, tears in her eyes. "I'm getting my camera." She strode to the plane.

Okay, so maybe she'd overreacted. Except Nina wouldn't have thought that if the plane had exploded in a fireball, would she?

"You did a brave thing," said Phillips from a few feet away. "*I* ducked."

He smiled at her, but Andee didn't reply. Instead she

stood and surveyed her passengers. "Listen, I know we're all rattled, but the first thing in survival is to not panic. God gave us brains, and that's our most important asset. Right now most of us are unhurt. Those who are hurt need the rest of us to be careful, to use our heads." She looked pointedly at Nina, now climbing from the plane with her camera bag. "I'm still the pilot, and I'm still going to get us home safely." She tried to steel her voice, but her words stalled on the thought of Sarah lying so quietly, almost peaceful in her slumber, save for the bloody socks wrapped around her head. *Help me get Sarah home safely.*

Andee noticed that McRae had opened the duffel and had begun pawing through the supplies. She knelt next to him. She'd seen panic before, and the way he followed her into the plane told her he might be starting to lose it. Keeping him focused would keep him calm. "We need to treat the injuries first," she said, trying to keep her voice steady.

He looked at her, then at Phillips and Flint.

"Are you hurt?" she asked.

"No."

"Then help me with Flint. We need to move him away from the plane. And Sarah needs to be covered with one of the sleeping bags to keep her from going into shock." She mentally ticked off the steps in warding off shock, then glanced at her other passengers for shallow breathing or signs of dizziness as she moved to help Flint.

McRae tucked a hand under Flint's arm, opposite Andee.

"Hey, I can move my own backside. I'm not helpless," Flint said, jerking his arm from McRae's grip.

Andee noticed, however, that he leaned on her as she moved him farther from the plane. Once Flint sat, Andee knelt before him to examine his knee.

McRae paced behind her. "What about the ELT? Is it working?"

"Mr. McRae, can you get me the first-aid kit?" Andee asked before she turned to Flint. "It looks like your knee is swollen. I'm going to have to cut your pants to get a better look at it."

McRae handed Andee the first-aid kit, and she used the scissors to open Flint's pants. A blue green bruise started at his patella, the knee swollen to nearly double its size.

"I hope it's not broken," she said as she prodded gently. The kneecap felt dislocated, but it could be broken, along with the proximal tibia or distal femur. Flint grunted as she probed. "I'm sorry. I just don't know how bad it is." She moved down the leg, felt for a distal pulse.

"I feel like I've been dragged ten miles behind a pickup."

"Can you straighten it?"

Flint gave her a look.

"I'm going to try just once. If you can't, we'll have to splint it as it is." As gently as she could, she tried to straighten the limb. His howl could probably be heard in Juneau. "Okay, we'll splint it bent."

Flint leaned back, sweat beading along the rim of his renegade-label cap. At least he'd rescued *that* from the plane.

"I'm going to check on Nina's head wound; then I'll come back and splint your leg, Flint."

Nina had her camera case open, scrutinizing her equipment. She shoved it back into the case when Andee approached her. "Thanks for trying to . . . uh, save me. I'm sorry I . . ." She sighed and closed her eyes. "Do you think they'll find us?"

"We're going to be okay, Nina," Andee said, putting compassion into her voice. If she had children at home depending on her, she might also be a wreck. "Let me look at that gash." Andee moved Nina's hair, matted now with blood, and dabbed a gauze pad to clean it. "If we were in Fairbanks, I'd suggest a couple of stitches."

"But we're not in Fairbanks, are we?" Ishbane muttered.

"I'll have to dress the wound and hope someone picks up the ELT transmission and flies us out of here by tonight," Andee said, ignoring Ishbane.

"So the ELT *is* working," McRae said.

Andee glanced at him, saw his eyes fixed on her, and said, "Can you find me another cloth to dress Nina's wound, please?" She turned back to Ishbane. "How is your nose?"

"How do you think?" he snarled.

She sized up his wounds. He'd sustained a gash along the bridge of his nose. "The bone may be broken, but it looks like the bleeding has stopped." She noticed his leather jacket drenched with blood. Taking a gauze pad, she attempted to clean the wound.

He jerked away from her, glaring.

"We should probably bandage it, if not apply an antibiotic. Do you hurt anywhere else? Your neck?"

He snatched the gauze pad from her hand. "No. Not that it matters. We'll probably die out here."

She wondered if perhaps he might be going into shock. Feelings of impending doom preceded weakness, nausea, and clammy skin. She reached over to touch his forehead, but again he jerked away and glared at her. Apparently she'd assess from a distance. "Try to keep warm, Mr. Ishbane."

McRae stepped into her path as she returned to Flint. "Did you get a response from the Mayday?"

She stepped around him. "Please, Mr. McRae, I know we need to address our location and situation, but I'm serious about treating injuries first."

Despite her words, even she could admit that her busyness kept her from facing the reality of Sarah's injuries. She looked at Sarah, watched her chest rise and fall. Rise. Fall. *Please, please wake up, Sarah.*

She felt McRae's eyes on her while she searched for something to splint Flint's leg. Stubborn Scot. He needed to get out of the way and let her do her job.

At this altitude and surrounded by tundra, sticks to splint Flint's leg were scarce. She stood, studying the plane. In the tail section, where she stored extra cargo, she'd rigged two PVC pipes to hold the fishing gear of the early summer clients. Andee hiked around the plane, found the tail section, then climbed inside. Mounted to the bulkhead with nylon straps, the PVC pipe would make a decent splint, despite its cumbersome length. At least for now.

She took it back to Flint. McRae stood not far away, watching, his gaze cool. Rolling up a sweater, she shoved it under Flint's bent knee, then secured the pipe to his leg so he couldn't move it. Much. "I'm sorry, Flint. That's the best I can do. You'll just have to stay off it."

She knew the others stared at her as she worked, psychological shock settling into their systems. As long as the shock didn't turn into a medical emergency, the injuries—save Sarah's—weren't life threatening.

Keeping warm seemed priority number two.

Although secluded in a bowl rimmed by peaks, the arctic wind sliding off the northern slope seeped through her clothing, lifting her hair on her neck, snaking down her spine. She guessed the temperature at a tame thirty-five degrees. But by nightfall, if they weren't rescued, it could drop to zero or below.

Finding shelter fell into the category of keeping warm.

McRae hovered just outside her line of vision, and when

she moved over to her duffel bag to open her supplies, he crouched beside her. "Listen, I don't know if you realized it or not, but we've crashed in the middle of nowhere. Do we or do we *not* have a hope of rescue?"

Andee tried to control her rising emotions. "*You* listen. Believe it or not, I know what I'm doing, and I promise we'll figure everything out after I take care of our basic needs."

McRae raised one cocky eyebrow.

She stood and brushed past him.

"Our basic needs are to get out of here," Ishbane growled.

"I don't know if anyone heard my Mayday," Andee continued. "But the ELT should be working, and any plane flying nearby should hear it. When we don't show up in Prudhoe Bay by nightfall, they'll come looking for us."

"Nightfall?" Flint's voice seemed strained. He needed pain medication. "We might need to spend the night here?"

"Aye. Maybe a few nights," said a voice behind her.

Andee whirled and met McRae's grim expression. "If you'll just trust me, I promise I'll do my best to get us out of here. But we need to work together. And you need to listen to me. One thing at a time."

Something flickered in McRae's eyes as he dragged his gaze over her, a look that told her just what he thought of her ordering him around. *Well, get used to it, laddie, because as far as I know, there is no one else driving this ship.* She alone was responsible for keeping them alive.

Andee shook her head and crouched to open the bag. "At best, we'll spend the night here. Worst-case scenario has us hiking out." She glanced at Sarah. "Then again, depending on where we are, I could start now for Wiseman or Disaster and maybe bring back help. It might be faster than waiting on the ELT."

McRae knelt in front of her. "Are you talking to me? Because you're mumbling."

A blush burned her face. She did that—thought out loud in a low mumble. Sometimes even answered herself. It helped to get a couple different perspectives sometimes. She raised her voice. "I have two bags, enough provisions for six, plus tarps and blankets. We need to gather as many supplies as we can—"

"But there are seven of us!" Ishbane said. "There isn't enough food—"

"Well, the girl isn't eating, is she? She'll probably die—" Nina looked at Andee. "I'm sorry." She put a hand over her mouth. "I'm really sorry . . . I didn't mean . . ."

"Sarah's not going to die. No one is going to die," Andee said tightly.

She didn't know how to read the silence of the passengers as they watched her. She returned to the duffel bag and noticed her hands shook, just enough to betray the adrenaline that filled her veins. More than all of them, she longed to believe her own words.

+ + +

Mac noticed that Emma's movements seemed quick, jerky, as if she was trying to hold back the emotions that he'd heard in her voice. She may be small and seem well-attuned to emergency situations, but he noticed the tremor leaking out in her hands.

He had to admire a person who pushed past her fear and took command of a situation. Only he should be the one in charge. He had survival training and had spent too many nights in the bush to remember. With her cute curly hair, her freckles, her lithe form, Emma looked like a city slicker who'd signed up for an Alaskan summer-flight internship.

And she talked to herself. He couldn't decide if that was unnerving or attractive. For now, he'd find it intriguing. Informative. And just for the record, all he'd wanted was an assurance that she hadn't forgotten an important aspect to their survival—namely turning on the ELT. Was a straight answer such a problem?

Lightning flashed, followed by another peal of thunder. This late in the year, he expected snow, but then again maybe it would be icy rain.

Spending the night on this mountain, soaking wet and cold, sounded like the perfect way to spend the first day of his vacation, pondering his future. *Oh, joy.*

He watched as Emma pulled out supplies from her emergency kits. A signal mirror, whistles, a multitool knife, a compass, waterproof matches, a flint-style fire starter, tinder, and a survival candle.

He picked up a roll of wire. "What's this?"

"A snare wire," she said without looking at him. "In case we have to catch our food."

He envisioned a field mouse dangling on the other end and made a face. "Let me help you."

She faced him, surprise in her eyes. "Okay, lay these out in piles so we can assess what we have."

Precisely what he'd have done. Or maybe he'd already be leading them in a hike out of these mountains, heading south. With the ELT tucked under his arm. They came with batteries and a remote transmitter.

Except for the basic desire to sleep in a warm bed, exactly what did he have to hurry home to? His brother's grave? Awaking each morning to the choking weight of failure? Maybe he should be joining Ishbane with chills and feelings of doom. He should step aside and let Ms. Pilot Extraordinaire do her thing. Especially if he wasn't planning on being an FBI agent anymore anyway. No need for heroics.

She added a flashlight and four chemical light sticks to the pile, then a tarp, two space blankets, a spiral of climbing rope, a bag of climbing paraphernalia, two ponchos, a pair of gloves, and sunscreen.

"You seem prepared," Mac commented.

She said nothing and added a thermal cap and two pairs of wool socks and a couple packets of chemical hand warmers.

"Were you planning on crashing?"

She stopped, and he instinctively braced himself. "Yeah, absolutely because I think it is oh so fun to be out here, my friend seriously injured, the responsibility of six people on my shoulders. I do it for kicks—take passengers out with the promise to get them to their destination safely, and then I purposely crash the plane. Actually I'm writing a book on psychological responses to stress. Consider yourself a test subject."

"Sorry . . . I was joking."

"Not funny. We're in a world of trouble here, Mr. McRae, and my one thought is making sure no one dies. So, please, help or get out of the way."

"You're not in the least interested in anyone else's ideas? On what we should do to get out of here?"

She actually frowned at him, an expression of confusion that he would have thought funny if she wasn't so serious. "Yeah, sure. This is a committee. What do you think we should do, McRae? Fish? Hike? Maybe sing camp songs?"

He held up his hands. "Sorry. I just thought maybe we could talk about what we need to do."

"We will—after we figure out how bad the situation is." She sighed, and he saw her shoulders sag a little. "I'm sorry,

McRae. I know you're trying to help. Right now, just sit down and try to stay warm. I promise I'll take care of you."

Whoa. No one had ever said that to him before with such seriousness. He felt like a first-grader, outside in his shirt-sleeves during a fire drill. Everything inside him simply stilled, confused. He'd never *not* taken charge, and he didn't do help-less. Never had.

Still, he could see stress shimmer off this woman, and while he'd had his doubts about her abilities, she did appear to have her wits about her, even if she did wear her prickly side out. Besides, he was on vacation, not responsible for anyone, right?

"Call me if you need me." He sat beside her, watching, wrestling with his ego. He had nothing to prove to anyone.

She pulled out a canister of water, four survival bars, a packet of coffee, a pot, a ministove, and a metal canister with what he assumed held camp gas. She sat back, her hands on her legs. "Oh no."

"What?" From his first glance, it seemed she'd brought everything but his aunt Brenna's canning kettle.

"I thought I'd packed a tent." She put a hand to her fore-head, then absently ran her fingers along the bruise. "What was I thinking?"

For a moment, past the can-do attitude and the snippy way she'd drawn the line in the sand, he recognized regret. The expression that said *why am I so stupid?* zeroed in on a tender place inside him and squeezed. *Wow. Okay, just breathe through it.* Regret did that—snuck up on him when he least expected it.

Thankfully he was a lifetime away from his job now. The plane crash felt like an abrupt dividing line between the man he'd been—pushed by his job, his goals, his duty—and the man he might be if he gave it all up.

Nobody. Just another dazed passenger emphasized by the way Emma talked to him. He was a guy with a future hauling in salmon or crab fishing on the open sea. Although he respected his sisters' husbands for their choices and hard work, something inside him had wanted more. To save the world evidently.

In the end, those hopes had only gotten his brother killed. He didn't know how he expected to face that grief. Or recover and go on doing his job.

Maybe if he finally faced Andy MacLeod and demanded some answers from the pilot, he might begin healing. Maybe he'd quit the bureau, find a wife, start a family. It seemed like a goal Brody might smile at from the heavens above.

His new life could start right now, right here. Learning to live in the shadow. Learning to take orders. Learning to survive, not conquer. Learning to dodge the pain and settle into the cold, dead landscape that was his heart.

Most of all, learning how to exorcise from his life this burden that hovered—more than worry or regret over his choices—the weight of *responsibility*. The fear that if he didn't get it right . . . then who would?

Not *him*. Not anymore. He should keep that thought paramount, especially now.

Emma pushed herself to her feet. "Everyone, listen to me. We need to get to shelter before the storm breaks. Then we'll figure out where we are and what to do next. Did anyone bring a tent?"

Silence.

Emma winced. "All right, then we need to find shelter."

"What about the plane?" Ishbane asked. He still held his nose although it had stopped bleeding. Mac noticed him shaking slightly.

Emma must have seen it also, for she grabbed one of her

emergency blankets and draped it over his shoulders. "We can't go back into the plane until we know it's safe. With all the leaking fuel . . . well, I don't feel comfortable. Besides, if it starts to snow, we could get snowed under, store up carbon monoxide, and suffocate. Not only that, but it's liable to get cold tonight—really cold. And the plane won't keep us warm enough—"

"What if we build a fire inside?"

Emma closed her eyes, as if drawing patience from some deep well.

Mac shook his head. Apparently no one besides him had taken basic chemistry. Spark plus fuel equals big bang. Maybe someone should say that aloud a few times.

Emma sighed. "It would be better to find a cave or construct a shelter."

Standing there, her hands balled in her pockets, she looked every inch the Scottish lass, her face into the brutal wind as she gazed out onto the Highlands.

What a dunderhead! He was starting to think like his father, who still had pieces of his heart back in the old country. Mac and his siblings had grown up on tales of famous Scottish heroes like Robert the Bruce and Mary, Queen of Scots. This pilot reminded him of Flora MacDonald, a heroine of the eighteenth century. Resourceful and feisty, she dressed an English prince as her maid and helped him escape the clutches of his family's rule.

Just like this lady might help them escape the clutches of hypothermia.

As if reading his mind, Emma turned and caught his attention. "See what you can find from the debris. Anything. A tarp, a sleeping bag, clothing, rope. Even books. We can use them to start a signal fire."

The wind picked at the litter, sending papers scattering.

Mac walked out into the debris field, found the cover to the belly pod and another sleeping bag. He noticed books fluttering and wondered who among them was the reader. He picked up one that lay open, its torn pages fluttering. *Last of the Breed* by Louis L'Amour. Yes, they might need that one for reference if they hoped to find their way out of here. Despite what Emma had said about the ELT working, he saw a long hike in their immediate future.

More papers blew at his feet, and he stomped on them to keep them in place. They crinkled under his feet, and a torn corner caught his eye. A map. He leaned down, picked it up, and stared at it. He recognized the Trans-Alaska Pipeline System quickly, having memorized the area. Three points were circled in red.

Realization came slowly. The circled areas were weak points in the pipeline, the places due for overhaul. Places where a saboteur might place a bomb or two, enough to blow the line. Horror dried his mouth. *No.*

He looked at the passengers—Flint leaning over his bruised knee; Nina, now picking through the debris like a woman searching through the remains of her charred home; Ishbane, who sulked under his emergency blanket; and Phillips, diligently searching for a place to huddle for the night.

He glanced again at the map of the pipeline, noting how it had been marked with repair updates and shut-off valves. A route had been highlighted in yellow, another in blue. And right in the middle, northwest of Wiseman, someone had penciled in a large gray circle around Disaster.

He closed the map and shoved it into his jacket, feeling every nerve tingle, his instincts firing for the first time in three months.

Maybe paranoia had taken over.

SUSAN MAY WARREN

He racked his brain for the truth. Hasid had disappeared in June and hadn't been caught. More than that, many members of his cell had never been fully identified. More and more, terrorists from all walks of life, sharing the same agenda, bonded over one goal—cripple the war on terror. England and America had become their favorite targets, and nowadays customs officials and Homeland Security struggled to sketch an accurate profile of the everyday terrorist.

He or she could be anyone—a hunter, a photographer, a skinny businessman . . . a bush pilot.

Mac glanced over at Emma and her friend, saw the worry etched on the pilot's face. He wanted to feel sympathy. Instead he felt only dread.

Cold, dark dread.

And from overhead, sleet began to fall like pellets from the sky.

Chapter 4

ANDEE FLASHED THE beam of her flashlight across the crushed instrument panel, examining wires. She'd dug out her radio from the debris, followed the wires into the panel, and spent an hour trying to rewire the radio to no avail.

Outside, sleet had turned to snow, and it sifted from the gunmetal clouds, dusting the hull of the plane. Wind seeped inside through the cracks in the broken windows and made Andee shiver. She should get out of here, but with Phillips and McRae constructing the shelter, she thought she'd attack priority number three and figure out if help might be on the way soon. Not only that, but the panel had stopped sparking, and the threat of explosion seemed more remote. Apparently she'd overreacted when she'd tackled poor Nina.

"Did you get the radio working?" McRae stuck his head through the cockpit door and settled beside her. The cut on his forehead had dried, his bushy hair now hung in tangles about his head. Melting snow in his brown hair glistened in the fading light.

"No. But the ELT is working." She'd debated taking it out of the plane, but with the electrical panel now quiet and no danger of fire, perhaps it would be safer to leave it in the plane away from the elements.

McRae nodded without smiling. "The shelter is almost done."

"Great." Andee squeezed out of the cockpit door after him and trekked thirty feet down the tundra bowl, where Phillips had found a slight indentation in the rocky wall. Flanked on either side by a tumble of large boulders, the enclave made an adequate overnight shelter for the whole group. But with the wash of sleet and now the snow, she didn't hold much hope of long-term accommodations. *Please, Lord, send help.*

Someone like her SAR pals Jim Micah or Conner Young.

She shook the thought away. Micah and Conner weren't here, and just because they had the alpha-male tendency to lead their SAR team's call-outs didn't mean that she couldn't think for herself. Her father had taught her to survive in more ways than even he realized. She simply needed to keep one step ahead of panic.

Thankfully, McRae had calmed down and focused his energies on helping. "I'm sorry I barked at you earlier," she said to him as she surveyed his work.

With her instructions, Phillips and McRae had used an edging of metal they'd torn from the broken wing and propped it against the top of the rocky wall. They'd draped one of the two tarps she'd brought over the wing piece for a roof. Wedging it into the rocks, they'd hung the other tarp over the entrance, securing it with the duct tape in her bag. It wouldn't win any survival-school awards, but for now it would keep the passengers out of the wind and snow.

"It's not pretty, but it'll hold," McRae said, voicing her opinion.

She quirked an eyebrow at him, aware that his attitude had changed in the last hour. Hopefully their predicament had subdued him, and he'd start listening to her.

*Now that would be a first. A stubborn Scot bending his will
to a wisp of a lady. Wow,* she thought she'd forgiven her father,
Gerard, for his heritage. Apparently she still harbored latent
grudges.

She knelt before Sarah, who lay zippered inside her sleeping
bag. Flint watched over her. "How's her breathing?" she asked.

"Okay."

Andee felt for a temperature, took Sarah's pulse, checked
her eyes. One pupil seemed slightly larger than the other, but
in the dim light she couldn't be sure. She refused to jump to
conclusions. With a head trauma, it wasn't unusual for a victim
to fall unconscious, but with each passing hour Sarah's injury
seemed more profound.

She checked Sarah's bandage. The bleeding had stopped,
and from a cursory glance the wound seemed superficial. Still,
she could have hit hard enough for an intracranial hematoma,
and hanging upside down certainly had to have increased the
pressure. Which meant Sarah needed medical assistance,
maybe even emergency surgery, as soon as possible.

"Has she made any noises?" Andee asked Flint.

Flint nodded. "Groans mostly now and again."

Andee felt a flare of relief. Groans or any reaction to pain
she'd sing hallelujahs over. "Let me know if anything changes.
And if it looks like she might vomit, turn her on her side and
get me immediately."

McRae and Phillips were dragging supplies inside the
shelter. Andee ducked her head inside and saw Nina trying to
assemble the stove.

"I thought we might need heat," she said to Andee. Nina
seemed to be trying to conquer her fears, and Andee couldn't
help but admire her. She'd be a good ally once the adrenaline
and shock wore off.

The gray overcast sky along with the gray tarp turned the inside to shadow. The space inside the embrace of rock allowed for the group to sit comfortably. With Sarah lying prone, it would be a tight fit. Body heat could raise the temperature inside a snow cave up to forty-five degrees. Only they weren't in a snow cave, and Andee feared for the heat loss as the night closed in.

"We should get inside and stay there." Andee glanced at Nina, still trying to assemble the stove. "Let's run the stove only when we're cooking or melting snow for water. We need to conserve the gas."

Nina nodded.

"Just how long do you think we'll be here?" Ishbane entered the shelter, shivering under his blanket.

"Sit down and get warm, Mr. Ishbane," Andee said. "When we have everyone inside and a fire going, we'll discuss options."

"Our only option is to get out of here fast," he said.

Oh, sure. I'll just call 911. She battled frustration as she crawled out of the shelter. However, one look at Sarah and Andee had to agree with Ishbane. She briefly surveyed the map. According to her calculations, it was a two-day hike to Disaster Creek. Possibly three.

Sarah could be dead in three days. Andee would give her entire life savings to know if someone had picked up their ELT transmission. Her flight plan didn't have her checking into Prudhoe Bay until well after noon, and no one except her father knew she was headed to Disaster. Officials in Prudhoe Bay, not to mention her experienced father, could easily surmise, with the temperamental weather, that Andee had landed to wait it out. If she guessed the time correctly, it was nearly four, with night descending fast.

Her thoughts tumbled over each other and threatened to

steal her breath, her action. *Make a fire. Determine your assets. Concoct a plan.*

She breathed through the cascade of events, piecing them out, weighing her priorities. *Get the injured inside.*

"Mr. McRae, can you help me move Sarah inside?" She turned around and was surprised to see him standing arms akimbo, staring at her. As if before she'd even spoken, he'd already been fixed on her, studying her with a pensive expression. He'd put a fleece pullover on under his lined canvas jacket. The wind shifted and tangled his hair, and she couldn't put out of her mind the image of some outlaw from the days of legends and Wild West cowboys—or maybe the age of lairds and wars with England and Robert the Bruce. He certainly had the aura of a man on edge.

She'd make sure he slept on the other side of the cave tonight.

"Mr. McRae?"

He raised an eyebrow as if only just now hearing.

"Can you help me lift Sarah?"

"I'll help." Phillips appeared from the shelter and took one end of Sarah's board. Before Andee could react, McRae grabbed the other end. They carefully maneuvered Sarah into the shelter, while Andee helped Flint. She hated his moans, wishing she had something to give him—even whiskey at this point.

But she needed clear heads and cooperation, and whiskey didn't exactly encourage sane behavior.

Inside the shelter, the barest of lights lingered to outline faces as people clumped around Sarah and Flint, tucking in their legs so as not to jostle them. The ground, wet from the sleet, felt like a sponge, and dampness seeped into her knees. They needed dry ground. And they needed to eat.

Yes, she needed to figure out what to do if the ELT didn't call in rescuers. Heaviness loomed over the quiet shifting of snow overhead. Andee tried not to let it find her spirit, but as she slumped against the boulder near the opening, feeling the wind flap the edges of the shelter, she fought the sudden burn of tears. *I'm in over my head here, Lord. Way over my head. Please help me.*

"We need to get supper going," she said softly. No one moved. Not that she expected them to, but still, if Micah and Conner were here, they'd already have a blaze heating the shelter like a cabin in the north woods.

No, that wasn't fair. Micah and Conner had been Green Berets, and Phillips and McRae had both obeyed her instructions without grumbling. Sorta.

But with Micah and Conner she felt safe. Even if the world fell in, they'd be there to help hold it up.

As the wind whistled through the opening and Sarah breathed quietly and five pairs of eyes peered at Andee through the darkness, she had the sudden and overwhelming urge to let weariness overtake her, to put her hands over her head and hide.

Andee had tried to hide from her misery after the high drama of watching her life shatter, the day when her family finally fell apart, when her mother had packed her bags and Andee's and demanded that Gerard fly them to Fairbanks so they could check out of his life. Andee had felt numb as she watched her father fly away, leaving them on a wet and cold tarmac, seeing the only life she'd ever known or loved disappear with him.

In the childish places of her heart, she had just wanted someone to tell her that someday, somehow, this nightmare might end, that they might be a family again, that everything would be all right. Sort of like she felt now. *Please, Lord.*

"Nina, hand me the stove. I'll show you how to light it." Andee took the stove from her and dug out the canister of gas from her duffel bag. She lit the stove with her lighter, adjusted the flame. It growled and flickered out, grabbing at them with fingers of warmth.

"Is anyone feeling like they might be running a fever?" Andee put a hand on Sarah's head, then checked her pulse. She scanned the group.

Nina shook her head.

"Do you know where we are?" McRae spoke out of the semidarkness. He'd taken the place across from her, so his feet nearly bumped hers. She saw his dark profile and for a second felt an odd burst of relief that he'd taken the place near the opening. Just in case the wind decided to attack their shanty.

"For guys who have just been in a plane crash, Mr. McRae, you and Phillips think well on your feet. You did a superb job on this shelter."

"Thanks, Emma," Phillips said, although he sounded exhausted.

Andee took the pot out of her duffel and filled it with water from the water canister. "I have six soup packets and enough water for three days if we ration. We'll have to share the soup. The good news is that we have enough Sierra cups."

Silence.

"That was supposed to be a joke. I was thinking that you might not care about sharing at this point."

"I care," Ishbane said.

O-kay. Andee nodded, smiling in his direction. He shivered, and she instinctively reached out to check his temperature. He slapped her hand away.

"Hey!" McRae barked from his corner. "Back off, Ishbane."

"She got us into this mess. I don't want her near me."

"She may be your best bet for survival. Hit her again, and you'll wish you hadn't."

Andee felt the tension snap and coil around her. "All right. Sorry. I . . . ah, just wanted to check your temperature, Mr. Ishbane. Tell me if you're feeling hot, okay?"

He only grunted.

Andee shot a glance at McRae. He didn't meet her gaze, and she couldn't tell if she was grateful for his words or annoyed. She needed these passengers to see her as a leader. To trust her.

Not to have to protect her.

Then again she didn't really need protecting. She had walrus-thick skin after fighting for a place in the bush-pilot world of Alaska. She'd seen Ishbane finishing his smokes in one long succession after the crash, heard his litany of descriptions about their plight and his opinion of Andee's flying skills. So what? If it helped him slough off stress, he could call her any adjectives he could string together.

Good thing they didn't know her real name. For now let them think of her as Emma. Somehow it felt safer, like their accusations and fear couldn't penetrate her exterior and mix with her own fear. As Emma, the pilot, she'd make wise decisions, take care of her passengers, and get them to safety.

Even if the Andee inside wanted to hide.

McRae seemed in control, unflappable as he sat in the corner, watching her stir the soup. As if it might be just another event in his daily routine as a . . . "What do you do for a living, Mr. McRae? Salmon fisherman? Pipeline inspector . . . ?"

She wouldn't peg him as an executive—he bore a roughness around the edges, a barely contained energy that made her suspect he liked to be in the middle of the action. Or perhaps he simply hid his residual panic very well. After all, look at her.

Emma on the outside, high-adrenaline Andee on the inside. She made a fist to hide her tremors. It wasn't every day she crashed a plane. She'd been sixteen the last time she'd landed in a panic. And then her father had been driving . . . kind of.

"Aye. Something like that," McRae answered quietly. "Why?"

"Ever spent time in the bush?"

He met her gaze, and she found it quiet and unsettling. Something about him said secrets. Lots of secrets. "Aye."

Andee touched Sarah on the forehead, cupped her hand over her mouth, waiting for breath. In. Out. Yes.

She sat back and pulled out the aerial maps she'd dug out of the wreckage and shoved into her jacket. Unrolling them onto her lap, she flicked on the flashlight and ran the beam across them.

"I've been looking over the maps, and I think we veered northwest." Andee traced the path with her finger, thankfully now steady. "I adjusted for knots and dive speed, and my best guess is here on Foggytop Mountain."

McRae clenched his jaw, but he gave no other outward sign that he understood exactly what that meant.

"We're in the Brooks Range, maybe thirty miles from the nearest outpost of civilization," she explained.

"That's quite a walk." McRae's hint of accent seemed more pronounced with the night pressing against them, shadowing faces, blurring forms. The way he said it—emphasizing his consonants, tightening his words, the hint of Scottish brogue—somehow calmed her, reviving her memory of the man who'd taught her how to survive in these very mountains. The memory and the accent should also elicit some sort of defense mechanism, especially with her history—or rather her mother's history.

A Scot rubbing shoulders with her. Trouble wrapped in

unruly brown hair, a five-o'clock shadow, and dark, impenetrable eyes. If McRae bore any similarity to her father and the few other Scots she'd known, he probably wore his stubborn streak on the outside of his body, tempered only by his rogue charm. Scots like him thought they held the market on bravery, loyalty, and the charm to win a woman's heart. McRae had certainly laid the groundwork by defending her against Ishbane.

Still, regardless of how gallant, Stirling McRae had better not call her lassie. Not even once. She didn't need a protector. Her father had also taught her that.

"Listen, I don't know how long we're going to be here, and Sarah is pretty banged up. I think—" Andee paused, weighing her words—"I think I should head east toward Disaster." She pointed to the dot on the map. "I know this area pretty well. I used to live at the base of this ridge here. I can probably make it in two days if I push hard."

"No, you won't," McRae said.

She frowned at him, his words jolting her. "I'm in good shape, and I know how to survive in the woods. Believe me, I can make it."

"You're not going anywhere."

She couldn't deny another flare of shock. "What?" She lowered her voice and involuntarily glanced at Sarah. Although her pulse and breathing seemed steady, she still hadn't awoken, and every minute she stayed unconscious, the greater the chance her head injury inflicted permanent damage. "Sarah needs help. She could have a concussion or even swelling of the brain. Every minute we wait is one more percentage off her chances of survival. We don't have time to sit around and wait for someone to figure out we crashed."

"You're not going anywhere alone." McRae's voice also lowered, and she detected a hint of warning.

She sighed, fighting a rush of words. "I appreciate your gallantry, Mr. McRae. But I can make better time alone. Trust me. I really do know what I'm doing. I do SAR work in the Lower 48, and I've done more than my share of solo camping trips. Besides—" she scanned the other passengers— "who else would you send?" The only one who looked even remotely able to leave their bivouac and hike out was Phillips. Not counting McRae, of course. She half expected him to offer.

"No," McRae said. "We go together or not at all."

"But that's just stupid." She heard her voice rise, felt the tension ramp up in the shelter as four other heads swiveled in her direction. *Swell, Andee, make him mad.* She should have known better than that. Just what a stubborn Scot might need to fuel his dig-in-his-boots demeanor. Oh, well, she couldn't turn back now. "It doesn't make sense. Flint can't walk, and we shouldn't move Sarah."

It briefly occurred to her that she shouldn't even have to argue with him. She had piloted this plane and, according to the flight manifest, was still in charge. She alone bore the responsibility to get them to safety. With or without Mr. Stubborn's permission.

"No," he repeated quietly.

She bit back another retort. A little PR went a long way when huddled under a tarp on top of a mountain, thirty feet from twisted wreckage, cold and hungry. She needed McRae on her side if she left Sarah.

The thought twined around her heart and squeezed. "Why don't you want me to go?"

He ran his gaze over the other passengers, huddled against the freezing wind and snow.

Silence was accentuated by the shadows. Had he also

been injured in the crash, maybe a hidden head injury that turned him dangerous? He did have that cut. . . .

Andee tempered her voice. "Listen, I know you're . . . worried. We all are. But you're my responsibility, and I promised to get you to Prudhoe Bay safely. And by God's grace, I'll do it." She felt the hollowness of her words but hoped the others heard confidence.

"We go together," McRae said, his voice low but slow and distinctly hard. She noticed the slightest flicker of emotion in his eyes. "Together or not at all."

Andee barely reeled in a flare of frustration. *Remember he's in shock.* "Listen, McRae—"

"Call me Mac."

"Okay, Mac. I don't know why you're being so stubborn about this. It'll be faster if I go alone. Like I said, I know how to survive. I'll come right back, I promise."

"I'm not afraid, Emma."

He said it so softly that the others probably didn't hear, but it felt loud enough to resonate in her soul. Not only his words but his rolled *r*, the use of her call name, and his calming tone—it made her believe him.

So, if he wasn't afraid that made him *dangerous*. Why hadn't she seen that? He had all the marks—the cool demeanor, the dark eyes assessing them all. Underneath those rugged good looks lurked a man teetering on the edge. Over the last hour paranoia had set in.

She nodded but scooted away from him, blowing out a breath. "Right. Of course not." Her only hope was to sneak out tonight, hope that perhaps she could get away before Mac noticed.

But who would look after Sarah? Mac certainly wouldn't step up to the plate, especially now that she'd made him angry.

Andee leaned back, helplessness nearly cutting off her breath. What if Sarah's condition worsened, and no one knew how to help her?

What if Sarah died? Sarah was more than a friend. She'd been Andee's roommate, her SAR cohort . . . her *sister*.

Outside, the sky hovered close, darkness spilling into the shelter, along with flurries of snow and wind. *The temperature felt in the low teens, if not below zero. Why, oh, why had she insisted they get into the air, then above the storm? Lord, where are You? Help me know what to do here.*

"We're not going anywhere," Mac repeated as if she still harbored any doubt.

Andee flicked off her flashlight, leaving only the stove flame for light, and drew her coat around her. For the first time in hours she felt the fear hit her bloodstream, her marrow. *Please, Lord, I'm counting on You to make someone find us.*

✦ ✦ ✦

"Why not let her go?"

Mac could have guessed that Ishbane would be behind the mutiny. Mac pictured the guy huddled in his fancy leather jacket, shaking from cold—or probably fear—anger in his dark eyes. He'd been spewing nothing but hatred for their pilot since the crash, words Emma had dodged with admirable control.

As much as he could admire a terrorist, that is. He hadn't any idea whom the map, a two-way satellite radio, and the bag of flares he'd found after further searching might belong to. His suspicions had found his bones, settled into truth. As he searched the night for guilty faces, he had to start with Emma.

She would possess the greatest opportunity to tamper with the pipeline. She could even be a member of Al-Hasid's cell. If not, maybe she ascribed to membership among the Free Alaska purists who bemoaned the pumping of the earth's "blood" for man's consumption. According to these naturalists, they'd be better off on horseback or paddling up and down the rivers on log rafts.

Only Emma flew planes for a living—a hitch in that naturalist theory. Still, she may have other reasons, and the fact that she wanted to leave them and head to Disaster, the circled rendezvous on the map—using her *friend's* condition as cover—only solidified his suspicions. He wouldn't trust her as far as he could throw her.

No—wait, he *could* probably throw her pretty far. She seemed no more than five feet three and one hundred and twenty pounds, even with her fleece layers and hiking boots. So he wouldn't trust her as far as he could see her, which meant she wouldn't leave his sight. Ever.

"We're sticking together," Mac said into the near darkness. The stove's blue flame barely revealed profiles. "It's the safest way." *Safest for our country*.

"But she even said she knows this country and can survive. I don't know the first thing about tromping through the mountains," Ishbane said.

Mac clenched his teeth against the sudden urge to wrap his hands around the man's scrawny neck.

Ishbane wouldn't stop. "Did it ever occur to you that it might not be safe to stay? That if she doesn't make it, we'll freeze to death sitting here waiting."

"I won't freeze to death," said Emma. Her voice sounded clipped and a little angry. "I'll make it."

Mac ignored it.

"I could go with her," said Nina. Mac hadn't spent much time analyzing the woman, but she had the makings of a mother headed home, with a stuffed noise-making orca—just like the one he'd purchased for a niece in Anchorage—and a toy fishing ship packed in her backpack. And the way she took apart her damaged camera, scrutinizing the remains with a sickened expression—Mac judged her story sound. Still, the fact that she suddenly volunteered to accompany Emma had his instincts firing.

"No. We go together," Mac said. "Nina, you have a nasty cut, and you could have hit your head harder than you think. As for Emma—" His thoughts caught on Sarah, Emma's so-called friend. He'd call her bluff. "She needs to be with her friend." He considered Sarah's "surprise" late entrance. What if she'd arrived with the map, radio, and flares? What if she was Emma's accomplice? What if she wasn't nearly as hurt as she let on? "Emma obviously has medical abilities as well as survival skills. We'll need her to stay alive."

"I have survival skills," Flint said.

"How's your knee?" Mac asked pointedly.

Silence filled in the wake of his question.

"How about you?" Phillips's voice emerged softly, closest to him. "You and I could go. I've been camping a few times and learned orienteering. Emma could map it out for us. We could make it."

Mac let that idea roll through him. Phillips, with his linebacker build, probably could survive the hike over the peaks to civilization. Except two scenarios played in Mac's mind. First, Phillips trying to overpower him or, worse, succeeding, then returning to the plane to finish off the others and completing his mission to sabotage the pipeline. Second, Emma or Nina or even Ishbane out of his sight, seizing the opportunity and making a run for the pipeline—or at least to the rendezvous with his or her accomplices.

Mac pressed the heel of his hand against his forehead, feeling his brain thump against his skull.

Please, please let me not be overreacting.

Please, please don't let me be wrong and Emma's friend die on my watch.

Please, please let me think through the folds of suspicion and possibility to uncover the real saboteur and thwart his or her scheme before millions of dollars of oil can be emptied across the Alaskan soil.

He refused to be wrong. He couldn't be. Not with so many lives hanging in the balance of his decision.

He thought of the radio tucked covertly into his jacket. He could hike out of the bowl and radio for help. But what if he alerted the terrorists to their position? They could have a small army descending on them by morning.

No, better to stay in hiding, to ferret out the truth from a place of quiet. As long as the terrorist among them thought he or she remained unknown, the terrorist would stay his or her hand. Panic might set the terrorist off, maybe cause innocents to get hurt, lives lost.

Still, a little fear might rattle a terrorist who'd just survived a plane crash. Make that person show his or her hand. Mac would have to play a careful game. "We all go together tomorrow at first light," he said.

"Who abdicated and made you the king?" Ishbane snapped.

"The U.S. government," Mac said. "I'm FBI. And for our safety, we're sticking together."

He heard at least two people respond to his words with a huff of surprise.

"Well, well," Emma said. "I should have guessed. And here

I thought it was just the Scot in you suddenly turning this into an absolute monarchy. Turns out you're a Fed. Not sure which is worse."

What did he ever do to her? She peered at him through the semidarkness, and he had the feeling that if they'd been alone she might have slapped him. That felt weird. He'd had no problems attracting ladies during his stint with the bureau. Not that he particularly wielded his badge as a pick-up line—he had his own arsenal, one laden with charm and humor inherent in his family genes. But despite his ability to find a date for the occasional FBI event, he'd seen the wreckage of lives wrought by the career he shared with his fellow agents, and he had no desire to let someone into his life only to bring her pain. Case in point, his brother, Brody. No, after the agony of losing his brother, Mac knew he couldn't be both a husband and an FBI agent charged with saving lives.

Only he hadn't really saved anyone.

He stared back at Emma, trying not to rise to her words. He wasn't sure he wanted to be that FBI guy anymore, and for a split second the temptation called to him to take back his words. To just be a tired, hurt, and vulnerable victim of a plane crash.

If anything, he owed Brody more than that. He owed him a job well done. And if Mac wanted to get these passengers to listen and obey, he had to follow his instincts one last time.

He turned away from Emma, hardening his emotions to her indictment. "Sorry you don't like that, lassie, but that's the truth. I'm in charge here as of right now."

Her face registered his words, and her eyes narrowed slightly. Then she said, "Would you like some soup, Mac?"

She handed him a Sierra cup of watery chicken noodle soup. He took it, thankful for the heat that burned his hands, noticing the wary look she gave him.

She handed out the portions to the others. "It's not gourmet, but hopefully it will warm us."

Mac held his cup close, letting the aroma feed him as much as the temperature. The wind howled outside the shelter, and he sat on his end of the tarp to keep the air trapped inside. When Emma turned off the stove, darkness seeped into the crannies of their fears and the unknown hours ahead. He heard the other passengers hunker down in the cold, slurping their soup. Flint had a sleeping bag in his pack and extended it to Nina, while Ishbane wrapped himself in his space blanket. Phillips had a blanket around him, which left two for Mac and Emma. She looked frozen, huddled at the entrance only a few feet from him.

Phillips's soft, reflective voice came out of the darkness. "When the apostles Paul and Timothy were suffering in Asia, they thought they were going to die. The Bible says that they were under great pressure, far beyond their ability to endure. But they knew that God had put them there so He could reveal Himself as their Savior. They prayed for deliverance." He paused. "I think we should pray."

Mac felt an odd peace when no one objected and Phillips prayed for their safety and for Sarah. He felt like it might have been a couple millennia since he'd prayed—at least since the day he'd stood at Brody's grave. But he'd been raised in a Christian home, and the fact that he hadn't thought to pray sooner told him that perhaps Brody's death had sliced deeper than he'd thought. For a moment, he longed to have a relationship with God like the one the apostle Paul had. Trusting Him for every sunrise, despite the darkness.

"Amen," Emma said. Mac heard her move, assumed that she checked Sarah's breathing again.

"You should move away from the door," Mac told her. "Let Phillips sit there."

He heard her exhale deeply. Then, "I'm fine. I need to be here with Sarah."

He sighed. If Sarah and Emma truly had a friendship, then he didn't blame her for not wanting to leave her side. If Mac had been able to stay with Brody instead of trying to locate help, he would have chosen those moments in a heartbeat. Instead, he'd been on the radio begging some air jockey to land and save Brody's life.

He felt the familiar ache—now more than three months old—reach in under his rib cage and twist. He'd find Andy MacLeod, and when he did . . . well, he wasn't sure what he'd do. But the feelings that pooled at the end of that sentence felt dark and too enticing to be anything but wrong. He hadn't begun to offer forgiveness. Didn't want to. Probably that had something to do with why he couldn't pray.

Someone started to hum. He wasn't sure, but he thought he recognized Emma's voice. The song wheedled through his memories and found that place in childhood where he'd sat in his mother's lap, leaning into her embrace. He remembered the words:

> *"Jesus Loves me! this I know,*
> *For the Bible tells me so;*
> *Little ones to Him belong,*
> *They are weak but He is strong.*
> *Yes, Jesus loves me! . . ."*

A child's song for a child's faith. But he needed more than the Bible's word that God loved the world. Especially when the reality of terrorism and death argued against it. The place God had once inhabited in Mac's heart suddenly felt as cold and raw as the wind.

Mac's cynicism tasted bitter in his throat as he heard Emma's ragged breathing. She might be crying. Again he thought of the radio but pushed the thought away. He refused to care. His hunches about the pipeline and a saboteur among the passengers had to be correct. The country couldn't afford for him to be wrong.

Outside, the wind buffeted the shelter, blowing through the cracks. He shivered in his coat.

But beyond the shiver, Mac felt nearly on fire, knowing that God had given him a second chance to save the pipeline.

To be the hero he should have been.

Chapter 5

ANDEE WRAPPED HER arms around herself, shivering in the predawn darkness. She closed her eyes, willing herself out of the cold's embrace. Sleep came too easily perhaps. Sleep and summer and the hum of a Continental engine.

Periwinkle clouds hung over the snow-dusted peaks of the six-hundred-mile Brooks Range. Andee smiled into the memory of holding the yoke of the Cessna 185 amphibious float plane, her father's proud gaze on her, his brogue in her ears. She felt weightless.

"Watch your trim," he'd said, speaking quietly through the headset.

Below, she saw a herd of caribou so tightly packed that they resembled one long, brown-and-white carpet against the shades of green taiga. Cotton grass with its white tufted heads spotted the surface in patches and warned of soggy, wet tundra, unsuitable for landing. Arctic poppies, yellow bursts of color, and purple moss campion reminded her that summer stretched before her. A season of fishing on Disaster Creek outside their home, of berry gathering—blueberries and currants she and her mother, Mary, would can for winter and store in the shed off their two-room cabin.

The Cessna hummed so loudly that usually her thoughts and the rhythm of her body merged into the music of flight. But today as she helmed their trip to Anaktuvuk Pass, her nerves rippled with anticipation. She knew the wind gusts that raked the village nestled into the pass were unpredictable and potentially dangerous and could toss their plane the way she wrestled with Pakak, her malamute. She gripped the yoke through her gloves, switching her attention from the instrument panel to the scenery and back. Someday she'd be rated to fly with only the instruments, but right now she could only thank God for clear weather.

Wouldn't Mary be surprised to see Andee at the helm, landing like a puffin on the newly built runway?

She stole a glance at her father. His long brown hair was pulled back and tied with a lanyard. He'd turned up the collar of his flight jacket from Vietnam, and the headphones crushed the top of his favorite Yankees cap. His eyes twinkled. She recognized mischief—the kind that hinted at adventure ahead.

"After this peak, you need to descend to three thousand feet. The runway is at 2,200," her father said.

The snow became diamonds sparkling in her eyes, even though she wore sunglasses. Here in the high Brooks Range snow stayed nearly year-round, the earth thawing for only brief snatches of time. Even around her cabin, winter fought against the invasion of summer. Vanquished for only a month or two at best, winter lurked like a grizzly, waiting to close in and regain its ground.

Andee levered the flaps down and descended into the long valley toward Anaktuvuk Pass. She loved the trips to her mother's old village. The daughter of a French gold miner and a Nunamiut Indian, Mary MacLeod had met Gerard while working as a nurse in Fairbanks, when he'd been brought in for a broken leg. Gerard claimed she'd mended more than his leg, that something in his soul had been broken before Mary soothed it with her smile. Fresh from Vietnam and his job as a UH-1 Huey pilot, he'd escaped to Alaska in hopes of also escaping his demons. Looking at him, Andee wondered if flying also gave him escape.

Up here, above the jagged peaks with only the sky pinning her down, something inside her also felt free. She reveled in the glory of floating like an eagle.

A downdraft caught the plane, and it shook as Andee struggled to right it.

She noticed her father didn't even lift his hands from his lap. "Calm down, Emma. Don't listen to your heartbeat."

Andee swallowed back the rush of panic and kept the yoke firm while descending. The sky fell away, the ground rising to meet her. In the distance a dirt runway had been cut out of the tundra in a strip of brown.

Another sweep of wind took the plane, jerked it, and dropped it hard. Andee's stomach leaped to her throat. Splotches of black oil littered the front windshield as she fought the plane. The crankcase vent tube must have frozen, blowing the crankshaft seal.

Her father still didn't move. "Steady, keep her steady, Emma."

The plane shimmied and jolted. Why didn't her father take the yoke, guide them to safety?

She checked the instrument panel. The oil-pressure gauge had started to slide toward zero. "Gerard! The oil pressure." Even she knew that without oil pressure the engine would seize and they'd be a tin can in the air, plummeting to earth.

"Pull the plane up, Emma, and cut your airspeed."

Andee urged the nose up, climbing, bleeding off airspeed until she nearly reached a stall. Adrenaline ran through her veins, shaking out her limbs.

"Now put the prop in coarse pitch, cut your mixture back, then switch your mags off."

Andee's hand shook as she obeyed. *But without the mags—* Her father wouldn't let her crash the plane, would he? She glanced at him, and he gave her a slight nod.

The sudden silence as the prop sputtered and stopped, as the wind began hissing across the cockpit, turned Andee cold.

The airplane nosed down and began to plunge to earth.

Andee broke free of the dream and sat straight up, breathing hard. Dawn—or what masqueraded as the sunrise this far north—dented the misty gray of the shelter. Every muscle ached, and her head felt cottony and full. Where was she?

With the emergency blanket pulled up to her nose and the body heat of the other passengers, she'd lived through the night. *Oh yeah, plane crash. Sarah.*

Andee leaned over her friend, checking her pulse, her breathing.

"She was moaning in the night," a thin man said. He touched a cut across his nose, then moved his hand back under his blanket. Ishbane.

"Did she say anything?"

"Something. A name, I think"

Andee closed her eyes, relieved. She opened one of Sarah's eyelids. Pupils seemed normal. *Thank You, Lord.*

Sarah moaned.

Andee checked her other eye. "Sarah, wake up." She patted her cheek. "Wake up."

Sarah seemed restless, as if trying to escape the bonds of

her slumber. Andee took her hand and squeezed. Sarah squeezed back. Andee wasn't sure if the response was involuntary or a message.

She'd take it as a message. One of hope.

Please, Lord, send someone to us today.

She noticed Flint slumped against the back of the shelter, his back to the wall. He shivered slightly in his sleeping bag. She touched his forehead and found a slight temperature. She also noticed that Mac had vanished from his post. She'd slept soundly. "Where is everyone?"

"Outside," Ishbane said.

Andee couldn't believe they'd gotten past her position by the opening without her waking or that she'd fallen asleep in spite of her attempts to drive away her fatigue. She'd spent most of the night monitoring Sarah's breathing and devising escape scenarios. She had to help Mac overcome his fear or dementia or whatever held him back from taking a full panoramic view of reality and agreeing to let her hike out—and soon.

Twice she had caught Mac with his hand on Sarah's head, as if testing her temperature. It almost made Andee want to forgive him. But the fact that he'd bullied his way into command of their battered group with his FBI pedigree kept her from letting forgiveness take hold.

She couldn't believe he was FBI. What kind of dumb luck did she have to be trapped with a Scottish FBI agent? Her mother would be trying to immunize her from the Scottish charm while her father would slap an arm around him, reliving old times at the bureau. Andee considered it history repeating itself, a sort of heavenly joke.

As if things couldn't be worse.

She felt like she'd slept shoved into a tin can on a bed of

baseballs. Leaning forward on her knees, she pushed aside the shelter flap. A gust of wind nearly stripped the breath from her lungs.

Snow blanketed the bowl in which they'd crashed, a million tiny diamonds sparkling in the light. It might be pretty if she were soaring above it, enjoying the scene from her safe cockpit. But hidden beneath this morning's white blanket, the jagged rock, crevasses, and loose boulders lay in ambush.

Good thing Mac had collected much of their debris last night.

Andee scanned the pewter sky, with the sun melting away the night. It boded well for travel today, and she'd be able to make excellent time.

She heard popping and spitting, smelled smoke. Searching for the source, she climbed out of the shelter, pulled her blanket around her, and saw a pile of books and seat cushions.

Nina knelt before the pyre, blowing on the fire, coaxing it to life. Already flames licked the base, and black smoke, fueled by the vinyl seats, rose in a thickening trail into the sky. Sparks spat out, grabbed by the greedy wind and tossed hither. Andee watched in shock as they blanketed the crash area, some landing on the broken wings of the plane. What was worse, she saw Phillips shoving a seat cushion out through the cockpit door.

When Andee noticed a pile of used waterproof matches, she didn't have to ask how they'd gotten the fire going. Had she packed another canister? Thankfully, she still had her lighter.

"What. Are. You. *Doing*?" She tried not to sound appalled, but had they any idea the resources they were consuming?

"Making a signal fire," Nina said. Fatigue lined her eyes, sank her face, but her movements betrayed a woman on a mission. Apparently a mission to return to her children. "We figured that if they were looking for us, it would help to have smoke."

That's what the Emergency Locator Transmitter was for. The ELT operated on the VHF range of 121.5 kHz, with signals that bounced off satellites designated to listen for distress calls. Not only that, Andee, along with many other pilots, kept her radio receiver on "guard" frequency of 121.5, just in case. Even though no one had located them yet and they weren't on any normal flight path, someone could still hear them. If help didn't arrive soon, using up the matches was the first of many bad ideas.

Andee dropped her blanket and strode over to the airplane, grabbing the cushion just as Phillips emerged from the plane. "There is still avgas all over the place. This thing could go up." She shoved the cushion at Phillips. "Stay out of the plane."

When he blanched white, she felt instantly sorry. Out of all of them, Phillips seemed the one person she could count on. His prayer last night and his words about the apostle Paul and Timothy had touched her soul in a way she still couldn't voice. She hoped he'd keep praying for God's deliverance. She needed a reminder of God's presence right about now as she faced a day of keeping everyone alive.

As she moved away from the plane, her gaze fell on a backpack—Sarah's backpack—wedged against the instrument panel. It held Sarah's Bible and possibly supplies.

Andee took a deep breath and squeezed into the cockpit, reaching for the pack. Her gaze fell on the ELT, their only hope of—

She felt hands on her legs, pulling at her. "Let me go, Phillips! I gotta get the ELT!" The hands tugged at the back of her jacket. "Stop—" She turned.

Mac. And he had her by the arm, his face twisted in fury

or panic. "Get out of here!" He yanked her away from the plane, practically dragging her over the tundra.

She stumbled behind him and saw the blaze had caught, fueled by the wind and spray of gas on the vinyl seats. A bonfire of smoke and flames plumed, the fire hot and roaring, melting the snow around it, sparks showering down.

On the plane. And the damaged wings that stored fuel.

Run. She'd barely put thought to action when the plane exploded.

Ka-boom!

One second she was running, and the next she'd landed facedown in the snow while a scorching, roaring fireball rolled over her head. Andee couldn't breathe, let alone think. Atop her, she felt something—no *someone*—heavy pushing her head to the ground, breathing hard into her neck. *Mac?*

She listened to the flames growl around her as the fire consumed the plane in mini-explosions and found her extra gas can.

She shook. Mac's arm covered her head. He felt so close and so protective, she didn't know what to do with the feelings that rushed through her. His breaths came in ragged puffs. Then she lifted her head and looked at him. His blue eyes so luminous, so shocked, even worried. Another emotion followed. It dried her throat.

Anger.

He pushed away from her, turned on his hip, and stared at the plane. Andee's eyes followed his gaze. Flames clawed out of the windows, chewed at the cover, and peeled the paint.

Mac turned and looked at her. If she didn't know better, she'd think he blamed her.

"You okay?" he growled. He stood and pulled her up, staring at her for a long time.

She wasn't sure how to respond. She nodded slowly.

"So much for getting out of here," he said and marched away.

✦ ✦ ✦

Mac's suspect list had just expanded to three. His scrutiny ranged from Nina and Phillips, standing wide-eyed ten feet behind him, to Emma, who held a backpack in one hand as the flames roared through her plane. She seemed shaken when he met her gaze, and he saw fear ring her eyes. But terrorists were trained in deception. If he hadn't seen the sparks from the bonfire ignite the plane with his own eyes, he'd suspect sabotage, aimed at taking out the ELT and any threat of interference.

A warm-up to the big event.

The flames billowed to the sky, mingled with the gold sunrise dissolving the vault of gray. The fire growled and popped and heated his face, melting the snow thirty feet away, turning the ground black.

He'd barely yanked Emma out in time. His knees and elbow hurt from his racing dive into the rocks. Just think what would have happened if he hadn't looked up from his scrutiny of the map, only yards from the shelter, and spied Emma wiggling into the plane. He'd seen the bonfire erupt, the shower of sparks, and did the math on his way to haul her from the cockpit.

They'd barely escaped being charbroiled.

Then again one less terrorist to stop.

Unless she had an accomplice. She was probably meeting people, a scenario the two-way radio he'd found seemed to suggest. A pilot with connections and history on the North Slope wouldn't be suspected of treason—she could easily bring in supplies and deliver the goods into the hands of the saboteurs.

Especially since she'd been the one politicking to hike out. Alone. Toward Disaster and the circle on the map.

Emma turned, as if reading his thoughts, and he met her troubled look. She shrugged away from his stare as she stumbled over to the fall of rocks and leaned against them, dropping the backpack at her feet.

The slump in her shoulders and the way she closed her eyes as if defeated nearly did him in. She was a good actress. He nearly wanted to believe that she felt overwhelmed with responsibility, that she cared only about getting them all home safely just like she claimed.

She sighed, opened her eyes, and fixed her attention on the plane. The acrid smell of burning rubber, grass, oil, and paper singed the air. The thunder of the flames backdropped the silence.

"Oh no." Ishbane clutched his blanket around his shoulders, his face ashen. "How'd it happen?" he said to Mac.

Mac didn't know quite how to answer. "Fuel plus spark equals big bang."

Ishbane glared at him and mustered the energy to round on Emma. "Now what? How are they going to find us?" He sank to the ground, shaking. "We're all going to die out here. We'll freeze and start eating each other off, and in the spring only one of us will be alive. I don't want to die."

Me either. But right now that wasn't his highest priority.

"We're not going to die," Emma said quietly. She looked at Mac. "Because I'm going for help."

Oh no, not again. Mac blew out a long breath. Before he could answer, however, Phillips came to life. "I agree. Let her go. I'll go with her, help her—"

"We've been through this," Mac said. "We all stay, or we all leave. We stick together."

Nina rubbed her hands on her arms, her high cheekbones pronounced against her wool stocking cap. A long black braid snaked down her back. She appeared weary or hungry, probably both. She swallowed, as if summoning courage. "I'll go with you, Emma."

Oh yeah, sure. Like that was going to happen. He might as well give them back their map, make sure their two-way radio worked, and load them up with supplies. He even let out a grunt.

Oops. Apparently Emma heard that, for she approached him in fewer strides than he expected. Standing with her hands on her hips, she stared at him with that heart-shaped face, close enough for him to see the dark flecks in her brown eyes, her long eyelashes, and the angry set of her mouth. Her hair hung in dark ringlets around her face, and for a second it occurred to him that he'd label her as pretty.

And furious.

"I don't know what your problem is, FBI, but I hope you can see our dwindling list of options here." She flung one arm out in the direction of the fire. "We could hope that some pilot is out early this morning, hunting for us, and he'll see the signature in the sky. But our fire is going to puff out in a couple of hours at the most, and, sadly, Mr. Ishbane is correct. Our ELT was in my plane. So unless you have psychic powers or can make a snowball into a crystal ball, my legs are the only things getting us off this mountain."

He felt his traitorous mouth curling in a smile.

Her jaw dropped. However, she recovered quickly. "Nina, Phillips, c'mere. I need to leave you some instructions." She headed toward the shelter.

"Stop, Emma."

She ignored him.

Mac stalked past a shivering Ishbane and caught her arm.

She whirled and he took a step back, not sure which sparks might be more dangerous. Tears formed in her eyes. "My best friend is seriously injured. She could be *dying*. There is *no way* I'm not going for help, even if I have to shoot you to get by you. So unless you want to be in there next to Flint and Sarah, nursing your own wounds, *get out of my way*."

For such a petite person, she could command rapt attention. Mac couldn't take his gaze off her, hypnotized by the flash of determination in her eyes and her words. Shoot him? That wasn't a terrorist talking, was it? Nina and Phillips froze, staring at them. Only the sound of the wind whipping the shelter flap broke the silence.

"We'll all go together then," Mac said.

He could nearly see Emma forming a response, but he didn't wait to hear it. Instead he put every ounce of FBI training into his expression and lowered his tone. "I'm not arguing with you anymore. You're not leaving here, Pilot. Not alone. You and I will take care of Sarah, Phillips and Nina will carry Flint, and Ishbane will carry supplies. But you're not going alone. That's final."

Her eyes narrowed, and he could see her tremble, probably from anger. But he hoped she heard his words and his warning between the lines.

Just in case she didn't . . . "You're the only one with medical skills and knowledge of the terrain. If you leave and don't make it, we're all dead. As it is, if your friend wakes up or gets worse, not one of us would know what to do." He left out the part that said *except me*. While he hadn't had much training beyond first responder, he did know the basics of patient trauma stabilization and CPR. He also had done enough time in the bush to survive a hike out. But she didn't have to know any of that.

Emma stood there, breathing hard, her mouth a tight line of disagreement. She looked fierce, even resilient. Then the wind carried the scent of smoke to him, and for a moment he remembered the explosion and how Emma had felt in his arms. Like if he let her, she might fit there.

Maybe he'd hit the ground just a little harder than he'd realized.

He pushed that thought out of his mind. Just because she forced him to respect her a little didn't mean he should start trusting her. Start wanting to see her smile.

Besides he couldn't trust anyone but himself.

Chapter 6

GERARD MACLEOD WATCHED as Constantine Rubinov—convicted drug lord, murderer, and man with a slate to clean—paced the wood-planked floor of his cabin, jittery. Angry.

Gerard couldn't believe that after all these years the justice system had actually let him out. Or that he'd let down his guard. In his worst nightmares, Gerard woke to exactly yesterday's events—two thugs working him over and trussing him up like a piece of venison sausage. He should have guessed that Constantine would make good on his threats. Gerard mentally cursed his stupidity. Apparently, he'd been wrong to assume that he and Andee were out of danger.

Thankfully, the former drug lord and his dark-haired, foreign-sounding accomplice who sprawled on Gerard's sofa seemed to have a secondary agenda . . . something that had kept Constantine from gutting Gerard the first second he'd had him pinned. Gerard guessed it had something to do with the silent radio at which Constantine and his cohort kept swearing.

The first rays of light spilled into the window, dingy predawn that matched Gerard's fading hopes. *Please, Andee, don't come home today!* When she didn't appear on his doorstep last night, his relief nearly weakened him. But with the weather, she'd likely put down some place overnight. Which meant that she was just as likely to show up today.

There were moments when Gerard wished he hadn't followed his informant's tip so long ago and caught Constantine transporting one hundred kilos of marijuana. Of course he'd also found the source—the family farm just north of Fairbanks, tucked deep into the bush, where they thought no one would look. Gerard had helped put away Constantine, his brother, and their mother. A real family affair.

At the time, Gerard hadn't known just how far the "family" had extended or that he'd sparked the anger of the extended relatives in the Lower 48. Only after two of his partners had been executed and their families tortured did Gerard realize exactly how far the family long arm of revenge reached. Despite his best efforts to hide them, his family could be next. Gerard had been forced to make the first of his many painful choices— sending away his beautiful daughter and his beloved wife. A choice his wife, Mary, approved of after discovering his clandestine profession. Another of his grand mistakes—keeping secrets from his wife. After so many years when he finally thought he was in the clear, he couldn't bear the thought that Andee might end up dead.

Please, don't come home, honey.

Constantine glanced at Gerard, looking just as happy to slit his throat now as he had been twenty years ago. Except for the man Constantine called Juan, Gerard felt sure he'd be a corpse for his daughter to find. That would be a fine welcome or good-bye. Maybe a more fitting one than the cryptic farewells he'd given her most of her life.

Choices. He hated how his had destroyed so much.

Gerard stretched his legs out along the floor, feeling them cramp. Lean, yet broad shouldered and fit, with long dark hair

SUSAN MAY WARREN

and eyes that some said could zero right through a man, he'd
cultivated a reputation in the FBI, one he'd hoped would deter
moments like this one. Moments when his past caught up with
him.

He strained to hear the conversation between the two
men. Constantine's agenda he understood. Vengeance. But
what was Juan's game plan?

Constantine walked over to Gerard, crouched before him,
holding a 9 mm Springfield pistol. He waved it at Gerard, who
clenched his jaw, refusing to flinch despite the close encounter
he'd had with the weapon earlier.

"When Juan told me to find an expendable pilot, I told him
that I knew the right man for the job."

"I'm not flying you anywhere."

Constantine gave him a wolfish smile. "Oh yes you are if
you want your daughter to live." He shrugged. "Of course, we
can have it your way too. In my wildest dreams I do to her what
you did to Leo."

"I didn't touch your brother."

Constantine ran the gun across Gerard's cheek, lowered
his voice. His eyes glittered. "I can still see Leo, every inch of
his body purpled by the beatings he got in prison." He shoved
the barrel of the gun against Gerard's Adam's apple. "You
remember my brother, don't you, MacLeod? Eighteen. Small.
Easy prey."

Grief flickered ever so briefly in Constantine's eyes.
"The day he died, I vowed that you'd pay. That you'd suffer, just
like I did. Like my mother did. That you'd watch your daughter
die slowly." When he smiled, Gerard noticed a gap where an
incisor had been. "And no one will even notice. Millions of
gallons of liquid gold spoiling the Yukon River and draining
Alaska of her piggy bank will divert the attention away from the

89

disappearance of a backwoods pilot and his daughter—don't you think?"

"Shut up, man." Juan strode across the room and grabbed Constantine by the back of his jacket, pulling him to his feet.

Gerard had watched the man leave after dusk last night, carrying a duffel bag, then listened to the motor of his four-wheeler evaporate through the trees. Juan returned right before dawn and had slept most of the day on the sofa.

Gerard had conjured up about every scenario he could and had solidified on one: terrorists sabotaging the pipeline. Now Constantine's words and Juan's glare confirmed it.

Gerard had spent enough time at the bureau to know the dangers. If they'd found those places that hadn't yet been refortified in the system's overhaul, weaknesses in the center that would do the most damage, they could cost America millions of dollars in resources and cleanup. It would even affect the war on terror, paralyzing equipment. In Vietnam he'd experienced firsthand what it meant to paralyze an army by cutting off supplies and support at home.

Righteous anger fired inside Gerard. This wasn't just about him and Andee. It was about his country. The one he'd served his entire life.

He'd fly them all to their deaths before he'd betray his country, unless . . . he shot a look at Constantine. The man stared at him, a smile on his face that turned Gerard's stomach. Andee. They'd use her to get him to fly them somewhere. And if he refused, they had his daughter as a backup pilot.

Please, Andee, don't come here.

"Why don't you just take my plane? Go. Do whatever you're going to do."

Constantine shook his head. "But don't you see, Gerard? You're our foolproof plan. You're our ticket out of Alaska. The

FBI won't suspect that one of their own men might be ferrying terrorists, would they? You'll be our cover, and no one will even know that we were here visiting. You'll simply fly us south, and when we're far enough away, we'll drop off your pretty daughter on some remote, safe landing strip. And you'll fly us to a happy ending."

Gerard knew he didn't have any sort of happy ending awaiting him, but he didn't care as long as Andee lived.

"Shut up, Rubinov," Juan said as he flopped back onto the sofa. Dark stubble covered his chin. Except for his dingy green army coat, he was dressed like the miners and trappers in these parts—wool hat, wool-insulated pants, insulated bunny boots.

"Anything?" Juan asked, nodding toward the two-way radio Constantine picked up.

Constantine sighed and shook his head.

Gerard stifled a smile, realizing that the static meant something had gone terribly wrong. Even he knew that TAPS security checked the line every week in progressive rounds. He could practically hear the tick of the clock counting down the hours until they found Juan's explosives.

"Don't worry," Juan said. "You do your part; we'll do ours."

Constantine looked at Gerard and smiled.

✦ ✦ ✦

"Like I said last night and according to my calculations today, we landed here, right past Foggytop Mountain in this valley." Andee sat in the shelter, running her finger over the aerial map she'd spread on her lap. She spoke between ground teeth, her best attempt at acceptance of Mac's coup. His FBI status meant diddly out here in the woods, and she was already kicking herself for giving in to him.

But in truth, he'd scared her. Behind those fixed, intense eyes, she saw something lurking—something that resembled an unspoken agenda. A look that seemed too painfully familiar to the ones lurking behind the eyes of her Green Beret pals Jim Micah and Conner Young.

Stirling McRae was up to something. The feeling had her every hair standing on end. Especially when she'd threatened to shoot him and he almost smirked.

Not that she would have, of course. But the fact that she hadn't even made him pause told her that she'd have a battle on her hands. She deserved some respect for her time spent in the bush, and she wasn't going to let an arrogant Scot run over her, even if he was FBI.

Besides, the Glock wasn't even loaded. She kept it mostly for an emergency, like getting caught in the woods between a grizzly sow and her cubs. But the .40 caliber 27-model pistol could hiccup a bear's attack and do serious damage to a man, so she kept the bullets separate from the gun unless absolutely necessary.

She didn't really consider shooting Mac to be absolutely necessary. Yet.

The truth was, she wanted to trust him. To believe his bullheadedness was more about getting them all to safety than about his heritage or shield. And the fact that he'd pulled her out of the airplane and saved her life, well, that counted. She shook off the idea of being in his arms as he protected her; the way, for a moment, she felt not alone, not overwhelmed, not so deeply afraid that she might shatter.

Until, that is, she saw his expression and he began his fresh crusade to undermine her leadership.

And then, right in the middle of his mutiny, he'd offered to carry Sarah. His words had bit into her anger, deflated it. The idea of leaving her friend alone, without a soul with medical training made Andee feel weak. Maybe hiking out with everyone meant they'd all live.

Or die.

Clearly there were no easy choices.

"Survival protocol says to always stay with the plane," she told Mac. "Even if it is only smoldering remains, we have shelter, and overhead searchers have a much better chance of spotting a downed plane than a clump of wounded trekkers." She rubbed her eyes with her thumb and forefingers. "However, it's getting colder, and in two days our food supply will be gone. Add to that the threat of hypothermia, and at this altitude, fluid in our lungs or altitude sickness. We might not be able to travel in a few days if they don't find us."

She surveyed the group, saw their worried expressions, and tried to inject calm into her words. "I guesstimate we could make it in two days if we push hard." She swallowed, hating the next part. "Here's the bottom line. My gut says in two days of waiting, we'd have to start walking out anyway without food and possibly with life-threatening sickness."

Flint seemed to follow her line of thinking. "So you're saying if we go, we go now. We're our best chance of gettin' off this mountain."

Andee nodded. "That's where we're at. But we have to leave before another storm blows in." The clouds seemed to gather in the spiral of black smoke, and her best instincts told her they'd need to get out of this bowl to lower elevation, find shelter, and build a campfire. Soon.

"What if we stay?" Ishbane said.

"What if no one picked up the ELT transmission? We could be here until we freeze or starve. Or eat each other," Nina said, quirking a small, tremulous smile at Andee.

It reminded her of the camaraderie she shared with her Team Hope pals. Levity in the midst of tension helped keep them from combusting or burning out. She'd been praying that somehow, miraculously, God would alert her search-and-rescue pals and call them out. Sadly, Micah, Conner, Dani, and even recent addition Hank couldn't possibly have the faintest notion that she and Sarah were in trouble. Still, God knew. That was enough.

That thought bolstered her tone as she pointed at the map. "We'll have to hike over this ridge to the east; then there's a steep descent to this valley. From there we follow the valley to the Granite River. It's about five miles in all, but a lot of climbing and descending, and if there's snow cover it'll be slick. There'll probably be talus rock or scree on both sides of the climb so watch your footing. The chips of granite are slippery. I salvaged my climbing rope and gear from the plane, so I'll lead the way, and we'll rope up, especially on descent. Walk in my steps. We'll follow the Granite River south for about ten miles until it connects with Disaster Creek. From there, we'll be in my backyard. It's about ten miles to my old homestead."

"Do you have a telephone?"

"A HAM radio. But I can call in help. If my father is there, we'll have a plane and we can fly Sarah and Flint out."

"What about food?" Ishbane asked. He seemed like another good reason for Andee to go alone. He looked like he could be blown over by a stiff wind.

"Like I said, I have enough provisions to last us for two days. If it takes us longer, we'll have to improvise. But over this ridge, the land drops off, and we'll find water on the tundra as well as marmots, mice, and—"

"I'm not eating a mouse!" Ishbane said.

"You will if you're hungry enough." Flint's voice thickened with pain. "I'd do it."

Andee smiled at Flint. After his flirting at the beginning of the trip, she didn't suspect that he would be her greatest supporter. "There are grizzlies around, so be on guard. They don't roam at this altitude, but as we get closer to the river we're liable to run into one. If that happens, don't move. And if it starts moving toward you, make a lot of noise. Remember that grizzlies can't climb trees, so—"

"Maybe you should just go," Ishbane said. "We'll stay here."

"We're all going," Mac growled.

Ishbane stood, his eyes red-rimmed and sharpened by fear. He advanced on Andee. "Why didn't you take the ELT out of the plane? You knew how important that was! You just left it in there to blow up! What kind of pilot are you?"

Andee's own accusations echoed behind his words. "I'm sorry, Mr. Ishbane. It was a stupid mistake."

"You're going to get us all killed."

Andee sighed, softening her voice. "We'll be fine. We just need to stick together, use our heads, and not panic. If we happen to see or hear a plane, we have the flares and the signal mirror."

She glanced back at Mac. "The final thing we need to do before we leave is make a signal." She tried to ignore the way Ishbane glared at her. "Something that lets any searchers who find the plane know which way we've gone. We'll need the tarps and our equipment, so see what you can find to make an X—that'll tell them we need medical attention. Then an arrow pointing east. A pilot with any savvy will figure out our route."

Nina and Phillips nodded, new life in their eyes. Ishbane huffed and snatched up his blanket.

Mac frowned. "You sound like you've done this before."

Andee leaned back and stared at her passengers. "I'm an EMT and I work in SAR. In the Lower 48 I have a SAR team that I work with, and here I specialize in high-altitude rescues. So, yes, I do know what I'm talking about." She shot a look at Mac. "Which is why I should go alone."

"Not happening."

Maybe he had a touch of altitude sickness. Still, she didn't have time to argue with a person who seemed on the edge of control. Not when he stood six feet three, was built like a highland warrior, and had a touch of ferocity in his eyes.

"While I stabilize Sarah for transportation, I need you all to figure out a crutch for Flint. Nina, can you melt us more water and put it in the jugs?" Andee folded the map, met the expressions of her passengers, and tried to smile. But inside she couldn't deny the doubt that lurked behind every word, every decision.

What if she led them all to their deaths?

✦ ✦ ✦

Mac watched Emma slump back against the rocks, and as she scanned the faces of the others, he couldn't help but notice her expression momentarily morph from determination to defeat. He overcame the insane urge to reach out and tell her that he'd make sure they got home safely, that he'd take care of her friend.

That he'd trust her.

Sorry, but in his line of business he'd learned to trust, well . . . no one. He couldn't afford to believe that behind those worried eyes was a woman without a dark agenda.

Still, the way she'd trembled after he'd yanked her from the plane—it made him pause and consider his other suspects. What about Phillips or Flint? He'd ruled out Nina after watching how she stared at the fire, mesmerized with fear. No, she couldn't be a terrorist after she spooked that easily. Phillips seemed more likely, with his capable, linebacker size and his offer to accompany Emma on her jaunt. And Flint seemed like the type more than eager to jump-start America into a full-scale war with OPEC. Damaging the pipeline might be like poking a hornet's nest. Moreover, Flint could be lying about his injury. Even Emma couldn't be certain how seriously he'd been injured.

"What if the temperature drops?" Ishbane asked. "What if we freeze?"

"Then we freeze," Mac snapped. At least he could rule out Ishbane. The man had the backbone of an amoeba. If the skinny man didn't stop whining, Mac might be tempted to toss him off the first cliff. No, not really, but he didn't handle whining well. Never had.

"Let's get to work," Emma said finally as the smoke from the fire drifted into the cracks of the shelter. As she rose and stepped outside, she glanced at Mac, and her expression didn't say, *Let's be friends.* On the contrary, if he could count on his seven years of experience in the FBI, it read, *My friend better not die or else.*

He let the threat hang in the air, snap him to his senses. Remind him that he had to keep both eyes on her every step. Because the fact that she'd surrendered to his command only meant that she might be the type to slit his throat in his sleep to accomplish her agenda.

Aye, this will be a fun trip for everyone.

She met him outside the shelter. He nearly bonked her on the head. Her voice lowered, she spoke in an even, dangerous tone. "I don't know why you're doing this, Mac, and for now, I'll play along. But if my friend takes a turn for the worse, there's nothing you can do to keep me from hiking out to save her life."

Then she turned and stalked toward the debris of her still smoldering plane.

He stood there, the wind skimming over him, and for a second, doubt nagged him. What if coincidence had collected the clues of a saboteur and dusted them across the crash path for him to discover? What if his years of suspicion and a sense of duty had churned up real paranoia that dictated his every move?

Was he killing them—and especially the pilot's friend and maybe Flint—by his bullheadedness?

Mac shook the thought away, refusing to let paranoia sink claws in as he helped Phillips dismantle the shelter. They packed the tarps and the other supplies into one of the duffel bags, then emptied Nina's broken backpack and packed the heavier supplies into her bag. Nina didn't say a word as she hung her camera over her shoulder and tucked the soiled stuffed orca into her coat. *Let her have her gift,* Mac thought; *maybe it'll keep her focus on her family and her feet moving.*

Occasionally he stopped and scanned the sky, listening for rescue.

Always he watched Emma, as if he half expected her to make a break for open country. But she applied more tape around Sarah's head to secure her better to the backpack frame, then with Phillips's help moved Sarah onto an emergency blanket. After tying the corners over Sarah, Emma hiked around the smoldering hull of the plane to the tail section. She reappeared moments later with a slightly blackened PVC pipe that matched the one taped to Flint's leg. She wound both ends with duct tape—for cushion?—and threaded the pipe through the sack.

Mac and Emma would carry Sarah between them, one end of the pipe on each of their shoulders. It wasn't pretty and would probably be cumbersome, but it would work.

"Hey, Mac, I need your help." Flint motioned to him as

Mac used the last of the extra clothing to form the X Emma had requested. Against the snow and yellowing tundra, the jeans and shirts anchored with rocks would stand out to any pilot overhead . . . he hoped.

He trotted over to Flint. Sweat beaded below his cap. He'd unassembled the splint Emma had constructed. Mac crouched next to him. "What?"

"I need a favor." Flint's voice lowered, and he glanced at Emma, who was examining Sarah.

"What?"

"I need you to straighten my leg."

Mac met Flint's eyes. Until now the man had stayed in his corner, groaning, but Mac saw the expression of a frustrated man underneath that flannel-shirted, beer-drinking, trophy-hunter-wannabe exterior. "Even I know that's a bad idea."

"We gotta walk out of here. And I'm not going to lean on anybody. I gotta be able to walk."

"You could damage your knee permanently."

"Yeah, and I could be left behind, my carcass frozen for the wolves to gnaw on. Straighten it. I'll use the rest of that foam pad for padding. Tape it straight."

Mac was wincing already. "You sure?"

"Of course not. Straighten it." Flint leaned back, closed his eyes, balled his hands into fists, and Mac saw a new layer of sweat break out on Flint's forehead.

Mac's stomach turned. He grabbed Flint's ankle and, without hesitation, yanked.

Flint's howl echoed across the valley and turned Mac's blood to ice.

"What are you doing?" Emma materialized behind him. "Are you crazy?" Her tone said she wasn't really interested in his answer.

Mac turned and met her gaze, refusing to back off, despite her blistering expression.

"Knee injuries are incredibly complicated," she said. "Without an X-ray I don't have the faintest idea how bad it is."

Mac noticed that Flint was still breathing hard, trying to cut the pain. "He asked me to."

"If he asked you to push him off a cliff and end his misery, would you do that too?"

Mac blinked at her, calculating his response, wondering just how serious she might be.

Emma threw up her hands, made a sound of exasperation, and knelt beside the injured man. "Well, let's splint it." She shook her head.

"I did ask him," Flint said quietly. "I don't want to be a burden."

Emma used the piece of foam to wrap his leg, then taped it tight. "You're not a burden, Flint." She rose and walked away, not looking at Mac.

The sky darkened, and a stiff wind lifted Mac's collar. Or maybe the cold rush came from her demeanor and the fact that she made him feel a little ashamed.

Emma called everyone together.

Mac reached down to help Flint to his feet. The man groaned as he tried out his leg, but Mac had to give him kudos for his efforts. They'd need that kind of thinking out here if they hoped to survive.

Or . . . was Flint just trying to get back on his feet so he could complete his mission? Sometimes Mac hated the way his mind worked.

Emma again outlined their route. "We're going to try and get into the valley tonight. Ascending the talus slope won't be easy. Keep your weight on your feet, your soles flat on the ground, and take small, short steps. Talus slopes have larger rock pieces, so step on top of them, on the uphill side of the rocks. It'll keep them from rolling downhill and taking you with them."

Ishbane closed his eyes.

"We'll rope together about thirty feet apart. Follow in my steps. Mac will go second, Phillips last." She glanced at Phillips as if to ask his permission.

Mac noticed she didn't give him the same courtesy. She probably couldn't look at him without glaring. Oh, well, he didn't expect to make friends.

"Most of all, if you fall, dig your knees or your heels in to stop yourself, and everyone else sit, with your heels dug into the hillside. It'll keep us from going down together."

"I don't want to be roped up," Ishbane said. "Not if you all are going to kill me."

Emma sighed. "You can do this, Mr. Ishbane. I believe in you."

No one answered her, and for a moment he couldn't deny, Mac wanted to trust the woman who seemed to only want to keep them alive.

Chapter 7

"THANK YOU FOR carrying Sarah, Mac." Andee sat on the crest of the bowl in the shadow of Foggytop Mountain, four hours into their climb, eating a PowerBar. The sharp arctic wind had chased away clouds that had shadowed their climb for most of the morning, but sitting on top of the mountain, despite the semisecluded pass, the cold wind scraped away the veneer of perspiration on her forehead. Under her layers, however, sweat ran down her spine.

"Of course," Mac said, eating his own lunch.

Andee had driven them hard, although slowly, and with Flint leaning on a laboring Nina and Phillips, they'd made good time. She'd even heard Sarah groan more than once, and when Andee checked her pulse and her breathing, both seemed strong. *Thank You, Lord.*

Andee glanced at Mac, aware that she'd begun to count on him, especially the few times she'd slipped and nearly went down. He'd finally taken the lead, holding Sarah's head up, away from the jagged, snow-dusted rocks. Andee watched his steady step, his wide shoulders carrying the burden of her friend, and forgave him for undermining her leadership, forcing them to hike out, and putting Sarah's life in danger.

Basically for being a stubborn, know-it-all Scot with an FBI badge.

Her mother would be shaking her head in disbelief at her willingness to forgive him.

For the first time in twenty-four hours, Andee felt an inkling of hope. From where she sat, she could barely make out the Granite River winding through lush red and orange tundra. Unfortunately, they had to descend a scree fall that had received only a hint of sun to melt the snowfall from last night. Andee hadn't yet made out a sheep trail they might follow, and visions of them all tumbling over the mountainside took swipes at her confidence.

Still, they'd made it this far.

She inventoried their energy and spirits. Nina seemed set on making it to civilization, and with Phillips to encourage her, they seemed like a team that would survive. Flint was a fighter. Suffering and against the ropes, he'd gritted his teeth and muscled his way up the mountain. He reminded her of her friend Micah when he'd been diagnosed with cancer. Fighting for every step, willing himself to get better.

Ishbane, roped right behind Andee, cursed and moaned. She'd been thrilled to hand him a PowerBar, just to make him focus on something besides his misery. However, she deserved his criticism. If only she hadn't taken off in that storm . . .

"Have you been a bush pilot long?" Mac sat on the ground, his back against a boulder, rubbing his sore shoulder.

She nearly advised him not to do that—by working the muscles loose, it would only cause them to ache when they had to tense again to hold Sarah's weight. But considering the fact he wasn't snarling at her or bossing her around made her bite back her advice.

"I started flying when I was twelve. My father was a bush

pilot." He'd also been a few other things, but she'd been working at forgiving him for that lie for close to fifteen years. Bringing it up in a snide remark probably wouldn't help her forgive him.

"So you grew up here in Alaska."

Andee folded her PowerBar wrapper and put it into her pocket. "Until I was sixteen. Then I moved with my mother to Iowa, where she went to medical school. She's a family practice doc."

Mac faced her. He'd put on a wool hat, but his curly brown hair stuck out from the back and around his ears, blowing in the wind. He folded his wrapper into a straight line. She couldn't help but notice his hands—not wilderness roughened like her father's, but still dexterous, despite the layer of dirt. They spoke of a man accustomed to thinking through his problems. His initial stubbornness most likely had to do with his shock at being in the middle of a catastrophe. She wondered what he did as an FBI agent. Probably read reports and analyzed terror threats. Something cerebral and calm.

"So, I'm assuming that's where you got your medical know-how?" Mac asked.

Andee smiled. "No. I wanted to go to medical school, sorta following in my mother's footsteps. I didn't do well on my MCATs and decided that it was a sign."

He raised an eyebrow.

"Well, really, I don't believe in signs, because I'm a Christian, but I do believe in God directing, sometimes through circumstances. I knew I didn't want to be a doctor, even if I wanted to help people. So I became an EMT. And a bush pilot."

She felt a blush and ducked her head, realizing she'd told him more than he wanted to know. Usually she kept that kind of information—the kind that probed the mysteries of her heart—for Sarah or Dani.

"You must love flying." He didn't smile but seemed to study her. From this angle, she'd call him handsome, with a layer of whiskers on his jaw and a definite scoundrel cast to his features.

And his accent sounded like sweet music to her ears.

She was probably just tired. Didn't her mother's tears— or hers—teach her anything about letting a man under her defenses?

"I do love to fly. I love the freedom and maybe the dichotomy of power versus the awe I feel at being up there above the mountains."

She raked her hands through her hair, staring out onto the horizon. "Sometimes when I fly I can see herds of caribou thundering beneath me or a grizzly raise her head in the middle of a stream. I can trace my plane's shadow on a glacier field and count the Dall sheep that scatter upon these mountains."

She sighed. Other reasons she flew included wanting to be close to her father and trying to relive something she'd missed for so many years. Maybe even to regain that part of herself she felt had been stolen. Still, at the end of the day she was good at flying.

When she didn't crash into a mountain.

But being a bush pilot was only half her life. "In the summer I live in Iowa and work for a local hospital. I'm trained as a paramedic." She glanced at Sarah, lying within arm's reach. "She was a friend and college roomie, and then we began to work together on our SAR team."

Mac followed her gaze. "Do you know why she hasn't woken up?"

Andee shook her head. "I'm worried that she might have

had a severe concussion after the crash. She might have woken briefly in the plane. Then with the blood rushing to our heads while we were hanging upside down, it might have increased the pressure in her brain. Moving her and the flux of pressure might have complicated her condition. And the fact that we're at such a high altitude doesn't help. You don't have to be in the death zone to get altitude sickness or pulmonary edema. I'm hoping when we get lower, her body will readjust and she'll pull out of it." She touched Sarah's forehead, found it hot, and closed her eyes.

"What does she do for a living?"

Andee opened her eyes to his soft tone, aware of how it touched her. Amazing what a few hours and some gratitude could do to a relationship. Maybe she'd judged him too harshly. "She's a paramedic in New York City."

"Was she there when the towers went down?" Mac asked.

Andee nodded, remembering how Sarah had called her every night for months after that because she needed a voice that wasn't from New York, a voice that didn't live in the middle of the grief every day. Andee had flown out twice to help Sarah and the other volunteers dig out the wreckage. She'd been there the day Sarah had said good-bye to seven men from her station house.

"She'll make it, Emma," Mac said softly.

Andee looked up at him, his tone blindsiding her. She felt tears burn her eyes and blinked them back. Stress made her cry at stupid moments. She nodded, but the fact that he'd found not only the right words but the right tone, well . . .

He sounded just like her father—calm, sure.

She clenched her jaw, realizing just how dangerous Stirling McRae could be.

"How much farther?" Ishbane plopped down beside her. "I hurt everywhere."

"Why don't we just spend the night here then?" Mac said.

Andee fought a smile.

Ishbane glared at him.

"So, I guess you're a supporter of the war on terror?" Mac asked Andee.

Andee nodded slowly, not sure what he meant by that. "Let's just say that I don't like war, but I like terror even less. And I pray for wisdom for our leaders. Most of all, I believe in God and what He says in Psalm 146. 'Don't put your confidence in powerful people; there is no help for you there. When they breathe their last, they return to the earth, and all their plans die with them. But joyful are those who have the God of Israel as their helper, whose hope is in the Lord their God.'"

Mac stared at her a bit longer than she liked, as if he might be probing her words and analyzing them for truth.

She hoped so. She hadn't exactly stood on top of the mountain and declared her faith in God during this journey. Maybe she should start, because her belief in God gave her hope that He'd get them out of this mess, even though she felt like a failure.

Not that He'd be exactly thrilled that He had to bail her out . . . again. The story of her life—always letting the people and the God she loved down.

"We should get going," she said, pushing back despair. "Ready?"

✦ ✦ ✦

Mac hated the fact that under that gritty, can-do exterior he'd glimpsed a woman who was loyal and honest. And that she'd gotten under his skin.

Even if she did offer a rather vague answer to his even vaguer question about her politics. He'd meant it to give him insight to her beliefs, something to narrow down his suspicions. But she'd either been trained well or she believed her words of faith.

He had to admit that the words from the psalm found a barren, broken place inside him and nestled there, like water on parched soil. *"Joyful are those . . . whose hope is in the Lord their God."*

"He made heaven and earth, the sea, and everything in them." He'd heard that verse before. It had been one of those his mother had made him learn, one that he'd successfully avoided for so many years, especially after Brody's death. He should know better than to hope in God. Yeah, the Almighty might have the power to create the universe, but sometimes it seemed like He left the details of saving it on a daily basis to the fallible creatures who inhabited it. People like Mac who had to flush out a saboteur and stop a terrorist act from within the depths of the Alaskan mountains.

Without letting his emotions get caught in the cross fire.

Get a grip on yourself, Mac. It wasn't like he'd ever slowed down long enough for a woman to get her hooks into him.

If he were honest with himself, he could attribute his fear of getting close to a woman as what had kept him dodging and moving full speed ahead into his career over the past decade. It somehow seemed easier to focus on what he could calculate and conquer, instead of love—something that could trap him in a stranglehold when he wasn't looking. No, love was probably the truest terrorist of all—it blindsided a man, confused him, then drove him to stupid, panic-driven decisions that could cripple him for life.

He'd seen it happen to too many good men and women.

"Do you need a drink?" Emma asked. She rose, found the water bottle, then brought it to him.

"Thanks," he said as she returned to her spot behind Sarah's litter. He handed her back the water bottle and watched as she took a drink. Emma had Alaskan bush–style determination, and he couldn't tell if he respected that or if it raised every hair on the back of his neck. Because if his hunch proved true about the plot to take out the pipeline, she'd stop at nothing to finish the job.

The thought occurred to him that she might be planning on getting them to the valley where travel would be easier . . . then ditch them.

Emma capped the bottle and stood. "Listen, here's how we're going to descend. Scree slopes are dangerous. The rocks are flat and small and slippery, and this one doubly so not only because of the snow but because the slope dead ends on the north in what looks from here to be a cliff. If you fall, you could pull us all over."

Mac noticed how she didn't linger on that image but went right to explaining the route.

"We'll traverse until we hit the scree, then go straight down, digging our heels in, pigeon-toed style. Mac will lead. Stay close together to prevent rocks from sliding from above and hitting us."

"If we slip, should we sit down, like on the talus?" Ishbane asked.

"Yes, dig your feet in. And if you see someone going down, everyone else do likewise. We'll have to work together to get to safety. Check your knots, please."

Emma had performed some climber magic with one length of rope and fashioned harnesses that looped around their waists.

Mac checked her knot; then he and Emma lifted Sarah in one liquid movement and settled her upon his shoulder.

Ascending out of the bowl, he'd been painfully aware of the height difference between him and Emma, especially once they'd switched places. Now as he zagged toward the scree fall, he noticed that his height played to their advantage as Emma kept Sarah's head level.

The very fact he'd thought about that made him pause. Not that he didn't care, but perhaps for the first time in hours, he hadn't only been running terror scenarios through his brain; scrutinizing every passenger, his memory of their gear, their actions and reactions; or making assumptions based on outward appearances. For the first time, he also thought about descending carefully, with Emma's friend's life in his hands.

"Watch your step, people," Emma said. "Slow and alive is better than quick and dead."

She made it hard to accuse her, the way she cared for everyone, knowing each step to take, gauging their needs, even ignoring Ishbane's snide remarks. More than once he'd had to stop himself from about-facing on Ishbane and unloading some of his own frustration. Still, that wouldn't help him sleuth out his terrorist. He had to stay focused. The ability to focus was what made him good at his job. Well, until recently when he'd been a little overzealous.

Then again was it possible to be overzealous when it came to protecting one's country and family?

Maybe. If it cost lives. He had to admit, none of the passengers had *terrorist* written across their foreheads or even in their demeanor. But today's terrorists didn't ascribe to one skin color, one accent. They could be anyone. . . .

All the same, what if the map belonged to Ishbane or Phillips—as a pipeline inspector? The two-way radio felt like a dagger in his jacket. What if it belonged to Flint—for safety from his buddies down in Tennessee?

What if Emma turned out to be as loyal as she seemed?

Maybe it meant that guys like him could learn to trust.

Oh, brother. He probably had altitude sickness turning his brain to mush.

The snow creaked underfoot as he descended the scree. "You okay back there, Emma?" he asked, glancing over his shoulder.

Emma gave him a tired smile, her face tight with concentration and the burden of her friend.

The sun, already surrendering for the day, cast long shadows across the mountain as it slunk toward the Western Hemisphere. As he walked through darkened patches, watching his feet, feeling the pipe burrow into his shoulder, he considered his stupidity.

What if there is no terrorist?

If so, he'd hit an idiot low point for thinking Emma might be the ringleader. He flinched, wishing he could apologize.

He'd dragged them all on this trek based on a tight gut and a track record that should have sounded bells and alarms. And now he put Sarah and Flint at risk. What if Mac's paranoia got them killed going down this hill?

Mac felt like a bully. A paranoid, foolish bully. Emma and he or Phillips should have been allowed to hike out on their own to get help.

I suppose it's too late to turn back? The question nearly formed on his lips. So they'd have to descend the other talus hill they'd spent hours climbing. At least there they'd be in a known shelter. But no closer to help, and all this jostling couldn't be good for Sarah.

He slowed, intending to suggest turning around to Emma

when he heard a shout. Looking over his shoulder, he saw Flint tumble face-first down the scree. Sliding fast, Flint yelled and grabbed the rope.

No.

The momentum jerked Nina off her feet. She toppled behind him.

"Sit down!" Emma's voice galvanized him. He turned, grabbed the litter in both hands, and held it above his head as he sat down hard, digging for position before he settled Sarah on the hill, wedging her behind him. Emma followed. He watched over his shoulder as Phillips fell forward, pulled by the power of Nina and Flint. Mac heard Nina's screams, saw a plume of snow, scree dust, and spilling rock as they plummeted toward the bottom.

Ishbane tumbled down the slope.

Emma gripped the rope in her gloved hands and planted her feet. "Sit down. Get your feet below you!"

Mac seized the rope, his heart in his throat as he watched Flint slide over the edge and out of view.

Chapter 8

ANDEE BARELY STIFLED a scream of her own as Flint went over the edge. Instead, she sat and dug her feet into the scree. At this speed, if Nina and Phillips went over too, they'd all end up in a mass of blood and broken bones at the base of the cliff.

She leaned back, bracing herself and gripping the rope. "Ishbane, turn around! Stop yourself!"

Next to her, Mac had sat, and she knew that he'd braced Sarah behind him. *Thank You, God, for a man who listened to me. Finally.*

"Nina, dig your feet in!"

Nina and Phillips, skidding through the scree, sent up a wave of snow and rocks. The cascading debris sounded like a shower of rain hitting metal, despite the padding of snow. Phillips obeyed, digging his feet into the rocks, slowing his progress. Nina also fought for footing, although her screams had to cut into her strength.

Ishbane kept sliding and yelling as he neared the lip of the cliff. When he reached the end of his length of rope, Andee felt the line tighten. She fought to hang on, her back straining from the urge to lean forward, which would send her skidding face-first down the mountain.

"Help!" Ishbane hung on a jagged edge of rock, his legs dangling over the cliff. His blanket fluttered over the edge. "Help!"

Just above him, Phillips had his feet planted against the lip of the cliff on a wedge of rock jutting through the scree. He clutched the rope, straining to hold Flint's weight.

Below them, attached between Flint and Ishbane, Nina had slowed, her feet dug into the rocks. Andee saw her inching toward the edge as Ishbane's and Flint's weight pulled her closer to disaster.

In the wake of the showering rocks, the shrill cry of a hawk echoed through the valley below. It raised the hairs on Andee's arms. *Help us, Lord!*

Andee's thighs trembled as she clung to Ishbane's rope. "Climb up!"

"I can't!" His face was red with exertion.

Someone had to pull him up before he dragged them all over the edge to their deaths.

She could hear Flint hollering, a bellow of terror that echoed against the granite and into the darkening sky.

"I'm going after them," Andee told Mac, tracing her route. "I want you to stay here with Sarah." For a second, the argument building in his eyes shook her. She rushed past it, past the fear that always lined her stomach when she put herself on the edge of disaster for others. But she'd agreed to this responsibility. Mac hadn't. Besides, she knew what she was doing.

"I'll anchor around that rock—" she used her chin to indicate a jutting of rock ten feet down—"then cross over to Ishbane. Stay here and make sure Sarah doesn't fall—"

"I'm going. I'm stronger than you," Mac said, his tone almost angry.

"No. I need you to stay put." If Andee or anyone else died,

Mac could carry Sarah out to safety and medical help. Andee yanked her knife from her belt sheath and deftly cut the rope connecting her to Mac.

"What are you doing?"

"Watch Sarah."

"What about you? Ishbane could fall and pull you over the edge! Are you crazy?"

"No. Just . . . trust me."

"How can I trust you when you do stupid things?"

She ignored him. "Nina, dig in! You'll have to brace Ishbane as I move."

Nina nodded.

Andee felt Mac's gaze on her neck as she crept toward the jutting of rock. She reached the spire and braced her feet against it. Ishbane shouted. If he let go, she'd be dragged down the slope. Best-case scenario had her and Nina and Phillips holding both Ishbane and Flint. No, redefine that as *impossibly* best-case scenario. The probable outcome meant that her parents would finally be together in one place for the first time since that fateful day of her sixteenth birthday. This time, however, she wouldn't be forced to choose between them.

In all likelihood they'd still fight over where to bury my body.

Andee pushed that thought from her mind and grappled to find a place to anchor her rope, grateful that she always packed her climbing gear into their survival supplies.

She looped webbing around the spire, creating a natural anchor point, then clipped two carabiners into the loop holes. From there, she tied off the end of the rope into a double-knotted bowline and clipped it into the carabiners. With the webbing secured to the rock, she hooked another carabiner into the back of her sling and anchored it into the webbing. It was a lot of weight to put on the webbing, but she had little choice.

Turning, she sat and dug her feet back into the scree. Looping the rope leading to Ishbane around her back, she used her right arm as the braking arm, crossing it over her body. "I got you, Ishbane, but you're going to have to do your part. I need you to climb out."

"I can't! Flint is going to pull me down! Throw me your knife!"

"Nina and Phillips have a hold on Flint's rope, Mr. Ishbane. He won't pull you down, and you're not cutting your rope. Now I've got you. Climb!" Andee looked at Phillips. "How are you doing?"

"He's inching me over. But I think if you get Ishbane, we can pull Flint up."

Ishbane braced his arms over the edge, grunting.

Andee heard scree bounce over the edge and hoped none of it caught Flint in the face. She could nearly taste Ishbane's fear.

"C'mon, Ishbane. You're doing it!" As his rope slacked, she reeled it in, braking with her right arm. He slipped, and the weight caught on her arm, straining her shoulder, her body wrenched between anchor and Ishbane. But from this angle, she could hold a man twice her weight. Probably even Flint.

Ishbane slipped again and cried out, but she gritted her teeth, holding him. "I got you!"

"Emma, I'm coming down there to pull him up."

"No!" Andee shot a dark look at Mac. "Stay where you are!"

"This is stupid! You're all going to get killed."

Andee refused to hear him. No, they weren't going to get killed. She wouldn't go down in Alaskan bush history as the pilot who had killed herself and six other passengers because of stupidity and the desire to celebrate her birthday with her father and her best friend.

Lord, please help me!

Andee pulled with her left hand, and Ishbane eased up

farther. She raked in the slack, relieved when he gave another good effort, getting his hips onto the cliff. She snaked in the length and held it fast.

"Don't fall!" Nina shouted.

Oh, good idea, Nina. Still, Nina did her part to hold up Ishbane, her arms and legs shaking from the exertion. If it weren't for her, Ishbane would have slid off the edge into eternity. The young mother had a fighting spirit—one obviously fueled by her desire to see her children again.

Ishbane grunted his way to his stomach, then rolled over, breathing hard. Even from her position some ten feet away, Andee could see his exhaustion. She reeled in the rest of the rope.

"Now, let's get Flint," Phillips said. Andee saw perspiration trickle down the man's face from his black hairline.

"C'mere, Ishbane." She wanted him hooked into her anchor line. Then she'd help Nina reel in Flint. Ishbane moved over to the rock, inching his way up the scree. Andee grabbed his rope belt and snapped the sling around his waist into the carabiner before unsnapping herself.

Standing and wrapping Ishbane's line between her legs, around her right leg, and up across her opposite shoulder, she grabbed the uphill line with her left arm, faced the mountain with the line toward Nina in the other arm, and abseiled, or rappelled, face-first downhill.

Scree spilled out before her, the snow having been scraped away by Ishbane's descent. She reached Nina's side, sat, and tied off Ishbane's line into a figure eight. Then she anchored herself into Ishbane's line with a carabiner. If they went over, they'd have Ishbane's line holding them to the anchor of rock.

Please let this work. "We'll pull together," Andee said as she reached past Nina's hands on the rope. Her worst fear would be

Phillips going over in the attempt to raise Flint. The combined weight of Phillips and Flint might be too great for her equipment. "Phillips, I just want you to anchor Flint. We'll pull!"

She planted her feet into the scree, adrenaline like heat in her veins. "Okay, pull!"

She and Nina strained on the rope. Andee ground her feet into the rock, feeling her back muscles strain. Next to her, Nina grunted. Andee gathered in the millimeter of rope, then pulled again. Another millimeter. Flint must have the weight of a buffalo. Over the edge, she heard him breathing hard. "Try and get a foothold, Flint! Help us!"

The sound of spilling rocks made her glance up, and fear coiled inside her when she saw Phillips's foothold break off and shoot into the air. Phillips slid forward, barely catching himself against a jutting lip of rock.

Rocks spit out over the edge.

From the look on his reddened face, Phillips couldn't hold Flint much longer.

Which meant that in about thirty seconds everyone except Mac and Sarah would fly out over the cliff.

"Pull!"

✦ ✦ ✦

Did Emma seriously think he was going to sit here and watch them all tumble over the cliff to their deaths? Mac couldn't believe he'd sat still this long. Maybe he'd been mesmerized by Emma's coolheaded thinking, her attention to the rescue, in talking Ishbane up the cliff when he would have probably cut the guy loose.

Okay, maybe not. But he had little use for people who surrendered the fight at the first glimpse of pain.

Then again, perhaps it depended on the *kind* of pain.

"Pull!" Emma cried. The panic in her voice bounced against the mountain walls and right into his soul. He glanced at Sarah—eyes closed, breathing—and made a decision.

If they all went over, he wouldn't go with them. But he wouldn't sit here either. He kicked a pocket into the scree, securing Sarah into the well. Then he scurried down the mountain, feetfirst, toward the rock Emma had used for an anchor. Landing hard against it, he shinnied along Ishbane's rope toward Emma and Nina.

If Phillips went over, Flint's rope would hold him. And Mac and Nina and Emma would hold Phillips and Flint.

In theory.

"Hurry, Emma!" Phillips yelled as he moved closer to the edge. "I can't get a good hold."

Emma and Nina tugged together, but their progress, if any, seemed miniscule.

Mac reached the ladies, scooted between them, and gripped the rope. "All together now."

Emma said nothing as they heaved, finally making progress. While Emma and Nina held the rope, Mac grabbed a new hold. They rolled in the slack and pulled again. Phillips grunted, still holding Flint's weight. But as the trio hauled him farther, Phillips's load lessened.

Flint's hands came into view, and he gripped the rocky ledge. To his credit, he pulled himself up, resting on his forearms, breathing hard. His face dripped sweat, probably more from fear than exertion, but Mac also felt drenched.

Beside him, he saw Emma trembling.

They pulled Flint the rest of the way over the edge, and he climbed up, rolling onto his back and scooting toward them, favoring his busted knee. He lay there, still breathing hard.

Phillips backed away from the edge of the cliff and also lay on his back, breathing hard.

Emma braced her arms on her knees and shuddered.

Mac stared at the group. He'd nearly gotten them killed. He'd been so paranoid about a pipeline saboteur he'd practically herded them onto this mountainside, so they could slide off to their deaths. He felt sick and light-headed. "I'm so sorry, Emma," he said between breaths. "I'm sorry for making us hike out."

He couldn't tell her why, because then she'd have to know that he'd suspected her. And after what she'd just done, he couldn't bear to see the look of betrayal on her face.

In the span of the past fifteen minutes, he'd started to care for this petite pilot. He needed to get off this mountain and out of her airspace and fast, before she started edging in on the parameters he'd set for his life. "Maybe we should turn back," he mumbled.

Emma looked at him, a frown creasing her face. Her breathing was still labored, and she seemed to mull over his words. "We can't turn back."

"Why not?" Ishbane yelled from behind them. His voice cracked, and Mac recognized fear. Well, he'd nearly become granola. Maybe Mac should cut him some slack.

"Because we're over the hard part," Emma said, looking past Mac to Ishbane. "Because we're not giving up—" she paused—"I'm not giving up."

"Me either," Nina said. "I will see my family again."

Mac met Phillips's gaze, saw in his eyes determination and resolve. The resolve of a terrorist?

Mac wanted to fling himself off the cliff or at least give himself a punch in the chops. There was no terrorist here. He needed to get that through his head before he got them all killed.

"Let's get off this shifting mountain and onto solid rock," Mac said.

Emma's face clouded—partly in shock, partly in realization. "You left Sarah."

What?

His expression must have betrayed his confusion because she gave him a pay-attention look and pointed to her injured friend. "I purposely asked you to stay there so nothing would happen to her."

"And to take care of her if you died."

Bull's-eye.

She gaped, and he felt some of the hot wind escape from her demeanor.

He nodded. "I know exactly what you're up to, Emma. I know you feel responsible for us and for our safety. And especially for Sarah's injuries. But I wasn't going to stand back and watch while you and everyone else got dragged to your deaths."

She stared at him, and he saw doubt in her eyes. Yes, he'd given her plenty of reason to believe that Stirling McRae thought only of his higher—private—agenda. But the fact she'd believed that he didn't care . . . well, he'd never been that big of a jerk. At least not to his knowledge.

He lowered his voice, his eyes still on hers, hoping every word resonated. "I'm not hiking out of these mountains without you."

She swallowed and edged up her chin, but in her eyes— past the courage and the hard-edged refusal to let fear gulp her whole—he thought he saw a flickering of relief.

✦ ✦ ✦

"Where is your contact?"

Constantine's voice tugged Gerard from the precious blanket

of sleep that had soothed his wounds and the worry that gnawed at him. Late-morning sunlight seeped through the windows of the cabin, eating at the chill. Constantine and Juan had stoked the fire before securing his bonds. They'd left Gerard gagged and crumpled in the corner of the cabin, where his mind whirred, concocting escape scenarios until exhausted, he'd slumped over, out cold.

Gerard's face felt scraped and bruised against the wood-planked floor as he closed his eyes, hoping his captors hadn't seen him stir.

"Your contact should have checked in by now or at least turned on the GPS signal." Constantine's voice held impatience and a hint of disgust.

"Something's wrong, but my partner knows what to do." Juan walked over to Gerard. He felt Juan standing above him and braced himself for a kick to the face or the gut. "Maybe we should take a peek from the air. See if they went down."

"MacLeod will crash the plane with both of us in it if we don't have his daughter." Constantine's voice dropped to a low growl. "He's been waiting years for a chance to go out in glory."

Gerard kept his face expressionless, but it goaded him how close to the truth Constantine hit. For too many years after Mary and Andee had left, he'd taken the FBI jobs on the edge, the ones with high risk and low percentage of success. If only his colleagues at the bureau really knew what had driven him and his reputation, maybe they would have forced him to retire much sooner. Maybe change his name, his identity. He would have become someone different. An insurance salesman or a carpenter. Someone who lived a simpler life, one without people shooting at him or his loved ones.

He would have found Mary and stuck around until she believed his apology. And someday he would have driven that haunted, sad look from Andee's eyes. Instead he'd hidden his pain, his regret, and in the end had only caused more.

"She probably crashed into the side of a mountain." Constantine pushed back his chair, the sound grating against the floor. "Always trying to keep up with her old man."

No, Andee so far outpassed him. Even as a child, she'd amazed him. Like the time he'd guided Andee through a dead-stick landing at Anaktuvuk Pass. She'd been sixteen, so pretty, so ready to embrace life. She'd been copiloting for years, but when he finally handed her the controls, it felt as if he'd taken out a piece of his heart and tied it to the propeller.

His palms had sweat as he'd clutched his knees, and he felt her fear as she had eased the plane down, glancing at him for rescue. It took all his strength not to reach out and seize the controls. He'd gauged their altitude, judging the moment when he would take the yoke and land them safely. But he knew that she needed to learn to trust her instincts and her abilities, so he had fought his impulses.

She hadn't disappointed. Rather, he'd never felt so proud of her in his entire life as when they'd touched down on the runway. However, he bore the weight that she probably didn't see the lesson the same way. He'd disappointed her in so many ways it nearly crippled him.

"We'll just have to wait. At least another twenty-four hours." Juan walked away.

Gerard breathed a sigh of relief through his aching ribs. *Don't come home, Andee.* How it hurt to wish those words— again—for his only daughter.

Chapter 9

"I'M NOT HIKING out of these mountains without you." Mac's words resonated in her mind as Andee cooked supper on the stove in front of their makeshift shelters. She didn't know why, but for the first time since the crash she didn't feel quite so alone. Yes, she knew God had been with them—from the miraculous fact that they hadn't all been torn apart in the crash to the strength God had given them to pull Ishbane and Flint up the cliff today. But feeling that she suddenly had an equal on her side, helping her lead the passengers to safety, ministered to a barren place within her.

Who would have believed that God would give her a stubborn Scot to help her? Even though Mac had left Sarah when she'd told him not to, he had put his own life in danger when he'd skidded down that mountain to help her pull up Flint. Andee knew they'd all be a pile of broken bones tonight if he hadn't stepped in with his more-than-ample muscles.

It had taken them twice as long to descend the scree hill after they'd recovered. Flint, aided by Phillips and Nina, descended as a trio, belayed together. Ishbane was next, and Andee had to give the man credit for facing his fears. Mac followed, cradling Sarah in his strong arms. Andee's heart gave out just a little at that. Andee came last, unbelayed, rolling up the rope, knowing that they'd need it for crossing the Granite River.

They camped at the base of the mountain, the light having dissolved quickly during their descent. Andee had showed them how to secure the tarp at an angle into the hill and separated it into two, so the men could sleep in one and the ladies in the other. She'd fastened the tarp low to the ground with basket-ball-sized boulders around the edges. The tarp would protect them from the frigid wind that rushed up the mountain. Andee counted on their body heat to keep the temperature above hypothermic levels. She'd made the passengers layer their clothes before they'd left the wreckage, which would help them live through the night.

She stirred the soup, knowing that tomorrow their rations would have to be cut in half. Half a PowerBar. Half the soup. Half a cup of coffee for breakfast.

And twice as far to go.

Sarah lay in quiet repose, breathing steadily, her heart rate normal, her body caught in slumber. She'd nearly opened her eyes earlier, groaning and murmuring when Andee helped Mac set her down, but when Andee tried to rouse her, sleep reached out and tugged her back.

Andee should leave them, go for help. The fact that Sarah hadn't awoken scared her nearly breathless. She could make it—she knew it. She could take the flashlight, find the Granite River, follow it to Disaster like she'd planned.

She could be home by sundown tomorrow. Maybe.

In the meantime, Phillips could go for water, leaving the rest—namely Mac—to watch over Sarah.

After Andee poured the soup, she passed it around to the passengers seated around the darkened campsite. Few spoke, wrung out by exhaustion. Ishbane took his soup, greedily slurping it. Andee had surrendered her emergency blanket to him, knowing that he'd perish in the night with the cold. She'd snuggle next to Sarah. Besides, it wasn't like she'd sleep much.

Another good reason to leave tonight.

She put out the stove, and the night chased away the light. Stars winked at her, spilled out over the heavens like icicles. The wind whipped over the tarp, flapping the edges. Andee tucked her hands into her armpits, thankful she had her layers of silk long johns, fleece pullovers, and wool pants.

"I could go for a steak with fried taters and collards," said Flint. The big man hadn't complained once today, despite his brush with death.

"Or a big bowl of yellow curried chicken with honey and green onions and rice," Ishbane said.

Andee couldn't help but smile. Team Hope occasionally played this game when they were out overnight. Micah liked grits, Conner wanted flapjacks, Sarah loved pierogi from a deli near her apartment in Queens, and Dani would give her eyeteeth for hot buttered popcorn. It made Andee miss them all with an ache that went to the center of her body. She wondered if anyone would call her on her birthday and discover her missing.

"How about a stack of pancakes with pure maple syrup," Phillips added. "My mom's version of a Sunday night meal."

"My mother made haggis on Sundays," Mac said quietly. "Every Sunday after church we'd come home to haggis and stovies. Her nod toward our family traditions from the old country."

Andee glanced at Mac, detecting the change in him since yesterday. The outline of his face in the darkness spoke of strength. He sat with his back against a boulder, one leg drawn up, holding his Sierra cup in one hand.

"My mother made haggis once." Andee made a face.

Mac laughed, low and strong, and it warmed her. She saw Mac in her thoughts, how he'd been as they'd erected the shelter. Quiet, as if shaken by the day's events, he'd worked with precision as the night closed in. Wide back, strong arms, his eyes occasionally running over her, as if he too knew that for a moment he'd soothed the frightened place inside her. It made her that much more aware of the way she tingled when touched by his gaze.

"I wonder if they've figured out we crashed," Nina said.

That statement silenced the passengers and wound its way into Andee's thoughts. Would her father contact her mother when she didn't show up in Disaster? Probably not. He'd assume she had taken another charter flight and probably not check on her for days. Besides, he'd always believed she could take care of herself and never let himself worry, even when she'd needed him the most. But certainly the Alaska Mountain Rescue Group would search for them. If only the plane hadn't veered off in the wrong direction. It might take weeks for the rescuers to head west toward Foggytop, especially without the ELT working.

"How many children do you have, Nina?" Andee asked, hoping to fill the questions that lingered in the darkness.

"Three. Two boys and a girl."

Andee imagined them with deep brown eyes and dark brown hair, like Nina. "Are they with your husband? or relatives?"

"Yes. With relatives," Nina said. But something in her voice sounded unsure. It reminded Andee of her sophomore summer of college when she'd called her mother from Fairbanks en route to visit her father. Her mother had asked her where she was, and Andee had lied.

Of course, that hadn't stopped Mary from finding her a month later. Andee wondered if she'd known all along and couldn't bear the showdown.

"I'm supposed to be going home today," Ishbane said. His tone held surprise, as if normal life only existed in theory now. "My wedding anniversary is this weekend."

Ishbane had a wife? That surprised her. Not that he shouldn't, but she'd pegged Flint or even Phillips as married, not Ishbane. "She'll be worried," Andee said.

"Maybe. We're separated."

Andee grieved, cognizant of what those words meant, especially to a man so seemingly bereft of hope. She had the crazy urge to tell Ishbane that she'd been on the painful side of separation, watching her mother lurch through her day, feeling herself surrounded by shadow. She couldn't help but wonder if her mother might have chosen differently if she'd been given the foresight to see what leaving would cost them. Or if her father had chased them south just once, her mother might have returned with him.

"Where's home, Ishbane?" Flint asked.

"Toronto. I'm in oil, and our company is doing some drilling in the Yukon Territory. I was supposed to consult with some engineers at TAPS."

"Hopefully they'll miss you."

"How about you, Mr. Phillips?" Nina asked. "You aren't dressed for hunting."

"I'm a fisherman," Phillips said cryptically.

"Oh," Nina said.

Silence played a beat between them as they waited for Phillips to continue. He didn't.

"What about you, Mac?" Nina asked, rebounding.

He said nothing.

Occasionally, Andee had seen Micah or Conner go silent, caught in some dark memory or just keeping essential information close to their chest. She had learned not to push.

"I'm from Deadhorse," he said at last.

Deadhorse, Alaska, south of Prudhoe Bay. Despite the cold and barren climate, the people in Deadhorse had carved a life out of the snowfields, bonded by their work for the pipeline or their love of living on the last frontier. In such a remote place, people protected their traditions with the ferocity of a wolf. Clearly, his parents had clung to their Scottish heritage and given Mac his hint of accent.

"Do you have family there?" Flint asked. "Seems to me a lonely place to go for vacation."

Mac gave a low, wry chuckle, and the sound felt like a ripple under Andee's skin. Familiar yet new. "My parents still live there as well as four sisters, their husbands, my nieces and nephews."

"Poor bum. The only boy surrounded by girls. I'm sorry for you." Flint laughed.

Mac didn't. His silence felt thick and heavy. Finally he said, "I had a brother. He was killed last summer in a fishing accident."

No wonder Mac seemed far away, burdened. No wonder he wanted them all to hike out together. Andee's memory went to the many hunters and fishermen she'd airlifted to medical help. Too many bled out in her plane, something she hoped to fix someday by building an emergency trauma center/Fixed Base Operation (FBO) in Wiseman, Alaska, the halfway point between Prudhoe Bay and Fairbanks.

"I'm sorry, Mac," she said. Then, because she knew his words invaded their thoughts and would poke at them through the night, "We're going to make it, you guys. I promise."

"What if something happens to you—you fall off a cliff or something?" Ishbane asked. His voice lowered, as if, once the question had been breathed aloud, the cosmic odds might latch on to it and bring it to fruition.

"Mac will take care of you," she answered in an even tone. *Please, please, Mac, don't refute me.*

Thankfully, he stayed quiet. She'd take that as a good sign.

She got up and collected the cups. "I'm turning in. We have a long walk tomorrow."

Andee settled next to Sarah, listening to the group shift or groan, relaxing into slumber. She occasionally lifted her hand to check Sarah's breathing and her pulse.

Mac would take care of them. She knew it from the way he watched the group, had risked his own life today to save Flint—no, save them all. Deep inside that mysterious, quiet exterior she suspected a man who would surrender his life for others.

Which meant she could leave.

She waited until she heard Nina's deep breaths of slumber; then Andee eased out the flashlight, a flare, and a PowerBar and took a quick drink of water. She left her knife but tucked her gun into her jacket. Anything more would slow her down.

"Please, watch over Sarah, Lord," she whispered. Then she lifted the edge of the shelter and crept out into the night.

✦ ✦ ✦

Mac could hardly believe it. Here he'd begun to trust Emma, and then in a blinding moment of deceit she'd snuck out.

Mac lay there in the dark, his heart thumping against his ribs, tapping out Morse code for *fool*, listening to Emma's sure footsteps. Why did he so easily fall for a betrayer's smile?

Because she seemed to authentically care for her friend, for the passengers. Because when she'd risked her life for Flint, she'd done it with passion and 200 percent commitment.

Because in those pretty brown eyes, he'd thought he'd read honesty.

This time, he hated the fact that he was right. He'd found his saboteur. Why else would she sneak out in the middle of the night, nearly running as she escaped camp?

He waited until her footfalls dropped away and then quietly moved out into the night after her.

He'd drag her back to the shelter over his shoulder if he had to and tie her up with her own rope, then use the radio to call in the cavalry. If he could, he'd also get the truth out of her. Somehow.

Maybe he shouldn't think beyond right now as he followed her without a sound across the tundra. He could barely make her out in the darkness, with the sky speckled with stars, the moon full and bright turning the tundra to glistening silver. She moved with precision, slowing her pace slightly, but quickly enough to make excellent time. To where? Disaster? What if she'd landed purposely, if not gracefully, with the hopes of meeting her contacts in these hills? How far were they from the pipeline? From the map, he'd guesstimate maybe ten miles.

Ten miles too close.

Since 9/11, he'd tracked down two more scares, not including the so-called renegade hunter from last summer— the one who'd done real damage.

More serious damage to the pipeline would shut off supplies for months and skyrocket the price of oil. When winter closed in, medical and food supplies dependent on airplanes would be scarce in towns like Deadhorse.

His sister Maren, pregnant with her third child, wouldn't

be able to get to Fairbanks, and his niece Anna, suffering from diabetes, would run out of insulin.

Those thoughts fueled his steps, and he lit out into a run toward Emma. How dare she put those lives into jeopardy, play the heroine all this time only to betray her country.

If America was her country. With her dark looks, she could be from any of the South American countries vying for a place on the global oil market. Like Venezuela, for example. He'd read in one of the recent reports that the leader of Venezuela, Hugo Chavez, had actually teamed up with Iran to raise oil prices to America.

If Mac did the math, it seemed that Venezuela—number four on the world supplier's list—had much to profit from if America's wells suddenly dried up.

The tundra muffled his footsteps but not his anger, and Mac caught up to Emma quickly. She became more than an outline; she became a three-dimensional figure in the darkness, breathing and swinging her arms. She held a darkened flashlight in her right hand. Against the vault of night shining on her, she seemed like a blip of pure energy.

He sprinted up behind her, caught her arm, whipped her to a stop.

She screamed, one short burst, then hit him across the head with the flashlight.

Slightly reeling, he grabbed her other arm. *Wow, she can pack a wallop.* But her eyes were wide and her mouth open as if even she couldn't believe she'd hit him.

Or maybe that he'd caught her?

"Mac!"

"Yeah, that's right."

She sighed, as if she knew her plot had been revealed. "I'm sorry, Mac, but you have to let me go."

"Over my dead body."

"No, preferably not." She tried to twist out of his grip and frowned when he didn't let her go. "Let me go, Mac. I promise you I'll bring back help. But this is the only way. You saw the other passengers. They're worn out, and we're making horrible time. This time tomorrow we'll be out of food, and we might not be near water yet. I have to go."

She thought she could fool him with this story line? He shook his head.

Her eyes narrowed. "You don't think I can do it?"

He should have been prepared, but her momentary disbelief had him unbalanced. She twisted out of his grip and jumped away from him. He lunged for her, but she stumbled back and launched out with a kick at him.

"Leave me alone!" She backed up. "I might be small, but I promise you that if you touch me, you won't walk away upright." Despite her bravado, her voice shook, her emotions breaking through.

Oh no. His chest constricted, and a sick feeling welled inside him. Either she thought fast on her feet as a terrorist, or she believed he'd snuck out after her to attack her.

He held up his hands as if in surrender. "I'm sorry, Emma. I'm really sorry. I—well, I promise I won't hurt you. I would never . . . I . . . just can't let you leave."

She froze, staring at him with fear in those kind eyes.

He'd done some stupid things before—like chase after a terrorist without backup—and apparently hadn't learned anything from that lesson. This time he was accusing a woman who might be a hero of being a traitor.

No, she *had* to be a hero. After everything she'd done, how could he possibly still suspect her?

"Why not?" Emma's voice sounded so thin he could barely hear it in the night.

He wanted to tell her, but the truth on his lips would sound so incredulous he couldn't push the words out. "We . . . need you."

Oh no. That could be worse. Because it sounded more like "I need you," and while he'd begun to wonder—just a little— about that, he couldn't admit it.

Mac didn't need anyone. Or rather didn't *want* to need anyone. If he was honest, he did need her, not only as a trail guide but to keep everyone glued together while he figured out who owned the map and the radio he'd found. While he tried to find out who might be a terrorist.

She sighed and ran her gloved hands over her face. Her shoulders slumped, and her voice dropped to a murmur. "I'm so sorry that I got everyone into this mess."

He didn't know exactly how to interpret her words. He moved closer to her, his curiosity meter on high, but with enough wisdom to know when to mask it. "C'mon back." He reached out, as if to take her hand, but she moved away from him. Thankfully, she began to walk in the right direction. He followed.

"If I hadn't wanted to get into the air and get back for my birthday this weekend with Sarah, we'd be safe in the Fairbanks Airport right now. I'm such an idiot."

Her voice sounded so forlorn he couldn't help but touch her shoulder. She turned and looked at him, and he gave her a small smile. "You couldn't have known the clouds would turn to ice."

"A good pilot reads the weather. We should be prepared for anything."

"Seems to me you were. Look at us. Safe, fed, sorta warm."

"Sarah's hurt."

He nodded, realizing how prominent that thought hung in her mind. The top layer that eclipsed all other considerations, including her personal safety. Once he broke free of his suspicions, he wasn't so stupid that he couldn't tell she was putting her life in danger by hiking out alone. "She'll be okay. You have to believe that."

"I keep thinking about that Bible verse Phillips quoted last night," Emma said. "Something about Paul expecting to die and learning to rely on God, so He could deliver him. I keep praying that God is going to get us out of this mess, that He'll watch over us—"

"I think He did that today when we nearly went over the cliff. If you hadn't—"

"No, if *you* hadn't come down to help us." A smile flickered on her face. "You were an answer to my prayers today, the way you helped Sarah, put up the shelter, and saved Flint."

Mac wasn't sure what to say to that. Instead, he nodded. Or shrugged. "Do you truly believe God cares about the details, like our shelter or even saving Sarah's life?" He wasn't sure what allowed him to ask that. Maybe being out here alone, without anyone to shout recriminations at him. Without his mother to send him a frown of disapproval. He'd been raised never to question God. Yet when he'd stumbled upon a terrorist in the woods, only to sacrifice his brother's life . . . well, he'd had big, big questions for God.

None, it seemed, that had been answered.

"I do believe that," Emma said. "He'll get us out of these mountains."

"I . . . I want to believe that, Emma." He even lifted his gaze skyward, to where God lived, the void of space that separated the God of his childhood from the God he knew today.

The God that let "little details"—like his brother's life—
fall through the cracks.

But he hadn't come out here to confront the wounds in his
soul. "We won't make it if you leave us," Mac said. "We have to
stick together."

"Our safety doesn't depend on me." Emma shoved her
hands into her pockets. "Have you ever felt saddled with a
choice you couldn't seem to make?"

His mind swept over the terrain of his life, seeing places
and situations when he'd had to sacrifice time with his family or
dreams for the sake of his job. His fishing trip with Brody had
been an attempt to regain all that. Yet without a blink he'd
made the choice to race after Al-Hasid.

"I've made choices I regret," he said slowly, painfully
aware that he'd opened a corner of his heart for her to peek
into. But perhaps a new ordinary life meant letting someone
inside gradually.

Someone with sweet brown eyes, freckles, and a smile that
could keep him putting one step ahead of another. A smile he
could learn to trust. Maybe.

"How do you live with that . . . regret?" Emma asked.

Overhead, he saw a swirl of color—lavender, pink,
white—undulating against the night sky. "I guess I keep my
head down and keep going forward." No, that wasn't entirely
all—he also didn't stop long enough to get mired in the details.
Like relationships. Like broken hearts. "The northern lights
seem especially bright tonight."

Emma looked up at the sky. "I've always thought they were
a reminder of God, of His brightness, His creativity against the
bleakness of the moment." She sighed. "In the Lower 48, I
work on a search-and-rescue team. We call ourselves Team
Hope because we go in when all other hope has died."

He studied her, her profile. She had a small nose, a slight smile, a heart-shaped face perfectly framed by her stocking cap. He had the sudden memory of her in his arms when he'd pulled her from the plane, and he had to ignore the desire to twirl a finger into her curly hair. When she looked at him and smiled, he felt his heart leap.

It was such an odd, exhilarating, terrifying feeling that he nearly lifted his hand to his chest to calm himself.

"I can't help but think that I should go for help, Mac. But I'm afraid that if Sarah wakes up, I won't be there. That she'll need me, and in the end I'll fail her." She didn't look at him when she spoke, and he had the feeling that she might be speaking about someone else besides her friend.

He could relate. He'd had that feeling for the better part of his career. That if he didn't pay attention, something would spiral right out of his hands. That everyone he loved would be killed and he'd be left alone, staring at the holes in his life. At his failures.

"So, you really grew up in Deadhorse," she said, cutting through his thoughts.

"Aye. Why?"

"Frankly, your accent threw me off. My father's Scottish, but aside from the occasional *aye* and *laddie*, he sounds like an American. Although your accent is only a bit stronger, something about you seems fresh from the Highlands. I feel like I should address you as 'my laird' or something."

He smiled. "If you want to, my bonnie lass."

She studied him with the barest hint of a smile.

"The truth is," Mac said, "I was born in Scotland, and my father came over in the early seventies to work the pipeline. He had an engineering degree, and despite his love of the Highlands, he couldn't turn down the opportunity to work on the project. He's still one of the primary engineers."

He watched the lavender ribbon of the borealis curl in the heavens before he continued.

"Farewell to the Highlands, farewell to the North,
The birth-place of Valour, the country of Worth;
Wherever I wander, wherever I rove,
The hills of the Highlands for ever I love."

His words died out, taken by the wind, and in the silence he felt like an idiot. Where had that come from?

Emma wore an odd expression. "You're a poet?" Only she didn't laugh, and her voice sounded the slightest bit impressed.

He liked impressed. In fact, a strange warmth kindled inside. "My father loves Robert Burns. Made us all learn a few verses."

"Do you know anymore?"

"Aye." He smiled.

"As fair art thou, my bonie lass,
So deep in luve am I;
And I will luve thee still, my dear,
Till a' the seas gang dry."

Her gaze stayed on him, and he felt his mouth dry. He cleared his throat. "So, you really thought I was from Scotland?" he asked, his voice a little tight.

Emma shrugged. "I was trying to figure out how much time you'd spent in the backcountry."

"Hey, I did my time. Back when I worked for the police department and later as a TAPS security officer before I joined the bureau. Even barely escaped the claws of a grizzly sow once."

"All right, I'm sorry." Emma shuddered. "I hate grizzlies. They terrify me. One wandered near our cabin when I was about eight. It would have torn me to bits if my father hadn't been there with his hunting rifle. I stared at those glassy black eyes, those claws, those teeth, and just . . . stood there. Unable to move. I couldn't decide whether to run, play dead, or climb a tree."

"Climb a tree," Mac said. He had a hard time imagining Emma freezing in terror over anything after he'd seen her bolt into action today. "Always better to get up high out of reach."

"Can you fly a plane?"

Mac nodded. "Took lessons in Fairbanks a few years ago; the agency sponsored it."

"So you're really FBI?" She looked at him, and he sensed more in her question than just conversation.

"For now. I . . . I'm thinking of resigning." Somehow his family understood, but he'd barely been able to get his mind around his failure. He just couldn't spend the rest of his life seeing Brody's face every time he closed his eyes. Deep inside, Mac knew that until he got face-to-face with Andy MacLeod, show him exactly what his decision had cost Mac and his family, he'd never find closure. Never escape his demons, maybe never be able to do his job right.

"Is it because of your brother?" Emma's voice was quiet, compassionate.

Mac swallowed hard, caught off guard. Was he that trans-parent? He sighed. What would it matter if he told her, if he let her into his life just a little further? He knew it was an area he should work on anyway, especially if someday he wanted what his sisters had. What Brody should have had—a wife, a family, a heritage. "Aye, it's complicated."

She nodded. "All I can think about is being with my family right now. With Micah and Conner and Dani."

"You have a big family."

She gave a huff of laughter. "No, they're my Team Hope pals. But they feel like family. More family than I've ever had." She looked at him, and he saw sadness in her eyes. "My parents separated when I was sixteen. They never divorced, however, so I was left with that hanging hope they'd somehow reconcile."

"What happened?" His own parents had fought, sometimes raucous shouting affairs that raised the roof. But they also loved each other with a fierceness that had taught Mac exactly what committed love looked like.

"Me," she said simply. She stared at the sky, and he felt the loneliness in her voice.

Me. It occurred to him that maybe her lonely flights across the sky above the jagged terrain resembled his own escape into a career that kept him moving and above the pull of relationships and heartache.

"I'm sorry," he said.

"What was your brother's name?" Emma asked.

"Brody. He was two years younger than me. He died in my arms."

She blew out a breath. "I'm so sorry."

"The thing is, he could have lived. A pilot flew over, and I even radioed him, but he refused to land. Brody bled to death."

She gasped. Then she closed her eyes, as if bearing that pain with him.

Seeing her reaction ministered to the place his grief had rubbed raw. He couldn't stop himself from touching her hair.

She opened her eyes, frowning. He couldn't define it as fear or surprise, but he pulled his hand away. Still, the gesture lingered between them, and he felt something warm bloom in his chest.

Something warm and alive and growing in a place he'd long thought frozen over.

Chapter 10

SHE'D KILLED MAC'S brother. She'd *killed* Mac's brother. His story cut close—*too* close—and Andee couldn't bear to ask him if it had happened near the Dalton Highway. The truth gnawed at her as Mac herded her back to camp. She had no words for this intense grief.

She lay under the tarp long into the night, disbelief burning her eyes until tears ran into her ears. *"He died in my arms."* She couldn't bear to think how that felt.

Andee finally rolled onto her side, listening to Sarah breathe, praying that exhaustion might take over and plunge her into sleep. . . .

She dreamed of that moment when she'd felt alive and free and innocent, before her life had turned into a bad soap opera. The silence of a plane hurtling to the earth from three thousand feet, without a prop or any power to keep it aloft swept through her mind. Wind whistled against the cockpit window, and the little Cessna shook with the force of the turbulent descent.

Across from her, in the pilot's seat, Gerard MacLeod sat, his hands on his thighs, stone still, breathing in and out as if they were fly-fishing in Disaster Creek instead of plunging to their deaths.

Andee heard her voice, young and afraid, some ethereal part of herself caught in time. "Gerard, do something!"

"Keep your glide speed under 100 knots; cut your mixture. Turn off your master switch."

Andee's hands shook as she complied, holding the yoke as if it might offer her some control. They were falling out of the sky. Her heart had left her body somewhere up there in the firmament.

"Do you see the landing site?" Gerard asked.

Andee spied it, a strip of brown furrowed out of the tundra. She nodded.

"Keep your horizon level. Bring her in steady. Lower your flaps and cut your speed to 60."

Andee held her breath as the ground rushed at her. Beside her, Gerard made no movement to assist. Didn't he care that they were about to be crushed and turned into a ball of fire?

"Daddy!"

"Hold her steady, Emma. You can do this."

"I can't."

"You can. You have to." He left the rest unspoken, but Andee already knew the rest. He wasn't going to help. He expected her to face her fears, consider her options, and make wise decisions.

Their lives in the bush dictated that she learn to survive.

She swallowed, centered her plane on approach.

"Ease it down, tail slightly low."

They touched, bounced, landed again, jarring Andee's jaw. Her father didn't even flinch. "Brakes, Emma."

Brakes! She hit the brakes, fighting the yoke, the burn of her calves. The plane jerked, slowing too quickly. She eased up and let it bump and shake until it came to a stop.

Andee leaned forward, her head on the yoke. Euphoria bubbled out of her, a sort of heady, unbridled joy that started in her stomach and reeled out into laughter. She leaned back, tears streaking her face.

Gerard smiled. "You did it. Great job."

She looked at him, at the pride in his brown eyes, so much like hers, and felt more explosions of joy. She wanted to be everything he was and more. To be the best, the bravest, the most adventurous.

"Uh-oh," Gerard said, looking past her. His expression dimmed.

She turned to see her mother hurrying over the tarmac. Her dark hair streamed out behind her, her caribou jacket flapping open. Her expression turned Andee cold.

So, so cold.

"Emma, wake up!" The voice sliced through that moment when Andee saw her life separate into two pieces.

She blinked awake. The barest of light dented the gray pallor inside the tarp. Andee's nose felt stiff and hard, her joints ached, and her back felt as if a moose had trampled it. Probably from the strain of holding up Ishbane and Flint on belay yesterday.

"You were whimpering." Nina wore a motherly concern on her wide face.

"I'm okay, thanks. Just a bad dream." Andee pushed up, turned, and studied Sarah, who'd slept fitfully. The fact that Sarah seemed to want to break free of the cocoon of slumber buoyed Andee's hope. She checked her pulse and her eyes and nudged her. "Sarah? Sarah, wake up."

Sarah's eyes flickered, a groan emerged, but while Andee held her breath, nothing else happened.

"She made noises in the night," Nina said. "It sounded like

she said a name." She reached out to brush Sarah's hair from her face. "Frank, maybe?"

"Hank. Her boyfriend." Andee looked at the bandage around Sarah's head, then closed her eyes in repose. Hank would be beside himself with worry if he saw Sarah now. A Texan with a personality larger than his state, he'd courted Sarah without any stops and swept her clean off her feet. Andee wouldn't be surprised if the man proposed any day. No wonder Sarah dreamed of him in her darkest hour.

Andee felt a spark of jealousy. She hadn't had a boyfriend since . . . well, never. At least not like Hank. She'd had dates in high school, a close friend in college who'd wanted more. But she kept moving, always one step ahead of relationships that might suck her down to ground level. She couldn't bear to let a man not only deflate her dreams but wound her the way her parents' separation had wounded each other.

As it was, she'd inadvertently let Mac tread around the edges of her heart. It would help if he weren't so . . . unpredictable. Sullen and argumentative one second, brave and painfully sweet the next. Like when she'd caught him touching her hair, a look of concern on his face. It had found her unguarded soft spots and settled there. And his poetry-quoting moment didn't help in the least.

Who was Stirling McRae?

"We need to get going." Andee climbed out of the shelter, amazed at the difference in temperature. Inside, she could make out her breath with each word. Outside, the wind yanked it from her body, made her wrap her arms around her waist.

"Cold morning, aye?" Mac sat on the scree slope, his arms on his knees, booted feet digging into the earth, and a slight smile tipping his mouth. He wore three days' worth of whiskers on his chin, and his hair tangled in the wind, free of the cap now shoved into his pocket.

Oh no. Just when she thought she'd braced herself for the day. She wondered how long he'd been sitting here, watching the sky or her shelter. Protecting her?

The thought churned up a trampled longing inside her.

"We need to get moving soon. I'm going to heat some coffee." She had dragged her backpack behind her and now dug out the coffee, along with the gas container. "I think we have about six miles to the Granite River. From there, it's easy to navigate to Disaster Creek."

Mac nodded. "Flint's barely hanging on."

Andee added gas to the stove, primed it, then lit it with her lighter. "In this situation, pain is good. We need to know if he's getting worse. If I medicate him, he'll only push harder. Pain tells us when to slow down and ask for help."

Mac quirked an eyebrow. "I don't see you knowing when to ask for help."

Andee turned her back to him. Okay, yes, she knew she had some issues in the asking-for-help area. But out here, a person had to depend on herself. It had taken her years to learn to rely on her Team Hope friends. She wasn't going to dole out all her trust to the first good-looking Scot.

She knelt beside the stove and poured water into the pot. She had instant coffee, and today they'd share the packets. Maybe tomorrow at this time, she'd be having a birthday breakfast at Soapy Smith's Pioneer Restaurant in Fairbanks. Or with her father in Disaster.

And wouldn't that be fun? Her father probably wouldn't even remember that thirty years ago tomorrow he'd flown her mother to a doctor in Bettles, where she'd given birth to their only child. Or that fourteen years ago he'd helped them exit his life. Maybe she should delete tomorrow from the calendar.

Andee shook the thought away. She'd long ago surrendered her missed birthdays, Christmases, and major life events into the hands of the Lord. Just because she felt vulnerable, tired, and overwhelmed didn't mean she had to meander the road of what-ifs. She simply hadn't been gifted with people who readjusted their agenda for her. Except for Sarah. And look where that had gotten Sarah.

"How's Sarah today?" Mac asked, as if reading her mind. He knelt beside her, and his sudden presence, along with the breeze reaping his masculine scent, startled her.

"I don't know. She's breathing okay."

Mac nodded, took the packets of coffee, and emptied them into the cups. Apparently, he'd passed his math classes because he evenly divided the portions between the six cups. "When I was ten, my brother and I were wrestling. I dropped him on his head on the concrete floor of our house. He was in and out of consciousness for three days. Back then, we had a once-a-week flight out from Deadhorse, with the occasional medical flight."

As Andee listened to his story, his accent, his low tone, her throat felt scratchy. Her emotions simmered right under her skin today, and if she didn't watch it, she'd break into idiotic tears.

"My mom prayed and my father called in help. A low ceiling and temperatures below minus fifty delayed the flight. By the time they arrived five days later, Brody was better. They took him to Fairbanks anyway and then to Anchorage for a CAT scan. He'd had a slight concussion, but it had resolved itself. My father said it was because of my mother's prayers. It reminds me of what Phillips said—that God resurrects people from the dead because of our prayers."

"I didn't think you believed in God," she said, holding his gaze.

A slight smile flickered across Mac's face. "I believe in God. I'm just not sure He believes in me. Not anymore. But He'd probably listen to you."

Andee frowned, hoping he might elaborate, but Mac rose, carrying coffee to the men's shelter.

✦ ✦ ✦

Emma had the tenacity to rival any of his sisters, cousins, or the entire population of the McRae family still etching out life in the Scottish highland village of Dalwhinnie. Aware of the limitations of their scraggly group, she stopped often for short breaks, making sure everyone got a sip of water, taking pulse rates, and checking for dehydration. He felt like he might be with his mother or the bureau psychologist who'd taken her best shot at digging into his psyche after Brody's death. In front of Ms. Relax-and-Tell-Me-What's-on-Your-Mind, he'd felt numb and void of feelings, especially the kind he might spill into a report for his boss.

Without blinking, he'd revealed information to Emma straight from his soul, a piece of himself that he still hadn't gotten his brain around. God didn't believe in him? Normally he'd attribute those words to cynicism, but six hours of hiking and hauling a seriously wounded woman through the tundra of northern Alaska made him push that sentence around in his head for a good look.

He'd had a cerebral, wide-angle view of God pretty much since he was a teenager. Mac saw Him as the creator. The One to whom Mac would answer when the final note on his bagpipe faded. He'd made a profession of faith early on, had been baptized by a missionary, grew up on the meat and potatoes of Bible stories and the Gospels. Still, he had a hard time seeing God's touch in the every day. Yes, he could buy the occasional miracle—lives raised from the dead or even near misses that he felt pretty sure God caught in His capable hands. But God involved in his everyday life? If Mac still believed that, he'd chucked that belief into the wind the day Brody bled out in his arms. God could have deflected the bullet, tripped Brody, or even given him a willing pilot to help save his brother's life. How hard would that have been?

God didn't care about the big pictures or little details, and He didn't get involved in daily lives—at least not in Mac's. If He had, God would have heard Mac's cries as Brody's blood saturated his clothes.

Maybe, however, God heard the prayers of people like Emma. She deserved it, with her die-hard spirit, her patience, the way she cared for people. Obviously his now-discarded belief that Emma might be a terrorist only proved his abysmal skill at judging character. Perhaps that bureau psychologist should have probed a bit harder.

At lunch, Nina and Phillips lounged behind the rest of the group, propped against her backpack. Flint lay spread-eagle, staring at the sky. Ishbane sat farther away, his back to them. Emma had handed out PowerBars, half each. Mac watched her unwrap hers, slowly nibbling at each bite.

"So, what do you do when you're not flying or saving lives?" Mac had to admit, he had difficulty picturing Emma's life outside this wilderness.

She moved over to Sarah, checked her pulse, then tucked the sleeping bag around her neck. "I read a lot."

"No fishing or wrestling grizzlies with your bare hands?"

"I'm afraid of grizzlies, remember?" She grinned.

"I just figured a bush pilot would be busy doing something . . . rugged on her off hours."

"Oh, I love being outdoors. I lived for the days when my father would return after a monthlong absence, cash in his pocket from ferrying hunters or fishermen or flying the mail to remote villages. He'd plunk the money into my mother's tin flour can, then drag us out to the plane. It felt like Christmas unloading all those boxes from Fairbanks filled with food or clothing or books. But the best part was the next few days. Gerard would take me fishing or hunting, snowshoeing, or even mushing the dogs out to check the trap lines.

"I still love being outside. Sarah and I joke that our perfect vacation is a three-day backpacking trip. But I like a five-star hotel with a whirlpool, some honey-grilled salmon, and a decent Caesar salad on occasion. I *do* know how to use silverware and real linen napkins." She giggled, and he smiled at the sound. "Actually, I don't have much free time anymore. I'm saving for an airplane, so every last nickel goes toward a down payment."

"You don't own the wreckage we left on Foggytop?"

She shook her head, wincing slightly. "That belongs to North Rim Outfitters, and they'll be thrilled to know it's totaled. No, my dream isn't quite so fancy. I'd be happy with an old twin-engine Ottertail outfitted with an Automated External Defibrillator, a couple of epi pens, portable O2 tanks, spine boards, poison antidotes, and at least one obstetrical kit. And that's just for starters."

"I'm seeing a link between the EMT gig in the Lower 48 and your summer job."

He liked the fact that she smiled at his knowledge of her life. Well, a good FBI agent pays attention.

"I have dreams of opening a Fixed Base Operation—

a hangar and possibly a medical clinic—in Wiseman, a sort of midway medical-transport service that would reach the northern rim, the villages in the Brooks Range, and even towns along the Dalton. Fairbanks has some excellent medical services, but up here, weather and conditions are so temperamental, we could use something closer. There are too many people who need immediate on-site care, who can't wait until they get to Fairbanks for emergency attention."

Mac's smile dimmed, his thoughts going to Brody. "If there had been something like that three months ago, my brother might still be alive."

Emma's expression clouded. She looked away. "I'm so sorry about your brother, Mac."

She'd already said that last night. Still, her compassion touched him. "Thanks, Emma."

"So, what do *you* do when you're not bossing people around and saving the world from catastrophe?" Emma asked, obviously trying to push past the painful moments that surrounded them—from the injuries, to their dire straits, to his brother's death.

Okay, he'd take that. "I do some carving, fishing—outdoor stuff, you know. In keeping with my macho persona."

She nodded, fighting a sweet smile.

"I also love to cook. And . . ." He couldn't believe he'd actually started to say it.

"What?"

He looked away.

"You're blushing! It must be something horrible. Let me guess." She rubbed her hands together in mock anticipation. "You knit?"

He shook his head.

"You're an opera singer?"

He let out a bellow of laughter, then a long, low tenor that echoed across the tundra, against the far hills.

Ishbane turned, making a face. Phillips chuckled.

"Nice," Emma added. "Okay, how about finger paint?"

"What?"

"Oh, sorry, it's from a movie I love, *The Cutting Edge*. It's about a hockey player who takes a job figure skating with this really cantankerous girl who can't keep a partner. He's from a mining town in Minnesota, a real blue-collar haven, and when he returns to tell his bar-owner brother what he's been doing . . . well, he's so embarrassed, he mumbles 'figure skating.' The brother can't hear him well and asks, so that the entire bar can hear him, 'finger painting?'" Emma shrugged, but he could nearly see the moment behind her twinkling eyes. "It's hilarious. So, you do much finger painting?"

Mac shook his head. "I do skate, though. Played right wing, pond hockey."

"Figured that. But that's not what made you blush. I'll bet you . . . dance."

He opened his mouth, disbelief filling in where words might have been.

She laughed. "I knew it! Swing dance?"

He felt tiny explosions of warmth inside him at her smile. "Nope. Highland fling."

"That I'd like to see."

Hmm. Maybe someday. He let that thought linger as she rose and hustled the group out of repose. She'd fit right in with his sisters, with their feisty, headstrong spirits, their laughter.

Whoa. He'd gotten way, *way* too far ahead of himself. All the same, perhaps he could enjoy Emma's company just a little.

"How did you guess?" He took the front of Sarah's stretcher, hoisted it to his shoulder.

Emma picked up the other end of Sarah's stretcher and kept pace with him as they slogged downhill through the tundra. "Because you always have to lead."

Oh.

Well, that wasn't such a horrible thing, was it?

The day barely lingered to illuminate their steps as they picked their way toward the Granite River. Flint, draped over Phillips's and Nina's shoulders, moaned, despite his obvious efforts to rake in his pain. Ishbane stumbled in their wake, fatigue weighing his shoulders, his demeanor.

The tundra, although it looked like a plush carpet of grass, turned out to be a boggy mass of freezing mud that sucked at their feet, saturating their boots. Mac's legs burned, and his shoulder muscles bunched in little fists of pain.

Emma slowed. "Shh. If you listen, you can hear the river." Perspiration dotted her face, despite the cool breeze and the sun's descent into the horizon.

Mac glanced over his shoulder, silenced his thoughts, and heard only the rush of wind.

Emma's expression was lit up as if the sound of running water might be booming in stereo across the hills. "I think it's right over this rise." She motioned toward the shadowed hump that rose on their left. Covered in white artic cotton, it looked like snow against the reddish blaze of tundra grass.

With the night encroaching, she didn't wait for recommendations. She led them in a muddy hike across the swampy tundra, through icy water, and up the hill.

When they topped the hill, the smell of fresh flowing water caught Mac. He couldn't see it for the darkness, but he knew Emma had led them correctly.

Earning his trust.

He let that thought saturate him as they descended. Emma

turned on her light, surveying the path as Nina and Phillips picked their way down the hill, euphoria evident in their steps.

Ishbane practically ran across the soft ground to the river, twenty feet farther. As Emma shined her light to guide him, Ishbane made his way onto shore, cupped his hands, and drew water into his mouth.

"I can't believe you found it." Mac let the words spill out of his mouth before he had a chance to reel them in.

"Thanks for that vote of confidence," Emma said, but surprisingly, she didn't look angry. She must be very, very tired. "I'm just grateful we made it today."

Mac watched as she directed Phillips and Nina to erect the shelters, her soft tones gentle yet precise. She even helped Nina heat water; then the women washed and cleaned up the best they could.

Mac took the hint, located a bar of Ivory, his toothbrush, and toothpaste and did what he could to make himself presentable to the human race. He'd laughed at Emma when she suggested they bring the toiletries. Now it only added to his belief that he'd been a jerk.

When he returned from the river, feeling chilled but clean, he noticed that Emma had fired up the stove and begun cooking dinner. The light shone on the tight spirals of her dark hair. She made the last of the soup, passing it out and taking little for herself. She sat on a rock overlooking the river as she finished dinner, cradling a Sierra cup in her hands. The flow of the water, despite the sheen of ice caught in still pockets, backdropped the sound of the wind. The northern lights curled in a show of orange and red, a swath of fire across the sky.

"Sarah's still really groggy. She's moving some and groaning more but no coherent speech," Emma said, apparently noticing that Mac had edged closer to her. "She's getting dehydrated, and I don't have anything to start an IV. If we don't get help soon, she'll die."

She said nothing more, letting the wind and smells of the night fill in the moment. Then he saw a breath shudder out of her, a breath that look painfully like . . . crying.

The image he had of her—resilient, stubborn, solid—lurched inside him, nearly rocked right off its foundations.

She covered her face with one hand, and her shoulders shook. Emma *was* crying. She swallowed, as if fighting the tears, and the sound of it echoed across the tundra and into the places he kept barricaded.

"Don't . . . cry." The words felt so shallow in the face of her pain. Watching her try and hide her grief behind her hand made everything inside him hurt.

He glanced around to see if Nina might be around, but he couldn't see into the darkness. He was the only one within arm's distance.

He couldn't just sit there while her world crumbled around her. Besides, it rattled him more than he wanted to admit. He reached out, touching her shoulder. She didn't flinch, and he felt her body shake beneath his touch. "Emma?"

She breathed hard, ragged agonized breaths of pain that told him she bore so much more guilt and pain than he'd even guessed. Okay, he should inch out of his private world and really help her shoulder her load.

He scooted beside her on the boulder, wrapped one arm around her, and when she didn't resist, he used the other to pull her to his chest.

She curled into him. He rested his cheek against the top of her head, and for the first time in months—or maybe years—he let himself care about someone else.

Chapter 11

ANDEE DECIDED SHE must be having an out-of-body experience or something. She saw herself wrapped in Mac's embrace,
and everything inside her wanted to surrender and let herself
cling to the feeling of his strong arms around her. Only, she
couldn't fall apart. Deep inside she knew if she gave in now—
especially with Mac gently rocking, soothing, comforting—
she might never be able to pull herself back together again.

She wanted to cry for Sarah, for the unknown, and
because exhaustion filled her every pore. Most of all, she
wanted to weep for Brody, Mac's brother, the one who'd died
while she flew overhead. She wished she had the courage to
explain. But Mac's grief felt so raw, so fresh, and she couldn't
tell him. Not yet.

Especially with lives depending on her now. She needed
to keep Mac focused, keep herself focused. He had so much
anger inside—she heard it in his voice every time he mentioned
his brother. Who knew what would happen if she told him the
truth?

"I'm sorry. I'm okay . . . really," she mumbled, disentan-
gling herself from his embrace.

He let her go but looked at her, concern in his eyes. "It's
okay to cry, you know. You don't have to be invincible, Emma."

She shook her head, reining in the last of her escaping emotions. "I'm all right. I'm just . . . tired."

He reached up and ran a strand of her unruly hair through his fingers. "You're an amazing lady, Emma, but you are allowed to cry."

Her mouth opened slightly, and then she was fighting tears again. "I'm just worried about Sarah. She's like a sister to me. The only one I've ever had."

"You're an only child?"

She nodded.

He smirked. "Sometimes I wished I was an only child. My brother would get into trouble and blame it on me. Drove me crazy. When I was twelve, he accidentally set the barn on fire. We were making a fort out of old mattresses my mother had stored in there, and he was cold. We had an old stove my father used when he worked on snow machines, and Brody lit it. Only, the mattresses were too close to the stove, and about four hours later, they went up in flames. By the time we caught it, the entire building had turned into an inferno. My father blamed me." Mac shook his head, and she saw his eyes sparkle against the stars. "I couldn't sit for a week."

Andee smiled, grateful for the story that distracted her from her own turmoil. "Ouch."

"Yeah, well, Brody and I had it out. The thing is, after we'd smacked each other around, we always forgave each other. That's the thing about siblings. You can't choose them, but they become your closest friends."

She had another urge to apologize for Brody's death. Instead she looked away. "I always wished I had a brother or sister. That's how Sarah feels to me. Once when we were in college, I came home really late after a volleyball match. I'd gone out with friends and was a little . . . pickled. She locked me out of the dorm room until I promised to straighten up. Sarah was the one who got me going to church and in the end pointed me toward Christ. She knows me better than anyone."

"Then she knows you're doing everything you can to help her," Mac said.

Andee shrugged, but his words felt like a balm on her ragged nerves. "She's got a boyfriend. Hank will be beside himself when he finds out we've gone down."

"And your boyfriend—how will he feel?" Mac's voice sounded strained. It occurred to Andee that he might be having the same panicked feeling as she. He scooted away from her.

She cleared her throat. "How do you know I'm not married?"

She thought she saw him cringe. "I'm not married, Mac. If I was, I wouldn't have let you . . . ah, well, thanks for being there when I . . ."

"Cried?"

She made a face, aware that she probably looked a mess, with puffy cheeks and swollen eyes. Hopefully the darkness masked her. "Don't tell anyone."

"Your secret's safe with me." He crossed his chest in a childlike gesture.

"It's just stress. I'm sure we'll be fine. I've been on dozens of search-and-rescue operations that were far worse, with internal bleeding or people trapped on Denali, and we made it out."

"You're pretty adventurous. And you never answered my question about the boyfriend."

She met his eyes, saw in them something dark and curious. "No. No boyfriend. I can't see a man giving up his dreams for mine."

"What if your dreams and his are the same?"

Andee laughed. "I highly doubt some man is going to be

happy with me flying all over Alaska in the summer and living in the Lower 48 in the winter. It's not conducive to settling down and raising a family."

He caught a strand of hair blowing into her face. "And you want to do that? raise a family?"

How did this conversation turn so invasive? She looked away at the river, watching the water gurgle over the rocks, listening to it carve its way south. "Maybe. Yes. I guess. I don't know. With my history I'm not sure that it would be the best thing."

"Because your parents were divorced?" He said it so quietly that she thought maybe it had been only in her thoughts. But, no, as evidenced by the way he took her chin, drew her face to his.

"They're separated. For fourteen years now, but they won't get divorced."

"Why not?" He took his hand away.

She sighed. "I don't know. I think in some ways they still love each other. They just . . . can't live together. I don't know why. When I was sixteen, my parents had a huge fight. I know it had to do with my dad's job and my mother's dreams for me."

As she gazed into the sky at the unfolding of boreal lights, time reversed. She was back in her parents' cabin, eating her chocolate birthday cake out of a bowl, her spoon halfway to her mouth as her mother walked out of the bedroom, her suitcase in her hand. Gerard's spoon clanked into his bowl, and in that moment Andee saw everything she'd hoped and prayed for dissolve in the expression of anguish on his face.

"I need you to fly Andee and me back to Fairbanks," Mary had said, her voice tight, as if holding back a wave of pain.

Once reality sank in, Andee had begged, cried, pleaded to stay with her father. When she and her mother and father had finally stood on the tarmac beside the Cessna 185, the summer wind turning cold on her ears, disbelief had turned to fury.

"I told her I wouldn't go," Andee told Mac, "that I wanted us to be a family. That she couldn't leave, not when she loved him."

Mac had folded his hands between his knees, leaning into her story.

"She told me that sometimes love wasn't enough. That we had to live with the decisions we'd made, and I had to think about my future. Then she looked at my father, tears spilling down her face, and told me to choose."

"She asked you to choose? Between your father and her?"

Andee nodded, aware that her throat had tightened, that maybe she might not be able to speak. Especially when Mac reached out and threaded a finger through her closed grip.

"You chose your mother."

She shook her head. "I just stood there. Frozen. I couldn't choose. So my father chose for me. He got in his plane and flew away."

Mac said nothing, just swallowed, staring at her.

Andee pursed her lips. "I didn't see him again until my sophomore year in college. Sarah came with me, sorta to cushion the blow. We spent the summer here, flying. He was still ferrying hunters and working undercover."

Mac frowned.

"Oh, didn't I tell you? Yeah, my dad—he was FBI."

✦ ✦ ✦

"Is that some sort of crime?" Mac asked. The fact that Emma said it with such disgust made sense, but it also felt like a knife right in the center of his chest.

Her expression clouded. "Oh, well, no. Not really. I mean, of course not. Except my father worked undercover. My mother and I thought he was a mail pilot or was flying hunters, because he was gone so much. My mother hated it, worrying all the time, accusing him of putting his job before his family. Then one day she found out that he was really FBI. It was right before I nearly crashed a plane, and I think my adventurous spirit, along with his job, caused her to snap. She came home, packed my bags, and we left, just like that."

"Your dad didn't try to stop her?"

"Nope," she said. "He never wrote or called, didn't come and see me. I could only guess why, and the answers weren't pretty."

Sitting beside this incredible woman, watching the wind blow the hair on her hatless head, tears glistening in her beautiful eyes, he wondered how anyone could leave her and fly out of her life.

"I was sixteen," she continued softly. "My mother and I moved to Iowa, and she finished medical school. Looking back, I think it was a mutual decision—that my dad had a part in sending us away. My parents still write to each other, and they've never gotten divorced in all these years. For a long time, I've thought they would reconcile, but something holds them back. I think I need to face the truth that I've just been kidding myself."

"I'm really sorry, Emma. I can see why your mother felt betrayed. That had to hurt, not knowing who he really was."

Her eyes widened. Then she nodded and looked away.

"He probably wanted to tell you and your mom. He must have fought with his feelings of secrecy, maybe even hated himself for it."

She stayed silent searching Mac's face, as if for the truth.

He shrugged. "Just a theory, but as an agent, that's how I'd feel." How he *did* feel, suddenly knowing he'd hidden his reasons for forcing them to hike out. Still, the truth burned the inside of his mouth, and he swallowed it back.

"It's funny how the closest people to you can turn out to be the ones you know the least." Emma focused on her hands clasped between her knees. "Like my friend Micah, who thought the woman he loved killed her husband and for years blamed her for John's death. Only last year did he figure out who the real killer was. But he let the lie eat away at him for years until he was nearly numb."

Mac avoided her eyes. "Yeah."

"And another friend met this guy, who she first thought was a reporter. He turned out to be an undercover Homeland Security agent."

"I guess you can never know a person," Mac said.

"No, I think you can. If that person wants to be known and if you slow down, really care to see them. But we spend a lot of our time loving people as we want them to be. It took me years to forgive my father for flying away. For not coming after me. I finally realized that I can't make him be a dad. I can only be the daughter I hope to be. So I've spent every summer here since my sophomore year in college, flying and trying to repair those years of heartache. Looking past the obvious to what I know is underneath."

Mac was struck by Emma's faith in this man who hadn't proved it. She looked past the evidence to what she believed he had in his heart. Maybe that had been Mac's problem. He couldn't look past his suspicions—no, his *fears*—to see the truth. To see that Emma could never be a terrorist.

"Maybe you're right," Mac said. "Except that when I look at you, I *do* feel like what I see is what I get."

She sighed.

"I suppose Sarah knows the real Emma, aye?"

Emma nodded. "She came to Alaska because tomorrow is my birthday. I was going to spend it with her and my dad."

"I'm sorry you'll miss that."

Emma angled a look at him. "Maybe not. If we move fast we could get to Disaster by tomorrow night."

"Funny we haven't seen any planes overhead. I thought that with hunting season still open—"

"Most pilots don't like to fly hunters in after the middle of September. Too dangerous with the weather shifts. I was only doing it because I was bringing in supplies my dad would need for the winter. If they do fly, they stay nearer to the Dalton Highway."

"How far is that from here?"

"I don't know. About five or six miles, due east."

"Why don't we walk that direction then, instead of following the river?" He couldn't deny the litmus test embedded in that question. In spite of his belief that he could trust her.

"Because we'd still be twenty miles from the nearest town. We'd have to flag down a truck or a plane, and like I said, there isn't much in the way of traffic this time of year, especially north of Wiseman. Hence, why I want to start an FBO. We need medical services to the North Slope."

He felt a gust of relief. See, he *could* trust her.

"So, you're thinking of sticking around?" He wasn't sure why he'd said that, but somehow it felt very, very important. Enough to let the words settle between them and rustle the nerves down his spine.

Emma looked at him, then slowly shook her head. "I don't have enough money yet. I have a job waiting for me in Iowa. I'll leave with Sarah. . . ." Her expression dimmed. "I hope."

Mac saw the tension written on her face. He could use the radio. He'd let that thought free a few times over the course of the day but now really took a good look at it. If the two-way belonged to Flint, then Mac should be able to climb the hill they'd just descended, fire it up, and even if he couldn't raise the North Rim Outfitters hunting lodge, he might be able to scan through the channels and find . . . someone.

He'd been selfish not to think of it sooner. To consider that saving the pipeline might be more important than saving Emma's best friend. Only . . . was the safety of a nation worth more than one woman's life? It felt ugly to even think it, but the question lingered, unanswered.

"You need to get some rest." Mac brushed Emma's hair back from her face, tucking it behind her ears. "Put on your cap; you'll get sick."

She smiled at him, and it made him hurt a little with its sweetness. "Aye." She put it on, looking out into the sky. Again he realized how pretty she was. Petite, tough, feisty, but pretty in a natural, take-his-breath-away sense that did just that.

"I'm sorry I crumpled on you, Mac," she said finally. "I usually don't do that."

He let those words sink in, running his mind over the past two days, how she'd galvanized them all into action, teaching the others how to survive. She'd conquered any normal fears to help them all dig deep and unearth courage. He wondered just how much coping with her heartbroken parents had taught her to hold her chin up and continue on. To protect herself and keep people at a distance, in case they found her cracks.

In fact, that was how he'd lived most of his adult life.

"You're a real toughie," Mac said, "but I meant it when I said you're not hiking out of here without me."

She gave him a sad smile. "I'm supposed to be taking care of you—not the other way around."

He shook free of the inane urge to slip his hand around her neck and kiss her sweetly. "I don't need you to look after me."

She shook her head in mock disgust. "Of course not."

He rose and held out his hand. She took it and he helped her up, catching her in his arms when she stumbled against him, then holding her away because for the first time in Mac's life a woman had sneaked under his calluses to the soft place of his heart.

Talk about a woman crash-landing at his feet. He sucked a calming breath. "Good night, Emma."

"Thanks, Mac. For listening—" she paused—"for caring."

He could only nod. It had been a long time—way, way too long—since anyone had said that to him.

He watched her make her way to the shelter and disappear under the tarp that protected Sarah and Nina.

He pulled out the two-way radio, held it in his hand for a moment, then stood and looked toward the hill that overlooked the sparkling Granite River.

Chapter 12

ANDEE LAY IN the quiet chill under the shelter, listening to Nina and Sarah breathe. *"What you see is what you get."* She'd tried not to let Mac's words unravel her, but thinking of his kindness and the way he'd wrapped those muscled arms around her made her feel horrible.

She had to tell him the truth. That she'd been the pilot who'd cost his brother his life. She owed him that much after he'd . . . what? Stood by her? Helped her with Sarah? That and more.

Mac, with his soft brogue, his listening posture, his story of his brother meant to cheer her—he'd been a friend to her.

She wiped the tears from her cheeks. A friend? Oh, she even lied to herself. Settled inside his arms for that moment, she'd even contemplated letting him into her life. Because whether she wanted to admit it or not, she felt protected around Mac. With the wind buffeting the shelter, the cold seeping into her bones, her best friend in a near coma next to her, and ten miles to go to safety . . . she needed protection. Or instead *wanted* it.

Could it be that God had looked deep into her heart and sent her not only the one person she'd be least likely to trust but whom she intrinsically needed more than anyone else? A man stubborn enough not to give up on her?

She wondered what Micah and Conner would think of Mac if they ever met him. They'd probably like Mac—his save-the-world demeanor would be a bonding agent with her two Green Beret pals. Micah and Conner cornered the market on protectiveness, but it felt different with them. When Conner or Micah gave her a hug, it didn't make her want to lean into his embrace. And why had Mac asked if she had a boyfriend? That felt . . . unsettling. Like a million sparks had jolted through her body.

If only she weren't leaving. She *would* be back next summer. And if Mac was still around . . .

Her mother's warnings replayed in her ears, almost an echo in time:

"Gerard MacLeod, what are you doing?" Mary MacLeod's voice could be heard through the Plexiglas windows of the airplane even before Andee cracked open the door. The wind tore at Mary's jacket, yanked her dark hair from its braid, and wrapped it around her face. Andee felt heat radiate off her mother's countenance and recoiled. Mary stalked toward the plane. "You let her land?"

"She needs to learn how to take care of herself. To land a plane dead stick." Gerard didn't raise his voice, just kept it low and simmering. Yet his gaze never left Mary's face.

She grabbed Andee's jacket, pulled her out of the plane. "You know how I feel about this. You teach her to fly and I'll lose you both in a fiery crash." Her eyes filled. "No. I'm not doing that, Gerard. She's too young—you can't treat her like one of your rookie pilots."

"Mary, she's *sixteen!* She can do this! Besides, how will she learn to survive out here if we don't make her—?"

"She won't learn." Mary's fist balled on Andee's coat, burning her upper arm as she pulled Andee along.

"Mary—," Andee started.

"You hush. You know how I feel about you flying."

"Mary!" Gerard's voice boomed over the runway. "Mary, come back!"

She stopped and rounded on him, her voice cold. "I'll get my own ride home. With Andee." She jerked back around, glancing at Andee.

Andee shrank under her mother's glare but didn't miss the tears edging her eyes.

"He's the worst mistake I ever made," Mary said simply. "I hope you never make the same."

Now Andee rolled over on the ground, feeling the ache that had taken possession of her body. She nestled her head in her arms, listening to the night. Outside, a wolf howled a lonely song that echoed through her cold body. The river gurgled, splashing against rocks. She heard the thump of feet against rocks—probably Mac climbing into his shelter.

Except the footsteps led away. She strained to hear. Was someone leaving? Phillips?

She scooted to the edge of the tarp and lifted it, staring out into the night.

Mac's outline against the velvet of night dissolved as he walked in the direction of the hill overlooking the river.

Her curiosity piqued, she climbed out and stole after him. Where was he going? Did he think he could hike out? He'd get lost and die. Especially since he was going in the wrong direction. Yeah, *sure,* he'd spent time in the bush . . .

She stayed low, remembering Micah's and Conner's stories of their Green Beret days. When Mac climbed the hill and stood on top, like some highland laird surveying his land, she had to duck, blend into the landscape.

She watched as he lifted something to his lips. And then, because the wind carried it, she heard static.

He had a radio.

A *radio*!

She wasn't sure what ignited first, her anger or her feet, but she closed the space between them before he could turn. She would have tackled him if she hadn't been breathing so hard. "You have a *radio*?"

So much for not keeping secrets, for trusting people. She wanted to slap him.

He stared at her as if she might be an apparition from the depths.

"You have a *radio*? What are you doing, FBI? Why didn't you use it earlier?" She shook her head, raising her arms in exasperation. "I can't believe it. All that talk about helping me. I cried in front of you, worried about Sarah. *And you have a radio!*"

He looked stricken, just standing there staring at her, the static of the radio buzzing in the background.

She grabbed for it. He yanked it away, taking a step back, now breathing hard. He still said nothing. She wanted to strangle him. "Well?"

He looked at the radio, then back at her, as if realizing for the first time that he held it. "It's not mine."

"Then whose is it, Mac? And why exactly does that matter? Were you afraid that one of our starving, cold passengers might be upset that you found their *link to the outside world*?"

"I thought it might be yours."

"What?" She put her hands on her hips. "Yeah, it's mine. And I've been looking all over for it—give it back!"

He actually looked at her as if he might believe her.

"I'm *lying* to you," she said. "Do you think if I had a radio I wouldn't have used it the *first* second I could? What kind of person do you think I am?"

He cleared his throat. "You . . . the thing is, Emma, I thought someone aboard might be a terrorist. I found a map of the pipeline, with weak points in the line marked. I thought that maybe one of the passengers—"

The air puffed out of her. "That's why you made us stick together." She put her hands on her head to keep it from spinning. Maybe she should sit and put her head between her knees. "You forced us to stay together because you thought someone was going to blow up the *pipeline*?"

"It's not so far-fetched," Mac said, his voice rich with passion. "The pipeline is a vital source of energy for the U.S. Just this year we arrested two groups we believe to be saboteurs, and we have an entire department dedicated to protecting the pipeline, plus TAPS has its own security. There are a number of domestic groups—from environmental terrorists who want the oil harvesting to stop, to militants who want us to carpet bomb the Middle East and take possession of her assets—who would sacrifice their lives to blow up the line. Not to mention a dozen countries that would spend their national treasure to see America crippled financially and on her knees.

"Take Venezuela, for example. They're the fourth largest producer of oil, supplying America with 15 percent of her oil. But they're aggressively seeking a bigger share of the market, making alliances with Iran, China, and Russia—all with an eye to jack up barrel prices. If the pipeline was taken out, we'd have to turn to them for help—their wildest dreams come true."

Andee gaped at him. "Venezuela? Okay, take me to your leader, because c'mon, Mac, listen to yourself. You sound like a CIA world report! You don't actually *believe* what you're saying, do you? We're stuck out here in the middle of nowhere—do you seriously think we're caught in some sort of terrorist plot?" She let loose an angry snort of laughter.

Her voice tightened as fury took over, spiking her nerves, turning her nearly inside out with frustration. "You put Sarah in danger, *knowing* that I could hike out and get help because you thought there might be a Venezuelan terrorist among our passengers? Who was it, *Nina*? She's probably lying about those kids—no, wait, the Shamu whale she sleeps with is really a *bomb*."

He winced. "I didn't suspect Nina."

Who did he think . . . ? "*Me*? You thought *I* was the terrorist?"

Mac put his hand to his head, as if trying to lift the thought from his mind. "I know . . . I know . . . I feel sick."

Something about his tone made her slow, take another breath. "How could you, Mac? After everything I've done to take care of us. Did you think a terrorist would have a sudden change of heart, maybe a soft spot? You just might be the worst judge of character on the entire planet! Why did you think—?"

"That's how I'm trained to think! Because I've spent the last three years analyzing rap sheets and faces and scenarios, and everything about this screamed that something wasn't right! And because I swore to protect my country, regardless of the cost."

"Like my best friend's life?" Andee's voice lowered.

He looked away and nodded.

She had the desperate, crazy urge to hit him really—*really* hard. She balled her hands into fists and turned away.

"I'm sorry. I'm so, so sorry, Emma. I didn't want to deceive you. But I thought . . . well, I was wrong."

Until this moment, every time he'd called her Emma today had made her feel sick, like she'd deliberately lied to him.

Now she just felt even.

"Does the radio work?" she said coldly.

He looked at it, as if just remembering he held it in his hands. "I got a signal and some static, but no one responded to my call. I thought maybe I could get different channels, but this is tuned to only one, and I can't seem to change it."

"Maybe it was damaged in the crash." She reached out for it. He met her eyes as he handed it over, and she saw his shame.

Then it hit her. "You came out here because of Sarah, didn't you? Because you're worried about her."

She glimpsed the truth on his face, and suddenly much of her anger disintegrated like the fine particles of an early autumn frost at dawn.

"I don't want her to die, Emma. I don't want any more people to die because of me."

His voice sounded so tortured that Andee closed her eyes against a wave of ache.

"I'm such a fool." He made a fist and pushed it against his forehead. "I'm doing it again. I can't believe it."

Andee couldn't stop herself from touching his arm. "I don't understand."

He stood there, unmoving, but she thought she saw him shake his head. Then he sighed and rubbed his eyes with his thumb and forefinger. Emotion filled his voice. "Three months ago, I was fishing with my brother when I saw—" his jaw clenched—"a terrorist. It was a guy we'd been tracking for years, part of a terrorist cell. The FBI had him under surveillance, waiting for him to reveal his contacts. I ran after him and took him down. But not before he blew a hole in the pipeline and . . . in my brother."

"Brody," she said, feeling herself go weak.

"Aye. And the worst part is we lost our link to the cell."

"No, the worst part is that Brody died."

Mac closed his mouth, pursed his lips in a grim look, and turned away.

Lord, why didn't I listen to his call? land on the highway?

"You know," Mac said, "for the longest time I thought if I could just get in the face of MacLeod, the pilot who let my brother die, and tell him what he'd done—I might have some closure."

Andee felt cold, right to the center of her body.

"But I know now that it's not about Brody or MacLeod. It's about me. I was so consumed with being someone who might make a difference." He shook his head as he sank down onto the hill, his knees up, head hanging. Defeated.

Andee stood over him, feeling like she might cry. *"I believe in God, but He doesn't believe in me."* Mac's words came back to her, and suddenly she understood.

"I didn't expect to change the world. But the last thing I expected was for it to crumble in my hands. Brody's death is my fault." He hung his head. "I'm an idiot, Emma. I'm so sorry."

Andee sat next to him, close enough that their shoulders touched. "You know what I think? I think you're trying too hard. God does believe in you, Mac. That's why you're here with me. He knew that Sarah needed you." *That I needed you.* "You don't have to be a national hero to be used by God. You can simply carry Sarah's stretcher or help haul Flint up a cliff."

He stared at her. "I guess I was hoping for more."

She gave him the kindest smile she could find. "To Flint and Sarah and . . . me, it is more."

For a second she saw emotion in his eyes. Fear or maybe gratefulness. It swept out the last fragments of her anger.

She nudged him with her shoulder. "You just don't want to admit that you're afraid."

A slight smile played on his lips. "You're talking to a Scot, lassie. We don't get afraid."

She held the radio in her hands, turning it off, then on. "Yep, FBI, you're afraid. You think that God is going to drop the ball, so you need to step in. You *do* think you can save the world."

He didn't move. "You must think I'm the most arrogant man on the planet."

"No. Just one of a few I know who sometimes think that way." Andee handed him back the radio. "You may not believe this, but I trust you, Mac. And I'd like you to trust me too. I'm not a terrorist. And I don't think Nina, Flint, or Phillips is either." She nudged him again with her shoulder. "Ishbane, however . . . I'm not so sure about."

✦ ✦ ✦

"*I trust you, Mac.*" The words resonated in Mac's head, saturated his sleep, filling him with warmth that edged out the cold. Not only the cold seeping inside the tarp, but the cold that had numbed him for far too long. The cold perimeter he'd constructed around his life. Only Emma had somehow snuck under that perimeter to attack those walls from inside.

No wonder he felt off balance, out of control.

He heard movement beside him and woke to see Flint rising, grimacing, probing his knee.

"How is it?" Mac asked, sitting up. The morning sun barely fractured the gloom inside the tarp. Mac felt achy and chilled. They should get a fire going before starting today's hike.

If only the radio had worked, they might have hope of

rescue. He and Emma had tried for over an hour before giving up.

Ishbane lay in a heap, the emergency blanket pulled up to his chin, and Mac remembered Emma's words: *"I'm not so sure about Ishbane."*

He knew she'd been kidding. Even Mac could hardly believe he'd suspected any of the passengers of sabotage. He needed to quit the FBI and start a new life, like his father had suggested.

His father's suggestion had also included finding a wife and starting a family. Until today, he'd shrugged that thought away, not giving it time to take hold. Now as Mac climbed out of the tarped shelter, letting the brisk wind blow away the last vestiges of sleep, a smile emerged quickly when he saw Emma working a flame out of a pile of kindling she'd scraped together from the scrub willows along the river. She wore a red fleece pullover under her leather flight jacket, and it only made her that much more striking.

"You're up early," he said.

Emma looked up, and despite the lines of fatigue framing her eyes, he saw hope in her pretty face, in those incredible eyes that last night had held trust, even redemption. "The sun is shining, the air is warming, and I caught two graylings." She held out two fish on a stringer. "I'm going to go clean them. Can you tend this fire?"

Who is this woman? She'd risen early to go *fishing*. To catch breakfast. She seemed one step ahead of him at every turn. Mac stood in frozen disbelief as Emma picked her way along the rocks. He guessed that she'd clean the fish far enough away from their camp that if a fox or even a bear caught the scent, the animal wouldn't be a threat.

"Need some help?" Phillips emerged from the shelter.

SUSAN MAY WARREN

"I smelled the fire." He knelt beside it, feeding more kindling wood into the flame. Next to the fire, Emma had piled more willow. Exactly how early had she risen? It brought to mind that mythical perfect wife he'd read about in the Bible.

Okay, Mac, shake that *thought away.* Mac crouched beside Phillips. "How are you feeling today?"

"Ready to get moving." Phillips stood and stretched. "I have a mission, and I'm anxious to complete it."

Mac tried not to let that comment ignite his reflexes. "Really? What's that?"

"I'm a missionary headed to Resurrection for a month to relieve the missionaries working there."

Mac sized up the man. With his dark looks and his sturdy build, Mac would have placed him as a hunter. Or a lumberjack. Not a servant of the gospel. Except Phillips had been the one to pray, to suggest that God could get them out of this mess.

"We used to have a missionary in our area," Mac said, "but he had a hard time of it. Our community had a mix of people from so many backgrounds, he fought against denominations, paganism, tradition."

"Sounds like the same thing the apostle Paul dealt with. He had denominations within Judaism, and the pagan religions of the Greeks, and of course his own traditional upbringing. Yet he found the balance of fitting into the world he ministered to while still preaching the truth."

"I recall him ending up in jail a lot." Mac poked the fire.

Phillips laughed. "That too. But I think that was God's design more than any fault of Paul's. I think God put him into those painful places so God could prove Himself faithful to Paul. Something Paul needed, especially at the end of his life."

"Sorta like, what doesn't break you makes you stronger?"

"Well, more like, everything we do matters to God, and each step prepares us for the next."

"Even if our steps seem to accomplish nothing?" Mac ran his thoughts over his past, the plans he'd thwarted, the fear that terrorism could never truly be wiped out.

"But do they accomplish nothing? Consider Jericho. For six days the warriors marched around the city, blowing the trumpet of victory. Six days they did nothing, so to speak— nothing but walk in faith. But on the seventh, they gave a great cry, and God imploded the walls. Or think of the Israelites following God's cloud and pillar of light through the desert for forty years, every day packing and unpacking their tents. Was their journey fruitless? Or did it create a generation of faithful followers ready to enter the Promised Land?"

Phillips crouched, warming his hands before the now blazing fire. "Perhaps the great thing isn't found in the walls coming down or in the claiming of the Promised Land. Maybe it's every step taken on the way. In the end, God has to empower both the vision and the steps."

Mac massaged a muscle in his neck that had been cranked by sleep. He'd spent his life with his eyes fixed on the prize—a safe America, a secure supply of oil, thwarting terrorist attacks. But perhaps just as important were the everyday activities— training, analyzing potential threats, even maintaining the pipeline. It was similar to their hike back to civilization—wasn't getting there in one piece, healthy and sane, just as important as getting back at all?

"Even Paul's darkest moments were used by God to build his faith, prepare him for the next step. When Paul and his partner Timothy sat in prison and thought they would die, Paul said, 'In fact, we expected to die. But as a result, we stopped relying on ourselves and learned to rely only on God, who raises the dead. And he did rescue us from mortal danger, and he will rescue us again. We have placed our confidence in him, and he will continue to rescue us.'

"Those verses aren't just talking about deliverance from death, but deliverance from bondage. Like fear and fruitlessness and despair. Paul wrote that they 'learned to rely only on God, who raises the dead.' That's not only people who *are* dead, but those who *feel* dead. As if life is over. God raises those walking corpses and gives them new minds and bodies, frees them from deadly thinking. Don't you think that Paul and Timothy believed they had experienced a sort of resurrection when they were released?" Phillips looked at Mac and smirked. "Probably how I'll feel when I get a shower and a shave."

Mac gave him a wry smile. But the words bit at him. He had felt dead and trapped inside the overwhelming crest of responsibility. Emma had been right yesterday. He *did* doubt God. Doubted that He cared about people like Stirling McRae and the broken places inside him. Doubted that God would answer and save when Mac turned to Him in his darkest moment.

"Victory lies not only in the end goal but in the steps of faith we take every day toward that goal." Phillips poked the fire and sparks sprayed upward into the cloudless sky, pricks of warmth dissipating into the atmosphere.

Mac shivered, feeling damp. His stomach growled, and he felt grimy to his bones. To the north, he saw Emma, bent over a rock, cleaning the fish she'd caught.

She amazed him. And terrified him.

He wondered what his mother might think of her. Wow, how easily his thoughts fit her into his life.

"Emma!" Nina burst from her shelter, running toward the campfire. "Where's Emma?"

Mac stood and pointed toward the figure crouched onshore.

"Emma!" Nina yelled, her hands cupped over her mouth. "Sarah needs you!"

Chapter 13

THANK YOU, LORD, for the fish. Andee gripped the grayling by the tail, stripping off the meat as she filleted the fish, then washed it free from scales and dirt in the icy glacier water.

The sky above looked clear—a good day to travel, hopefully without snow. Her body still ached, her bones screaming as she pushed up from the ground this morning. Still, God had provided breakfast and another night of safety. He'd kept Sarah breathing and her pulse steady. And maybe today they'd get a signal on that radio Mac carried.

To whom does the radio belong? That thought had rattled about her head late into the night, pushing free of even the thoughts of sitting beside Mac, his muscled arm touching hers, his dangerous smile filtering into her thoughts. Around him, she felt not so alone, not so overwhelmed.

She couldn't bear to feel anything more than that. She could forgive him for thinking she might be a terrorist. Even forgive him for making them all hike out—they probably would have had to anyway. She'd forgive him for all of it because he'd have to forgive her for so much more.

Andee sighed, turning the fish over and stripping off the other filet of meat. She hoped that today they'd get close enough for her to leave Sarah and the others and hike to Disaster. She envisioned herself in her father's cabin, wrapped in a hand-knit afghan in front of his fireplace. Most likely, she'd be in Fairbanks, sitting in the hospital, praying. She dreaded the phone call she'd have to place to Sarah's boyfriend, Hank. He'd be on a flight to Alaska before she hung up.

What must it feel like to have someone care that much that they'd drop everything and stop at nothing to find the one they loved? Tears bit at the backs of her eyes. She'd never had someone like that in her life. Never.

Even now, if her father suspected her plane had gone down, yes, he'd call the authorities. But worry? He hadn't worried about her . . . well . . . ever probably. Not enough to turn his plane southward.

No, her father regretted nothing about the way he had raised—or *hadn't* raised her. While she regretted almost everything—her resentment, her lack of trust, her nomadic life that left her staring out the window at the northern lights most Saturday nights alone. She even regretted taking off in iffy weather three days ago and not listening to the pain in Mac's voice when he'd called for help for Brody.

If only she'd known then what she knew now. She would have been able to see that someday she'd be trapped on a mountain with a man who'd been devastated by his brother's death. A death she might have prevented if she'd taken the time to land. She had to tell him.

Mac looked larger than life this morning, his curly hair hanging rumpled around his whiskered face, framing those incredible blue eyes. When he'd lifted his mouth in a slight smile, her heart nearly leaped from her body.

Yes, she liked Mac. Liked his quiet demeanor and the way he measured his words, his brogue that hinted at passion beneath the calm posture, and the way his eyes twinkled under the northern lights. She liked the way he talked about his family. It made her ache for a family like his, a family who loved each other, who gathered for haggis and oat bread on Sundays, and who quoted poetry to each other. She liked how he respected her and especially that he'd hiked out into the night to protect her. Then again, maybe he'd only been spying on her, but it made her feel less alone all the same. She even liked the way he laughed and how he called her lassie.

Who would have thought she'd be a bonnie lass? Her mouth quirked up for a second, only to morph into a cringe. Yes, she liked him way, way too much for the secret she possessed. Even if they did manage to become friends—or more—when he discovered she had been the pilot who'd rejected his call for help, well, she could probably survive if they never had that conversation. *I thought if I could just get in the face of MacLeod, the pilot who let my brother die, and tell him what he'd done—I might have some closure.*

Andee had wanted to slink away then, to close her eyes and ears to the texture of pain in his voice. She'd wanted to climb into a plane and lift off, away from the earth and its pinnings, until the hum of the motor and the shiver of the cockpit numbed her mind and gave her heart a new rhythm.

Maybe she'd just keep flying.

I don't want to tell him, Lord. Please.

"Emma!" The panic in the voice made her pivot on the rock. Nina ran up the shoreline. "Sarah needs you!"

Andee stood, knife in one hand, fish in the other. "What?"

"She's awake!"

Andee dropped the breakfast and sprinted toward the shelter, wiping her hands on her pants. *Please, God, let her be okay!*

She saw Mac enter the small tarp she'd rigged against some rocks and his outline bump against the roof.

She lifted the edge of the tarp, letting in light. Mac was kneeling beside Sarah.

"Is she okay?" Andee let the tarp fall from behind her, blanketing them in semidarkness. She knelt beside Mac, felt for Sarah's pulse.

"Andee? Andee?"

Andee leaned forward, tears scraping her eyes. "Yes, yes, I'm here, Sarah. Do you know where you are?"

Sarah's eyes were open and searching for her.

Andee leaned past Mac into Sarah's view. "You're okay. You hit your head, so don't move. But we're going to get you out of here. Just hang on."

"What happened?" Sarah's voice sounded feeble and scratchy.

Andee reached for water, attached a straw, and ran it into Sarah's mouth. "We crashed. But we're all alive." She pressed her lips to Sarah's forehead. "We lived." She closed her eyes, feeling those words to her marrow. *We lived.* So far.

"I'm cold. My head hurts. And I can't move."

"Can you feel my hand on your leg?" Andee asked.

Sarah held her gaze. "Yes. Yes, I can."

Andee felt Sarah's legs move, and relief filled her eyes. "I'm leaving your neck braced until we get to safety." She took Sarah's hand, held it in hers. "We'll take care of you, I promise. I'm not going to let anything happen to you."

"Andee, what about Hank? Does he know?"

"No. We haven't been able to get help. And the plane exploded, so the ELT blew up. But we're hiking out. We're about a day away from Disaster. Just hang on, okay?"

Sarah closed her eyes.

Andee turned to Mac. "We need to get going."

Mac didn't move. His eyes were dark, holding hers, void of emotion. His fierce expression sent a shiver down her spine. "Andy MacLeod," he said evenly.

She blinked at him. Then dread filled her body. She sank back onto her ankles and sighed. "Yeah. That's me."

Mac stared at her for a sharp and brutal moment when she felt everything sweet and warm between them shatter like the ice on a highland stream.

Then he stood, flung back the tarp cover, and stalked away.

✦ ✦ ✦

"Mac!"

Mac kept walking, past Phillips tending the fire, past Ishbane huddled on a rock, past Nina standing with a worried expression and rubbing her arms as she watched him.

"Mac!"

He felt like a fool, and he let that moniker fuel him as he ground his teeth and walked downriver away from them all.

Women were terrorists to the heart. He couldn't believe he'd lowered his defenses to cautionary instead of high, where they should be permanently affixed. Obviously that crash had knocked loose more than his grip on reality. It also jarred his common sense.

"Mac!"

Andy MacLeod. No . . . Andee MacLeod. Female. He didn't know why he hadn't considered that before. It felt deceitful—her calling herself Emma all this time and hiding her identity. Yes, he knew that most pilots went by a call name when they flew. Crowbar Pete or Aces or Buckeye Joe. But Emma? He thought it was her *name*.

Not only that, but she knew about Brody. Knew that he grieved his brother, knew that he'd wanted to confront the pilot— He'd told her that he'd blamed himself, that Brody's death was his fault. No wonder she hadn't come clean. He'd enabled her lie.

He needed therapy. What was it about him that the first woman he let into his life betrayed him? Independent and feisty only translated into deceitful and heartbreaking.

"Mac!" He felt a hand on his arm, gripping, yanking.

He let himself be turned, fury still fueling his steps, his expression.

He stopped short at the look on Andee's face. Tears streamed down her cheeks, her expression torn. She stared at him, shaking her head.

He saw her struggle for words. He said nothing.

"Mac," Andee whispered, her voice shaking, "I wanted to tell you."

He felt his anger simmer right below his skin.

"I felt sick about your brother—then and now. You have no idea how I wanted to land that day to pick him up. And when I found out he died, I . . . I couldn't go to bed at night without asking God to forgive me. I felt sick."

He felt sick listening to her relive that day. He heard himself again, pleading for her to land.

"You have to know that I was faced with an impossible choice. I had a woman on board who'd been mauled by a grizzly. She had four little children. She was bleeding out, and I had to get her to Fairbanks. She had already arrested once. There wasn't time to pick up your brother—she would have died." She put her hands over her face. He watched her shoulders rise and fall. "I had to choose."

You chose poorly, he wanted to say, but he couldn't

dredge the words from his mouth. They felt sour in the face of her obvious grief. Still, he couldn't reach out to her, couldn't release the anger that pinned down every other emotion inside him.

He'd longed for this moment, an opportunity to face the person who'd killed his brother.

For the first time he realized that maybe it wasn't Andy/Andee MacLeod he had to face at all. And maybe it wasn't Andee he had to forgive—at least for Brody's death.

"When I realized you were the man I'd talked to on the radio, you have to know I died inside. I wanted to tell you, to explain and beg your forgiveness, but I needed you. I couldn't risk having you hate me so much you wouldn't assist me—or worse, try to get help alone. I had five other lives at stake, and I gambled." She looked away. "Maybe I didn't make the right choice. Maybe I should have trusted you. I know it wasn't right to deceive you. You have to know how I longed to tell you." Her voice dropped to a soft, nearly inaudible rasp. "And how very sorry I am." She wiped at her eyes. "Please, please forgive me."

He listened to her apology, to her broken voice and realized he'd heard it before. Many times, in fact, over the past few days. Yes, she'd known who he was. What she'd done. And in spite of her choice to keep it from him, she had started apologizing long ago.

He felt something unwind from his soul. Still, he couldn't speak. Instead, he turned and walked away from Andee MacLeod and everything she'd done to him.

"Mac!"

He let her voice bank against the mountains, echo down the flowing river. The air smelled of fall, with a hint of snow. His feet already felt damp as they crunched on the broken rocks. He stuck his hands in his pockets and stopped walking, stood on the edge of the river, not looking back.

This really hurts, Lord.

He didn't know exactly where those words came from. They bubbled up from some stopped-up place inside, some long-ago wound he'd thought he'd stitched over but had only poorly bandaged.

He closed his eyes, probing for a place that *didn't* hurt.

"I'm so sorry, Mac," Emma—no, *Andee*—had said as she sat on the scree hill watching the northern lights. He'd heard the pain in her voice even back then.

"Do you ever regret the choices you've made?" she'd asked as the night had enfolded her. He'd watched her shiver, knowing that she'd given her blanket to Ishbane.

"God does believe in you, Mac. That's why you're here with me. He knew that Sarah needed you." She'd leaned back on her hands, tugging up a smile as they sat in the grass on the hill overlooking the camp under the fall of stars.

He saw Andee, thanking him for carrying Sarah, putting up their tents, making dinner, caring for Flint and Sarah.

"I trust you, Mac. And I'd like you to trust me too. I'm not a terrorist."

Mac ached with each memory, aware that, despite his best efforts, he'd let another kind of terrorist sneak inside to blow to bits with her servant's heart every line of defense he'd built over the years.

She'd made him slow down, see her as a friend, trust her.

Lord, I believe everything happens for a reason. But I admit I have a hard time seeing how things fit together from this viewpoint. I thought You'd put me on that plane for a second chance. His eyes burned. *But this wasn't the second chance I was looking for. I'm not ready to forgive anyone . . . yet.*

Mac crouched on the rock. He splashed water on his face, letting the shock reawaken him and wash away the realization that for the first time in years he had to forgive the terrorist in his life.

Chapter 14

ANDEE PUT ONE foot ahead of the other. She hated her chapped cheeks and the way the others looked at her, especially after Mac had returned to camp without so much as a glance toward her. She'd cooked the fish she'd filleted, and after eating in a silence that felt colder than the descending front, they'd packed up camp.

Thankfully, Mac had resumed his post at Sarah's head, taking his end of her stretcher onto his wide, capable, unforgiving shoulders.

At least he hadn't left them all alone in the woods for her to take care of by herself. Then again, with this cold demeanor, she shouldn't count on him for help. She swallowed a rush of pain and kept her eyes fixed on her footing.

She still couldn't believe that he'd suspected her to be a terrorist—or any of them for that matter. However, with her little news bomb, he could label her a terrorist, on a par with someone who inflicted pain and chaos.

"How long have we been traveling?" Sarah's voice lifted from her stretcher.

"This is day three." *Or four? Or two?* Andee frowned at her own answer. It seemed every day of struggle had merged into the next. "I think."

"Then I missed your birthday."

Andee let that thought bring her upright, and then she smiled. Trust Sarah to remember the one day Andee always tried to dodge. "No, actually, it's today."

"Happy birthday, Andee. I wish I had a cookie for you." Sarah had started a tradition years ago of sending an oversized chocolate-chip cookie in the mail to the Team Hope members for their birthdays. "I'd get one that read *My Hero*."

"Wait until I get you out of here before you start singing me anthems."

"I think she's a hero," Phillips said from behind them. He and Nina held Flint between them. Ishbane trailed them, picking his way on the rocks, bemoaning his wet feet. "Happy birthday, Emma."

"It's Andee," Mac growled so low that probably only Andee caught it.

"My name's Andee," she corrected Phillips. "My call name is Emma. It just seems easier in the summer for people to call me Emma." And it perpetuated the feeling that here in the northland, she could be someone different, perhaps someone she'd always wanted to be, at least part of the time. Someone who didn't let people down or destroy their lives.

"Her friends call her Andee," said Sarah, a little bird of information. "And I'll bet that Conner is waiting for you when you get to Fairbanks. He mentioned your birthday in his last e-mail."

"Conner isn't coming to Alaska, Sarah," Andee said. Conner Young, former Green-Beret-turned-computer-whiz had left the army five years ago to start a computer-security consulting company. In between tending his IT company in Montana and the various SAR jaunts he took with Team Hope, he lived very comfortably on a five-acre plot on Ashley Lake. He had little incentive to trek two thousand miles north for scenery. Or the birthday of a friend, even if it might be a good friend.

"He would if he knew our plane crashed. He worries about you, you know."

They all worried about her. Andee, the nomad. "He doesn't worry about me any more than Micah or Dani do."

"Sounds like you have a lot of admirers, Andee." Mac's voice, again low, drifted back at her and stung.

She frowned at him, angry at his assumptions.

Angry and curious.

What did he care who her friends were?

"I don't have admirers," Andee said quietly.

Mac didn't stop walking or respond.

She watched how he climbed over the rocks, his steps sure, his arms easily balancing the weight of his burden. Apparently he hadn't heard the pain in her voice or her words of apology. How easy it seemed for him to assume the worst about a person. Obviously he hadn't the faintest idea what it felt like to look back on the choices you made—life-and-death choices, choices of the heart, even choices about your future—and wonder if you'd made them correctly. She'd give her next meal and a warm bed to have a God's-eye view on life and know that she was headed in the right direction. That at the end of the Granite River, they'd find Disaster Creek, and it would lead her home.

That goal felt like some sort of epitaph of her life. Hoping to head toward disaster. As if she couldn't hope for better. Well, with her history, maybe not.

She slogged on through the boggy riverbank and gnarled roots, searching for sure footing, listening to her stomach growl. Stunted willow, black and white spruce, and spindly birch clumped in welcome as the group descended toward the tree line of the boreal forest. The sun climbed as high as it could, then held on, fighting the pull to lower ground.

Andee finally called a halt a little after noon and passed around the water bottle, making sure Sarah got something to drink. Then, staring at the weary faces of her passengers, she grabbed the pot from the mess kit. "I'm going to look for food."

She walked away from the river, through whitened tufts of reindeer lichen, dissected with spruce. She startled a peregrine falcon, and it lifted off in a rustle of feathers and a cry. The thinly forested hillside gave little hope for food, but as she walked farther from the group, she looked for signs of blueberries. This time of year, perhaps they'd still be ripe enough. The smaller plants of this northern region produced the sweetest berries.

From the north, the wind rushed through the trees and brought with it the scent of the river. She spotted Dall sheep, white against the granite cliffs that bordered the valley to the west. She wondered what it might be like to be hind's feet on high places, navigating like a poet through the rugged Highlands.

My heart's in the Highlands, my heart is not here,
My heart's in the Highlands, a-chasing the deer,
Chasing the wild-deer, and following the roe,
My heart's in the Highlands, wherever I go.

Mac's voice turned her father's words through her mind. She'd learned too many Robert Burns poems on too many fishing trips. What was it about Scotsmen that turned their thoughts to poetry when they ventured out into the hills? Too much time around Mac would prove painful in so many ways.

She knew she should turn around, but the thought of

returning to Mac's angry airspace made her push on, over downed, decaying trees, stepping carefully over the knotted roots. The last thing she needed was a twisted ankle.

She came out into a clearing, a meadow seeded with buttercups, saxifrage, and mountain avens. Clumped among them she spied blueberries growing low to the ground. Her stomach tightened.

She walked over to the berries and picked a handful. After sorting through them and flicking away hardened, rotten berries, she popped the rest into her mouth.

Flavor exploded, sweet yet tangy, and her stomach roared with greed. She picked another handful, then started filling the pot. Perhaps it would get them through until supper. And then maybe they'd find a squirrel or a—

Andee froze, hearing a whuffing sound, then the sound of breaking trees and heavy feet crushing the forest floor.

Holding her breath, she looked up and turned. Time suspended into long, drawn-out gasps of fear. Some twenty-five feet away at the edge of the meadow and flanked by her two large cubs stood a grizzly sow. Her blonde fur, backlit by the sun, glowed with an ethereal, pagan power.

Andee's bones felt like liquid. *Move.*

She couldn't move. Couldn't even breathe. She stared at the hulking animal, at the black eyes boring into hers. Then the bear opened her mouth, baring fangs, pulled back her black lips, and roared.

✚ ✚ ✚

Mac stood at the edge of the river, scooping up a handful of rocks. He felt like a heel, arguing with himself that he should be following Andee into the forest and helping her.

Conner, Micah, Danny. How many men did she have in her life? He knew he had to drive Andee from his thoughts. He should have guessed that she'd have an array of admirers.

"I trust you, Mac. And I'd like you to trust me too." He pushed Andee's voice away, but it found footing and dug in. So she had a good reason to lie. . . .

He heard footsteps kick rocks out ahead of him and turned. Phillips approached him, hands in his pockets, shoulders slumped, as if Mac might not guess the guy had an agenda on his mind.

"Don't start, Phillips," Mac said in warning.

Phillips looked up, as if surprised. "I was just wondering if you might need a friend."

Mac narrowed his eyes. He didn't know Phillips's agenda, but he couldn't help but appreciate the man for his hard work. And that prayer he'd spoken the first night out still lingered in Mac's soul. Mac turned away, pitched a rock into the stream.

"I don't know what she did, Mac, but I think she deserves the benefit of the doubt." Phillips came to stand beside him on the shore.

"She lied to me." The words erupted in a bitter, surprising rush. Apparently three days in the bush had taken its toll on his ability to rein in his emotions. He threw another rock.

"Even so, everyone in Alaska can tell she's sorry. She won't even look at you. And I have to say, you seem intent on making her suffer."

Ouch. Mac sighed. *But shouldn't she suffer?*

"You have to know I died inside." Andee's voice, putting words to his own pain. Maybe she was already suffering. Mac pitched in another rock, then watched the sun ripple off the rock, the flowing water.

"Here's the deal, Mac." Phillips faced him, his dark eyes

holding Mac's. "I don't know what happened in the past, but you can't live there. You have to go forward. Consider not the woman who hurt you, but the woman who seems bent on taking care of you and all of us. I think she deserves it." Phillips paused, looked back out over the river. "I would suspect that based on what I see in Andee, she probably had a good reason to keep the truth from you."

"I'm not hiking out of these mountains without you." Mac heard his own words again to Andee. Emma. Whoever. He'd spoken them to the lady who'd nearly gotten killed trying to save the lives of her passengers. Whom he'd accused of being a terrorist. She'd needed him, and he'd led her to believe he'd help her.

Maybe he'd betrayed *her*.

That thought made him wince, one eye closed in realization. Perhaps he'd keep his promise, but only until they reached civilization.

For the time being anyway, maybe he'd try to forgive her.

Oh, who was he kidding? An empty, longing part of him wanted to forgive her. To see her smile and hear her call him FBI, even in exasperation. She'd been faced with hard choices—hadn't they all? And she'd made them regardless of the costs.

Regardless of her obvious struggle with regret.

Besides, holding on to anger only seemed to dig a hole through him, leaving him hollow. He could at least try to forgive her for the sake of their safety.

He sighed, feeling the tight knot of anger inside him loosen. He turned toward the group. "Stay here. I'm going to help Andee." He met Phillips's approving look and saw Nina glance at him. "I'll be right back."

As he plunged through a clump of willow, he heard a roar

shake the forest and echo against the mountains. His feet responded before thought kicked in, and he ran toward the sound. "Andee!"

He heard her scream, and every hair on his neck and arms raised. "Andee!"

Crashing through the forest, he felt his ankles bend on the gnarled floor, nearly catching him, tripping him. He heard another roar and burst into the meadow in a blur of fear.

A gunshot.

Reflex dropped him to his knees. Breathing hard, he heard another shot break through his thundering heartbeat.

A third shot, and he looked up to see Andee with a handgun. It shook in her hands as she pointed it skyward. She stared to the west, away from Mac, her gaze fixed on a retreating hulk of an animal breaking through the forest, two cubs on its trail.

Andee dropped the gun, shaking.

Mac stared at her, realizing two things: She'd just scared away a grizzly.

And she had a gun.

A *gun*.

If she'd been a terrorist, she would have used it on him days ago.

"Andee?" He found his feet and ran toward her, remembering her story of the grizzly. Only this time she hadn't frozen.

"Andee?" He put a hand on her shoulder, and she nearly jumped through her skin. "You're okay. It's gone."

Breathing hard, she turned toward him, her eyes glassy with fear.

Everything he'd been trying to bottle up or deny since she'd begged him to forgive her broke loose. He pulled her to his chest, nearly crushing her as he closed his eyes, letting his own relief rush over them and yanking the plug on the last remnants of his anger. How could he *not* care about her? *not* forgive her? "You scared me."

She didn't move, didn't speak. She trembled in his arms, and he held her tighter. "You're okay, Andee. It's gone. You scared it away."

"I did . . . ?" she said. It sounded more like a question. "I did."

"You did," he said, a smile finding one side of his face. "You're amazing."

"Or stupid." She shook her head and looked at him.

She was so close to him, so incredibly close he could see every detail of her beautiful brown eyes. Only they weren't just brown. They were brown around the edges with golden flecks inside that hinted at the treasure of knowing her. Long lashes outlined those eyes, and freckles dotted her tanned skin.

Wow, she is pretty. She fit into his embrace as if she belonged there, just like she had the first time. "Are you okay?"

She nodded, licking her lips, her voice broken and soft. "She just snuck up on me. I didn't see her until she roared, and then I knew I couldn't climb a tree fast enough."

He touched the side of her mouth, where tiny lines framed her smile. "Climb a tree."

She seemed startled by his touch, and her smile faded. "I . . . ah, well . . . I had the gun and I—"

He couldn't help himself. He sweetly touched his lips to hers. She stilled, then, amazingly, relaxed. He imagined her closing her eyes as she kissed him back. It lasted only a moment, but he let himself be inside this one perfect tick in time, isolated from the chaos and aches and journey that defined their lives. Andee, in his arms, trusting him. She tasted of blueberries, sweet and tangy, pure Andee.

When he pulled away, she swallowed, shock on her beautiful face.

He gave a sheepish smile. "Sorry, but I couldn't help it. Forgive me."

She searched his eyes, her face now cresting into a frown. "Forgive you? Oh, Mac, forgive *me*. Forgive me for Brody and for lying. . . ."

He cupped her cheek, running his thumb over it. "I forgive you." Then he kissed her on the forehead.

Her eyes glistened.

He heard crashing sounds in the woods, and for a moment he stiffened, afraid the bear might return. Then he heard Phillips and Nina calling, "Andee? Mac?"

Andee disentangled herself from Mac, her hands on his chest, staring at him with the slightest of smiles.

He met that smile and heard in it questions. What next? Was she in his arms because she wanted to be or because she'd been afraid? Did she really want someone in her life like Mac? What kind of future did he have to offer her?

The answers burned his throat.

"Andee!" Phillips burst through the forest wall. "Mac?"

Andee took a deep breath and looked away from Mac toward Phillips. "Here," she said, but her voice sounded fractured.

"Are you okay?" Phillips ran over to them, breathing hard, Nina close at his heels. He stared at Mac, then at Andee. "We heard gunshots."

"Bear," Andee said.

"She saw a grizzly. It would have mauled her if she hadn't shot at it. Scared it away," Mac said.

"You have a gun?" Nina said, her gaze resting on the Glock that now lay in the grass.

Andee glanced at it, as if just realizing she'd used it, and nodded at Nina.

"Okay, let's get Annie Oakley back to camp. *With* the blueberries," Phillips said.

Mac let the flint of jealousy pass. Because, as Phillips picked up the bucket only half full of blueberries and Nina took Andee's arm, Mac met Andee's eyes. For the slightest hiccup in time, she gave him a real make-the-world-stop smile.

A thousand explosions rocketed through him. It felt so good that for a crazy second he thought he might tear up. He watched her walk away with Nina steadying her. By the time they reached the edge of the meadow, she'd freed herself from Nina, and he could tell from her gestures that she was relating the story.

"Help me gather more blueberries?" Phillips asked.

"Aye," Mac said.

"That was a close call," Phillips said, shaking his head. "I don't know what we'd do without Andee."

Me either, he thought.

Chapter 15

"THE GPS LOCATOR has them heading east." Constantine Rubinov watched the blip over the grid, locating it on the map spread out over Gerard's table.

Late last night Gerard had watched Constantine and Juan jump like a couple of third graders when they heard static, then a voice come over the line. But before Juan could respond, Constantine had yanked the two-way from his grip.

Gerard hid a smile behind his swollen lips at their sudden confusion. Unless their partner had suddenly morphed into a Scottish-sounding male, their plan had taken a serious detour.

The light barely dented the chill gathering in the cabin, and Gerard's stomach roared with hunger. Constantine and Juan had eaten the last can of corn in front of him last night, and he'd gone to sleep dreaming of the venison steak he had secreted in the cellar behind the cabin. He only *looked* like he might be on the edge of starvation.

No, the emptiness came from the worry that turned him nearly inside out. *Where are you, Andee? Please, please don't come here.*

He'd taught her to use her head, to stay calm. If she was still alive—and the static on the radio seemed to suggest hope—Andee would eventually head to Disaster like a homing pigeon.

"What do you think happened?" Juan asked, leaning over Constantine. Even from ten feet away, Gerard could smell the man—sweaty and sour.

Constantine glared at Juan over his shoulder. "I don't know. Maybe they landed somewhere. But it looks like they're on foot, with the speed they're traveling. I marked the grid last night and today." He stared at the map, then got up and walked over to Gerard, who braced himself for pain. Instead Constantine grabbed him by his long ponytail and hauled him to his feet. "Where is she going?"

This close, Gerard saw the changes in Constantine—the speckled skin, evidence of alcohol abuse, and a scar that ran the length of his jaw. Gerard wondered if he'd gotten that in jail. "I don't know."

Constantine looked away, then struck Gerard across the jaw.

Gerard fell to his knees, his face exploding in pain.

"Here's the deal, MacLeod. You map this out for us and I'll let your daughter live. You know we'll find her. But if we have to do it the hard way, well—" he grabbed Gerard's hair again, made him meet his gaze—"all those things that happened to my brother Leo, I'll gladly revisit on her. You know, being in prison teaches a man a few things." He went quiet, letting images sink into Gerard's brain. "When Leo died you could hear his screams echo through the entire cell block."

Constantine's voice went low and tight. "Do you know what it feels like to listen to someone you care about die? listen to their screams for help? listen to them beg for their life? Do you have any idea what that is like, MacLeod?"

He didn't blink, didn't move.

Constantine smiled. "You will." He stood and looked at the map again. "I know you hope your daughter is tough like you . . . but I think that you might be disappointed."

"Don't you touch my daughter," Gerard muttered, hating how Constantine had gotten a rise out of him. But the idea of Constantine's hands on Andee—he thought he might wretch. He lowered his voice to a growl. "I promise you, I'm not the only one you'll have to worry about if you hurt her."

Andee had friends; Gerard knew that. She did SAR work with a couple of ex-military guys who acted like the big brothers she never had.

"Really? Because according to my information, your wife left you, and you have no other kids. So, unless she's hiding a bunch of big brothers in her flight pack, I don't think I'll have to look over my shoulder."

Gerard refused a smile. "She has nothing to do with this."

Constantine leaned close, his mouth near Gerard's, and whispered, "Oh yes she does, MacLeod. Yes, she does."

Gerard turned away. Why had he ever thought he could protect Andee, keep her safe from people like Constantine who wanted payback? His plan might have worked had Andee not tracked him down and burst into his life like sunshine after the dark solstice of winter. He ached with how much he'd missed her, despite the updates and pictures Mary sent to him.

For a blinding moment as they'd stood on that wet and windy tarmac, he'd considered rewriting his choices. Giving up his life in the bush, moving south, and starting a new one with Mary. He and Mary had even talked about it, and then in a blinding moment of pain, she'd demanded that he choose between the two lives he lived. But he knew that if Rubinov found him, he'd also find Gerard's family. So standing on that tarmac staring at his beautiful wife and his amazing daughter,

Gerard knew he couldn't live with himself if they died because of him.

Kind of like how he felt right now. Something hard and cold had solidified in Gerard's gut over the past thirty-six hours. If he lost Andee, he felt pretty sure the cold would take over his entire body.

Constantine stalked away from Gerard. "I'm guessing that they'd travel this way along the Granite River." He traced his finger over the route. "And then over to Disaster. Right here, in fact, running to dear old dad for help."

"My daughter won't come here. She doesn't need me to take care of her."

Constantine cocked his head. "All little girls need their daddies. Don't you know that? Can't you see that's why she comes back? After all these years, she comes back to *daddy*. How do you think I found you?"

Gerard forced himself to stay calm. "Andee is a bush pilot in her heart not because I want her to be. And she won't come here." *Please, please, Andee.*

Constantine smiled, because even Gerard heard the quiver of doubt in his own voice.

✦ ✦ ✦

The cold front had rolled down over the North Slope and followed the group through the river valley, turning the sky to chalky gray and blotting out the sun. Andee worked without pause to erect their shelters. Sarah complained that she could help, that she felt able, and Andee had to threaten to tie her to a tree. It helped that Sarah was still secured to the pack frame. In the end, her head still throbbed, crossing her eyes with pain at times.

They'd made it as far as the junction between the Granite River and Disaster Creek, where the two bodies of water flowed together in a roar. The water spilled over rocks and furrowed out the rocky canyon to the south. Andee had camped at these headwaters before and could find her way to her father's cabin and Disaster in her sleep.

Please let Dad be home. Or rather let his Cessna 185 be home. She had long ago learned not to expect anything from Gerard—he'd be just as likely to be out hunting as at the homestead. Or maybe he'd have taken the dogs or the four-wheeler into Disaster for supplies. Or he could be transporting—Gerard made a point of being one of the few guides who served the northern Brooks Range this late in the season. Days like this were one of the reasons pilots refused to leave hunters in the wilderness. Who knew when they'd get socked in by a storm and stranded or forced to walk out because of limited supplies before a pilot could return to retrieve them.

If Gerard had left his plane, she'd call in the distress signal while flying Sarah into Fairbanks. If he'd taken the plane, she'd use her father's HAM radio to call for help.

Either way, they'd be warm and safe by tomorrow. Flint would head home without his trophy but with a whopper of a story. Nina would be reunited with her husband and children in Prudhoe Bay. Phillips would go north to his mission work. Ishbane would return to Canada. And Mac . . . ?

Andee banked the fire, building a wind stop toward the north, protecting the flames as they chewed up the willow she'd gathered. Flint sat on the water's edge, hoping for a grayling or a trout, and Nina cleaned the blueberries they'd gathered en route.

It felt like a family of sorts.

Mac crouched beside her, holding his hands before the

flame. "You really know how to start a fire." A smile formed at his words.

She glanced at him. *As do you.* "Thanks."

He met her gaze with eyes that made her feel safe, as if the world might spin out of control around her, but as long as he looked at her like that everything would be okay.

She must be beyond exhausted, her mind turning to blubber, because not only had she let Mac kiss her, but she'd kissed him back. And now she smiled at him like a love-struck prom queen. She needed a serious dose of reality because even she knew they had zero chance at a future together. FBI agent. That fact right there should stop her dead in her tracks. She knew what that entailed, so no thanks.

Worry, more worry, and heartbreak.

Not only that, but according to her logbook she was supposed to head south in two days and start her fall shifts as an EMT at Des Moines Mercy Hospital.

Maybe she should check herself in and have her head examined. Because she couldn't remember ever feeling this out of sorts and confused. Or happy.

Mac broke into her thoughts. "I have a surprise for you. Will you come with me?"

She frowned at Mac, then glanced at Nina and Flint. In the graying light, they seemed okay, sitting onshore, Flint playing with his fishing line. She had just checked on Sarah, given her a drink, fed her some berries. "Where are we going?"

He held out his hand, and like magic, hers slipped into his grip. She stared at it for a second, thinking maybe it had a mind of its own. Her feet also seemed to succumb to his powers as they took her down shore, away from the group, up a fall of rock and onto a sheep path to an outcropping overlooking the river. Although hazy, she could still make out the lip over which the Granite, now combined with Disaster Creek, fell into a thunder of falls. To the east, she could follow the Trans-Alaska Pipeline System—the snake of piping that dissected the Brooks Range—to surge north.

"This is quite a view," she said, trying to be polite. But she'd seen this before, and as much as she enjoyed just being around him, this kind of activity wouldn't help at all when she had to tell him good-bye in twenty-four hours.

As it was, she'd be reliving that kiss for the next decade. Or two. *Wow*. Sweet and soft. She'd remember how good it felt to be in his arms. As if he'd needed to hold her as much as she'd needed to be held.

Mac still had her hand. He stopped, turned, and with gentle pressure made her sit on a boulder behind her. "Just . . . stay here, aye?"

She watched him as he traversed the path, then crouched to retrieve something. She couldn't help but notice his broad shoulders and the way the wind returned his scent to her. He smelled again of the biodegradable Ivory soap they'd used to wash in the river. Clean but enough Mac for her to smell the campfire smoke and his masculine scent. His stubble flecked red, especially when the light of the fire blazed against it. She had the errant urge to run her fingers through it, bristly and harsh, yet surrendering to her touch.

He turned, smiling, and his expression glowed in the light of a singular emergency candle she'd had in her pack. In a Sierra cup, he'd melted the candle into its wax and banked around it the pieces of a Hershey bar—she hated to know how long that had been in his pocket—and blueberries. "Happy birthday, Andee."

Her mouth dropped open, and for a glorious second, she couldn't speak. Her birthday. *He remembered my birthday.*

Mac knelt before her, grinning, his blue eyes alight. "Make a wish and blow out the candle."

Make a wish? She could hardly breathe let alone think. She took a breath, then shook her head. "I . . . I don't know what to say."

"Don't say anything. Just make a wish and blow out your candle."

She watched the candlelight as it bent and flickered in the breeze against the pane of night. "I don't want to, because if I do, I won't be able to see you. The night will close in, and it'll be dark."

Mac's smile turned wry. "Okay." He set the cup down and sat opposite her, his knees drawn up, his arms over his knees. "I wish I had a cake or something—"

"A cookie."

"A cookie?" he asked.

Andee picked out one of the blueberries. "Sarah always sends us cookies. Big ones, the size of a pizza."

Mac took a piece of chocolate. "My ma sends me a black bun every year, even though my birthday is in March. Wraps it up and sends it to Fairbanks or Anchorage or even out to Virginia one year."

"What's that?"

"Your mother never made you a black bun? Where is her Scottish heart?"

"My mother isn't Scottish. She's Nunamiut Indian and French."

Mac shook his head. "I'm sorry for you. Black bun is a New Year's cake made with raisins, currants, almonds, and spices. It makes a man want to go home."

"Your family sounds incredible."

"They are. My da is loud and raucous. Ma keeps him and

the rest of us safe and healthy. No matter where I go, a part of me will always be in our kitchen, watching my mother make bannocks or stovies."

Andee laughed. "Typical that you'd associate memories with food."

"Don't you?"

"No. I . . . ah . . ." She frowned. She associated memories of her father with flying and the woods, and her mother with late nights hovered around their rummage-sale kitchen table in their one-bedroom apartment. Later her mother's lab coat and the stiff smiles of her colleagues as she fought for a toehold in the medical community. She saw her mother wearing her mortarboard, their pictures side by side as college graduates. She looked at the candle. "Hard work, I guess. I remember a lot of lonely meals."

Mac's smile dimmed. He touched her hand when she reached out for a piece of chocolate. "I was thinking that maybe you could . . . uh, come to Deadhorse with me. After all this. Meet my family."

Andee stared at him, her breath tangled inside. "I . . . I don't know. I—" she shook her head—"Mac, don't you think maybe it's all just . . . being out here? I was afraid, and you were there."

She saw him look away and was suddenly afraid of the feelings she let accumulate, of those fairy-tale endings that had filled her childhood dreams. But Mac wasn't a knight in shining armor, and she'd never been a damsel in distress. Until now maybe. Her voice wavered. "Why did you kiss me?"

"Forget it." He stood.

"No." She grabbed his wrist, everything inside her aching to be back there in that moment when he'd held her and she'd been charmed by his wonderful smile. "Ever since I met you,

I feel like I'm in knots. One second you're arguing with me, the next you're helping me carry Sarah, the next you're saving Flint's life, and then you're accusing me of being a terrorist. And then . . . then you find out I was the one who didn't save your brother." She saw him flinch. Her voice fell. "Then you're kissing me like no one has ever kissed me before." She dropped her grip on his wrist. "I don't understand."

He remained still, the wind blowing against him, flickering the candle, snuffing it out until only a wisp of smoke spiraled and dissipated into the night. "The truth is, Andee, I don't understand either."

✦ ✦ ✦

Mac couldn't leave Andee sitting in the dark, although every instinct told him to run—far and fast. He wanted to bury this moment in his fleeting memories. Then he'd never have to remember that for a minute he'd thought he could have this woman who'd gotten so far under his skin that he might be ripped in half if he tried to pry her out.

He didn't understand why he needed her in his life.

But more than that, he didn't understand why she couldn't need him back.

"Mac, I'm not sure what to think. I've never been in this position before, I guess."

He looked at her, puzzled. "You've never . . ." What? Been in love? Did he have feelings of love for her? Admiration, yes. Respect, yes. Desire . . . yes, that had scared him the most. But love? He looked at the outline of her face, her luminous eyes.

She seemed to know what he might be thinking—or at least he hoped she did—for she shook her head. Her eyes glistened. "I have a pretty sorry track record when it comes to rela-

tionships. Not that I've had a lot of boyfriends. In fact, I
haven't. Yes, I got asked out, but I know how relationships end
up. And I can't be that girl who hopes for so much and in the
end realizes it was just a dream."

He sat before her, cupped her face in his hand, rubbed his
thumb along her cheek. "You're talking about your parents." But
he understood her words and knew how it felt to pin his hopes
on something, only to have it blow up in his face.

She shrugged and looked away. The grayness barely illumi-
nated her face, but he saw the pain carved into it. "When I was
twelve, four years before we left my father in the woods, my
mother got a call on our HAM radio. Dad had been working
undercover in Anchorage and had been shot. Of course, at the
time we thought a gun had accidentally gone off by one of the
hunters on his plane. My mother got a flight to Fairbanks, and
we left within the hour.

"I'll never forget seeing him, a central line protruding from
his chest and an oxygen machine breathing for him. He'd been
shot in the stomach, and it dissected his liver. My mother got
us a room at a hotel, but we didn't use it once. We stayed by his
side, sleeping on a cot or in a chair until he was well enough to
be released. We lived in the hotel for a month, my mother nursing him back to health. I remember it as a happy time. We
played chess, and when I had him in check, he'd wiggle his
knees and upset the board. My mother cooked all his favor-
ites—oatcakes and porridge—on a hot pot. A couple of times
they sent me out to get pizza."

"Sounds like they loved each other very much. What
happened?"

"Love was never their problem. I found out not long ago
that they corresponded for years—still do. My dad just couldn't
give up his career."

Suddenly the pieces fit into place. "As an FBI agent."

He saw the sadness in her eyes. She nodded. "Gerard loved his job. But more than that I think he felt compelled to do his job."

Gerard? Mac searched through his mental files. *Her father couldn't be Gerard MacLeod, could he?*

"I told you he was a Vietnam vet. Only after I did SAR work and watched victims cope with the deaths of their friends did the connection spark. He saw so many of his friends die and couldn't figure out why he wasn't among them. I guess he thought he had to do something extraordinary to justify his shame of living.

"I'm not sure why he couldn't choose my mother and me. Maybe he simply couldn't accept that God had chosen him to live, and he had to somehow prove his worth to the world. Prove that saving his life had been worth it to God."

Mac rolled her words through his mind. He'd always held a pragmatic view of life—the good of the many outweighed the good of the few. But since Brody's death, that theory hadn't helped him cope with the loss of his best friend or accept the man he saw in the mirror.

He might be more like Andee's dad than he wanted to admit. Only, from his recollection, Gerard had been labeled a hero.

Nothing at all like Mac.

"In the end, though, I think it was their pride that kept them apart," Andee continued. "Neither could say the words *I need you.* Or *please don't go.* It broke my mother's heart and turned my father into a bitter, driven man."

As Mac ran his thumb down Andee's cheek, her words burned. Anyone who needed him was going to get hurt, just like Gerard had hurt Andee and her mother. Most of all, if he slowed down enough to need someone, that would only get his attention off what was most important.

Andee smiled at him sweetly, sadly.

A woman would have to crash-land at his feet to get his attention. He'd joked about that to Brody so many times he'd actually started believing it. Only Andee had done just that. Crash-landed in his life, blowing apart his defenses. Somehow over the last few hours, he'd lulled himself into believing that maybe he could start over with Andee. Build that life his father had painted.

"My dad gave up a thousand moments with my mother and me for his job and the big picture," Andee said. "And even though I hang out with him every summer, probably trying to recapture those happy times, I know what I missed. I can't live like that, Mac. I can't be the girl you leave behind."

"But maybe I won't be FBI anymore," Mac said. "I'll resign, go home, fish, or work the pipeline. Or something." He cradled her face with both hands. "You could come home with me. Start that FBO you've been talking about. We *can* have a happy ending here, I promise." He hated the desperation that filled his voice, wanted to strip it away, but it had already tumbled out. He tightened his jaw against another flood of emotion, aware that he'd just made a fool of himself.

Especially because she shook her head. "Mac, whatever drove you to be an FBI agent is still part of you. You might think you've given that up, but I know better." She touched his face, ran her fingers through his beard. "The thing is, I like your dream. You have no idea how much I'd like to meet your family." She swallowed, leaving the rest unspoken. "But I can't compete with that place inside you that will look for terrorists in every person you meet or imagine scenarios whenever you see a marked map or a gun."

He began to protest, but she stopped him by laying a hand against his cheek. "I can't take loving another man who lets me down."

He closed his eyes, just concentrated on breathing.

"We'd better get back." Andee stood, and with careful steps, she found her way to the jagged path and right out of his life.

Chapter 16

"YOU LIKE HIM, don't you?" Sarah's voice filtered through the early morning, hushed against the snappy air.

Andee let herself come fully awake, realizing that she'd been semiconscious for a while now, listening to the wind in the trees, shivering under the blanket she shared with Sarah.

"He carried you down the mountain," Andee said by way of an answer.

"That's not what I asked. I see the way you look at him. All that toughness drops from your eyes, and inside is the Andee that laughs at Conner's jokes or buries her face into a child's neck. You want to trust him."

"I do trust him. I mean, enough to help us get out of here. He saved Flint's life. He ran toward the sound of the bear instead of away. He's a good man; I know it."

"Of course he is. But I think he wants to be more for you."

Andee lifted her hand to feel Sarah's forehead.

"I'm not hallucinating the way he looks at you, Andee. He likes you. You should have seen him watching you put up the shelters last night. Every time I look at him, I see Mel Gibson in *Braveheart,* with that long hair, the half smile, those blue eyes, watching everyone like a protective warrior. He's got the stuff."

"He thinks we're all terrorists—that's why." Andee kept her voice low.

"What?"

"He's FBI. He thought that one of the passengers was a terrorist, going to blow up the pipeline. That's why he watches everyone like a hawk." She cast her gaze onto Nina, who lay with her back to them, rolled up in a sleeping bag.

"You're kidding me."

"No. He found a map marked with drawings of the pipeline and a two-way radio. We tried to contact help but got nothing. He, of course, thought it was part of some sinister terrorist plot. That's why we had to hike out, although I'm thinking it was the right decision. I haven't seen any planes overhead in the last three days, which means that the rescue teams don't know where to look. We could be ice cubes sitting in that bowl, without food or water if he hadn't forced us off the mountain."

"You wanted to hike out alone, didn't you?"

Sarah knew her too well, knew that she'd risk her life before she risked the lives of others.

Andee said nothing, tucking the blanket around Sarah's shoulders. "You need to get some rest. We'll be at the homestead by this afternoon and in Fairbanks by tonight."

"You know, you could stay in Alaska, Andee. You don't have to go to Iowa."

The statement stopped her movements. She studied Sarah's face and saw she meant her words. "My mother needs me."

"Your mother is the head of family practice of her own clinic. Somehow she'll survive."

Andee closed her mouth, looked away.

"I think you need her more. This running back and forth between your parents has to stop. And don't tell me you're not doing that. Everyone can see between the lines, trace the paths of regret. The fact is, you can't erase time. Or heal your parents' hurts. Maybe you can learn from them. In the end, you can only go forward and trust God that He'll take care of it."

Andee closed her eyes, wishing Sarah's words didn't burn.

Sarah continued. "When I think of people with past hurts, I think of Rahab, the woman who hid the spies. She heard of God and wanted to trust Him. Even though everyone around her told her she was a fool, she acted on faith that God would save her. And God took her and her entire family out of Jericho and put her right in the middle of the lineage of Christ. Transformed her and gave her a new life despite her ugly past.

"Don't you think we all have regrets—choices we wish we hadn't made or that others hadn't made for us?" Sarah said. Her eyes shimmered with memories that Andee knew gave her a foundation from which to speak.

"But we have to trust that God's going to redeem us, our mistakes, and our choices," Sarah continued, her voice soft. "Lacey and Micah are learning that. Dani and Will are learning that too. You can't let regrets—yours or others'—keep you from going forward. You gotta trust God one step at a time, expecting Him to work it out. Remember our psalm?"

Psalm 42. The one they quoted when life got darkest, when after fifty hours of searching they still hadn't found the victim. "'Why am I discouraged? Why is my heart so sad? I will put my hope in God!'" Andee quoted.

"Hope in God, the One who has a perfect view of our lives. You need to face the sunrise, Andee, not the shadows behind you. God loves you, and you can expect Him to guide you because you're His child. If you seek Him, He's not going to let you screw up."

"I like what I do," Andee said. "I like flying, and I like being an EMT—"

"I know. But you also want a family, Andee. Dani and I know that better than anyone. We saw your face when Micah and Lacey got married, when Emily jumped into Micah's arms. It made me hurt for you."

Andee swallowed through her thickening throat. "I'm happy for them."

"Of course you are. But be happy for yourself too. Out there is a great guy. And after the chaos clears, he might just be the one. But not if you don't give him a chance."

Andee sat up, making ready to leave. "It's not about chances. Mac is an FBI agent, all the way through to his bones. I don't think he's going to give that up for me, despite what he says."

Sarah caught Andee's arm and pulled her back into her line of vision. "Don't judge Mac by Gerard's standards or weaknesses. Have a little faith."

Andee smiled and patted Sarah's hand. Faith. It wasn't that she didn't believe God, but she'd seen what faith in her father had done to her mother.

She climbed out of the shelter. The rising sun had begun to burn off the clouds. The cool air raised the hair on her neck, but the day looked hopeful, with a swipe of lavender across the sky. A day for hope, for going home. The sound of the river flowing against the rocks and the smell of the campfire still lingering in the air gave a surreal picture of a family camping trip. She stretched, working out the kinks in her arms, feeling a little like a mole with all this dirt caked on her. She needed to wash her face, brush her teeth, and hopefully soon she'd be able to take a whirlpool bath some place with room service.

She looked upriver, wondering about breakfast, and was surprised to see a large figure sneaking northward. The person disappeared behind a spruce tree, then moved away.

Mac. What was the man doing? Creeping up on a caribou? Or on another wild-goose chase?

See, she'd been right to believe that the sly FBI thing wouldn't leave his body on a whim or a command. She turned away, intending to bank the fire and start the coals when she heard movement behind her.

Nina probably. "Can you help me find some firewood?" she asked, turning.

"No, I'm afraid I can't." Nina held the killer whale for her son in one hand and Andee's Glock in the other. "Because, you see, we have other plans for today."

✦ ✦ ✦

Mac should have suspected Phillips had an agenda the moment the big man started spouting off missionary speak. All that mumbo jumbo about breaking free of bondage, of resurrection of spirit. Mac should have seen through it to the code. New world governments, breaking the bondage of American capitalism, raising the spirit of revolution—that's what Phillips had meant.

Mac watched Phillips steal through the morning mist, climbing over the rocks, escaping the riverbed and their motley cast of survivors.

Where was he going? Mac hated that his cynicism couldn't see past this little early morning excursion to some other excuse other than a rendezvous with Phillips's terrorist buddies. Maybe Andee had been right last night about the job being so much a part of him that he'd never break free.

Mac ducked behind a black spruce while Phillips topped the ridge above him and disappeared. He waited, counting his heartbeat, feeling the seconds spiral out, imagining Phillips as a terrorist, maybe even planted in New York when the towers collapsed. He wouldn't be surprised if Al-Qaeda, Hezbollah, or even the newest cell he'd read about, Hayata, had thousands of sleepers in America.

Waiting.

The thought spurred him to action, made him crouch and steal quietly up the rock. Maybe he did have FBI in the blood. Maybe he could never shake free of the desire to do something meaningful, to save lives, or—as Andee had accused—to save the world.

Was that so horrible?

"I can't take loving another man who lets me down."

He'd mulled those words over and over and over in his head during the night until they had finally driven him into a nightmarish litany of missed anniversaries, births of nephews and nieces, Christmases, and especially birthdays. A thousand memories he'd sacrificed for his job. Perhaps Andee had been right in turning him away.

What did he expect from her? Being in any branch of the military or protective government agency meant sacrificing for the big picture. It meant a guy sometimes missed out on the essentials of life. Like friends. Even a family.

Mac's foot spilled stones out, and he froze, listening to them bounce on the shelf of rocks.

Okay, he could admit that maybe he'd been about protecting himself also. He'd just never been any good at investing in someone, remembering their needs, thinking beyond himself. Because the minute he invested, he started to care. And when he cared, he left himself open for the sucker punches in life. No, Andee had hit right on the spot. He couldn't handle letting another person down either.

He climbed to the edge of the ridge, then shrank back. He saw Phillips not far away, sitting on a rock, his back to him.

Did he have a radio?

Mac eased over the edge, listening.

Aye, the man was speaking.

Mac launched himself over the top of the cliff and dived at Phillips, blitzing him. He landed with his knee in the man's spine, his arm pinning his neck. "Where is it?"

"Where's what?" Phillips choked out. "What's the matter with you?"

"Where's the radio? I know you're contacting your people."

Phillips lay there, eyes wide, mouth open in shock. "I . . . don't have people. I was praying."

Praying? Mac scanned the area, looking for the radio or a GPS. Nothing. He cringed and pushed himself away from Phillips. He couldn't even bear to give the man help up from the ground. He backed away from him, a hand to his head as he shook it.

Andee had been right. He needed to get as far away from himself and this job and who he'd been as fast as he could.

Phillips stood and brushed himself off.

"I'm sorry, man. Are you okay?"

"Are *you* okay?" Phillips asked. "I'm not the one sneaking up on people like some sort of thief."

"I thought you were . . . a . . . terrorist." Now that Mac said it aloud, he realized how stupid he sounded. He should go bury his head in a glacier or something.

"I've been called a lot of things. Nosy. Preachy. A wise guy. Even idealistic. But never have I been called a terrorist."

"Sorry." Mac stuck out his hand in apology.

Phillips took it, the expression in his dark eyes matching the forgiveness in his grip.

"So you were praying?"

Phillips nodded, turned, and opened his arms to the

expanse around him. In the west, the sunlight reflected against the jagged peaks, turning the snowcaps to glitter. Farther away to the east, a shredded veil of low-hanging clouds covered more mountains. In the valley below was Disaster Creek, a wild jumble of white water and rock, and just past that, the Dalton Highway, a strip of dirt that parted the mountains. "I thought this might be the perfect place to greet the morning with God. What do you think?"

Mac breathed in the pine-scented air and felt the sunshine warming the day. He nodded. "Looks like the perfect day to hike back to civilization."

"I knew God would save us. Can you believe that only four days ago Ishbane thought we'd freeze to death and eat each other?" Phillips said.

Mac chuckled. "Aye. Except Ishabane's fears were unfounded—he doesn't have enough meat on him to make an appetizer."

"Unlike me," Phillips said, laughing. "Only I was thinking a different kind of meat. I've been beefing up on Scripture for a year, getting ready for my trip."

"Where are you going again?"

"Resurrection, Alaska." He folded his arms over his chest. "Is that near Deadhorse?"

Mac sat on the boulder Phillips had been perched on before he'd tackled him. He scrubbed his face. "It's about forty miles west, I guess. I investigated a murder there once."

"Were you a cop?"

Mac nodded. "In a former life. I thought I could make a difference back then. Maybe help people."

"Why did you become FBI?"

Mac held out his hands in a sort of surrender. "Idealism. Again, I thought I could make a difference." But his words felt hollow. No, he'd become FBI because he'd wanted to be more than just a small-town cop. He'd wanted to matter, to be needed, to make a difference in someone's life.

"I know this is a personal question, but I thought I saw you sneak off with Andee last night. You and she . . . ?" Phillips raised his eyebrows and smiled. "She's a sweetheart."

Mac let a small smile escape. "Aye."

"But?"

"But she's not interested. Thinks I'm already overcommitted to my job."

Phillips shot him a look.

"Stop. The fact is, she's right. I can't balance both a job and a family. I've seen other guys try and get burned. Besides that, I'd make a horrible husband. I'm a big-picture kind of guy—not the flowers-and-chocolate type." Although seeing Andee's face last night when she saw his birthday treat had churned up a bevy of new feelings. Her smile had been worth his fear that she might break into hysterical laughter at his attempts. He'd never been a guy who remembered the details, but now he wondered if he'd just never found the right lady for whom he'd be the poetry-quoting kind of guy. The one for whom he'd make the effort to remember a birthday or anniversary. To whom he might come home to on a faithful, regular, first-priority basis.

The thought made him blink, and he stared at Phillips, who smiled.

"Andee's the one," Mac said quietly.

Phillips kept smiling.

Mac stood. "I've been thinking all these years that I couldn't balance the two—a family and the job—when in fact I couldn't face the risk. I didn't want to get that close to someone and let her down. Let myself down. So I turned to my job."

"Saving the world and tackling people on top of mountain ridges," Phillips said.

"Something like that," Mac said.

"Mac, at the risk of sounding too missionary, I have to say that we all want to do a good job at what we're about. But God gave us those people in our lives to show us why it matters. And when we get hurt or lose someone we love, it doesn't mean we shut down or stop caring. We keep moving forward in faith. Trusting God that He can take those moments that feel like death and bondage and free us. Give us a new life."

That's what Mac felt around Andee. A second chance. Someone who trusted him, whom he trusted in return. He breathed deeply the scents of the morning. "This is quite a view."

"Did you know you can see the pipeline from here? Nina pointed it out to me. She was scouting out the view from here." Phillips pointed through the trees to where Mac could make out sunlight glinting from a dark silver tube.

"Nina was up here?" *Scouting out the . . . pipeline?* Mac winced. *Oh, don't start that again.*

"Yeah. I guess I startled her. She was gathering firewood, I think, but she left part of her pile here when we climbed down." Phillips motioned to a gathering of willow sticks and brush.

Mac looked at the pile and something sparked. The feeling grew as he examined the hollow of kindling and tinder formed under a windbreak. It would only take a match, and in moments the pile would become a bonfire. . . .

Able to be seen for miles.

No.

Mac stared at the bonfire pile and tried to dismiss all his instincts that told him he'd been right all along. He'd blamed

Andee. He'd blamed Phillips. He wasn't going to make a fool of himself and call Nina a terrorist.

No.

Still, he turned, a low dread in the bottom of his gut pulling him back to camp. "Pray for us, Phillips," he said, meaning it as he climbed down the cliff.

He could see the campfire smoke rising from the camp, and the smell of it drew him into a jog. Andee had probably gotten up and started the fire. The thought made him smile. Somehow he'd figure out a way to prove that he wasn't going to do what her father had done and choose his job, whatever that would be in the future, over her.

He'd convince her that she meant enough to him to try and care about the little things, the things that turned a friendship into a romance. The things that showed her how much he cared.

His feet crunched over the rocks, but as he came close to the camp, he saw no one tending the fire. "Andee?"

Nothing.

He stood by the fire, watching sparks leap into the sky, crackling and dissolving into the crisp morning air. "Andee!"

He heard a groan and lifted the edge of the men's shelter. "Oh no." Ishbane and Flint lay facedown on their emergency blankets, hands duct taped behind them, tape muffling their mouths. Mac rolled Ishbane over and worked the tape off his mouth.

"It's Nina," Ishbane said, with more anger than fear in his voice. "She took the gun. And Andee."

Chapter 17

ANDEE TREKKED ALONG Disaster Creek, the sounds of the rushing water fading as she ascended the cliffs bordering it. Nina's steps thumped ten feet behind her. A quick glance behind confirmed that Nina still had Andee's Glock aimed at her spine.

"Why are you doing this?" Andee spoke in calm, even tones as they walked, grasping at her fading hopes that Nina had simply snapped, her common sense taken a hike off a tall cliff, leaving only panic to rule the roost. "Nina, I know we've had a rough trip. But we're almost to Disaster, and you'll be home to your husband and children tonight. Please put the gun away and let's go back."

Nina said nothing, just kept walking.

"Where are we going?" Andee stopped and faced Nina. Nina's dark eyes met hers with such ferocity that she felt her bones shake. Dropping out of the sky from four thousand feet didn't scare Andee nearly as much as staring into Nina's harsh expression.

"Keep going."

Andee climbed over boulders, deliberately crunching the dying purple buds of the Jacob's ladder that pushed out from impossibly barren soil. Maybe Mac would return and follow them. She flinched, remembering what Nina had done to Ishbane and Flint, how Nina had ordered her to tape them into submission. For the first time, when she looked into Ishbane's eyes, she was grateful he was a man who worried about details. He'd remember how Nina held a gun to Andee, how she'd taken the stuffed whale and her camera case, how she'd stoked the fire and poured a trail of camp gas from the fire to the shelters.

Most of all, she hoped he'd remember in which direction they'd headed.

Please, Lord, get Mac back to camp so he can put out the fire before it finds Sarah and the guys. The sun had burned off the frost lining the spruce and eaten the moisture from the rocks. Andee felt sweat slick down her back as she walked. For all Andee's hunger and fatigue, Nina seemed to have stores of energy that told Andee some great agenda kept her moving. *Lord, I know I've made a lot of mistakes over the last few days. But You've protected us all. I don't know what Nina wants, but I pray You'll save Sarah and Flint and Ishbane . . . and yes, me too.*

"Stop."

Andee stopped, bent over and gripped her knees, and breathed hard. From this vantage point thirty feet above the river, she could see for miles to the east. Dalton Highway, the pipeline, the pepper of spruce and birch against the colors of fall on the forest floor. The sky had turned pale blue, as if not wanting to make a decision between dismal and happy. Andee smelled smoke in the air and prayed it wasn't from the campfire burning the shelters.

"Sit down on your hands."

Andee calculated the distance between herself and the gun and sat on a boulder, her hands tucked under her knees.

Nina pulled out her camera, screwed off the lens, cracked open the film case, and pulled out a small plastic box the size of a television remote. A GPS locator?

"Where did you get that?" *Okay, stupid question. Out of the camera-that-was-not-a-camera obviously, but really, what's going on?*

While Andee scrambled to sort out her guesses, Nina pulled the whale from her jacket and, gripping it between her legs, tore off the tail.

Andee stared at her, dread fisting her stomach. "What about your son?"

Nina gave her an are-you-stupid? look.

Yes, apparently. Because until this moment, while she watched Nina tug another device zipped in plastic from the whale's body, she'd clung to the optimistic belief that Nina had just gone AWOL from her senses. Panic did that to a person—especially a mother—who was desperate and hungry and freezing.

This was not panic.

Nina tucked the device into her jacket, then held up the GPS locator. "Get up. Keep walking." She gestured with the gun.

Had Nina known where they were going all along? It made no sense. Until this morning, she'd acted like any other passenger—scared and willing to do anything to survive.

Andee traced back her morning. Remembering her conversation with Sarah made her feel sick. She'd told Sarah about the map, the radio, and Mac's suspicions. Had Nina been awake and listening? Or had she been planning this all along and only decided to take Andee along to keep Mac away, when she learned that Mac was an FBI agent? Why didn't she keep her big mouth shut? "Where are you taking me?"

"Over there." Nina pointed ahead, out over the water.

Andee's blood washed cold. A rope bridge hung thirty-plus feet over the gorge, the river below a snarl of freezing white water. A man stood on the other side of the rope bridge, waving.

"I'm not going across there."

"Yes you are, Andee. Trust me, you are."

Andee forced her feet up the path. At the top of the rocky path leading to the cliff's edge, another man waited for them. Wearing a dark green army jacket, a black cap, and bunny boots, he stared at her with black eyes that spoke of exasperation. He wore a semiautomatic weapon slung over his shoulder.

He looked past Andee to Nina. *"¿Qué le duró tan?"*

"I went out for pizza. What do you think?" Nina shook her head, glaring at the man. "Is everything ready?"

"Por supuesto," he snapped in return.

Andee listened to the foreign speech and felt ill. Why hadn't she listened to Mac? When he'd run that scenario by her about the Venezuelans, she'd actually laughed at him—laughed! And it felt way too creepy that she'd mocked him about Nina's whale. Her knees gave out, and she reached over to brace herself against a tree.

The man grabbed Andee's upper arm in a viselike grip.

"Ow," she said, too tired for bravery.

He yanked her toward a climbing harness lying on the ground.

"Put it on," Nina ordered.

Andee closed her eyes and just stood there, contemplating her choices.

"I know you know how. Do it."

"No. I don't know why you need me, but I'm not going to help you. I won't."

Nina stepped closer. "You might not think that. But the

fact is, you don't have a choice." She raised her voice, so it floated across the yawn of Disaster Creek to the other bank. "Show her, Constantine!"

Andee felt numb, right down to her toes, but couldn't stop herself from looking in the direction Nina had yelled.

The man on the other side pulled another man from the shadows. A lean man, with long dark hair pulled back in a ponytail. As she watched, Constantine leveled a gun at the man's head.

"Gerard!" Andee gasped. "Daddy."

✦ ✦ ✦

Mac watched the fire consume the second of the shelters, a plume of black tufting the sky. Thankfully, the rocky corridor that separated their campsite from the forest would keep the blaze from spreading, but the fact that Nina had tried to kill the others had him nearly blind with fury.

And scared. Because if she'd leave Ishbane, Flint, and Sarah to fry alive, what would she do to Andee?

He still couldn't wrap his brain around the truth. *Nina* had been his saboteur. Her tears, her seeming concern for her so-called children had thrown him off her scent, and he wanted to pound his head against the rocks. Why, however, hadn't she overpowered them earlier?

Phillips had helped him drag the others from danger and rescue their packs and supplies. Now Mac stood outside the ring of flames watching sparks escape, breathing hard.

"Which way did they go?" Mac asked Ishbane, who'd begun pacing. The man seemed to have conquered some inner demon, the one that made him pasty faced and weak. As if he finally realized that he might be a participant in his own survival.

Ishbane gave him a hard look, then pointed upstream along the Disaster.

Mac addressed Phillips. "Stay here. Watch over Sarah. And if Nina comes back, don't just pray."

Phillips met Mac's hard gaze with his own. "Listen to me. God already knows what is happening here. He knows how frustrated you are, and He knows where Andee is. I don't know what His plans are, but I know you can trust Him, Mac. Your job isn't to save the world here—it's to do your part and trust God for the big picture. In fact, God designs these moments so He can step in. *God wants to come to our rescue. So, frankly, my best defense is* prayer."

Mac wished he could embrace Phillips's words.

The sudden squawk of the radio nearly sent him through his skin. "Mac, I know you're listening." The static tried to blur the words, but as he grabbed it from his belt, he recognized Nina's voice. "I know you have the radio, and you think you're coming after Andee."

She has that right. Mac glared at the radio, as if willing Nina to materialize through it.

"Don't. I promise you, we'll kill her if you follow us or call the authorities. Stay where you are, and we'll keep Andee alive."

Sure, you will. Mac should have listened to his instincts, should have *never* let any of them out of his sight. He'd been lazy. Stupid. He listened to the static as Nina cut off transmission and nearly threw the radio against the rocks.

"Mac, calm down," Phillips said.

"You calm down! I can't believe I didn't see it!"

Phillips took a step toward him.

Mac held up a warning hand. "Don't. I have to go after her. I can't just sit here."

Ishbane stopped his pacing. "Yeah. You do. But leave the

radio. It'll be GPS tracked, and they'll know you're moving. We'll call for help."

Mac stared at him, frowning. GPS tracked. Of course. Nina hadn't needed the radio. The GPS tracking allowed her cohorts to locate her. No wonder she'd gone along peacefully, despite volunteering a few times to hike out with Andee. He thought of Nina's courageous, deceitful efforts on the scree slope. Imagine if she'd let Ishbane fall? It might have slowed them all down. And she'd buddied up with Andee because she'd needed her to stay alive. Until her fellow terrorists had located her.

Had he alerted these terrorists by turning on the radio, somehow activating an inbuilt GPS signal? He felt sick, nausea pitching his stomach. He handed the radio to Phillips. "I don't know if you can get any other channels, but try."

Phillips nodded. "God cares just as much about Andee as you do, Mac. Don't forget that."

Mac scrambled up the path in the direction Ishbane had pointed. *Please, God, don't take her away from me. I'm so, so sorry I haven't valued what You've given me. But I do now! I really want to be that guy who remembers birthdays and risks getting hurt just to see Andee smile.*

Before he'd met Andee he'd felt numb. Disintegrating. Andee had reached past the cold and made him feel alive.

"Joyful are those who have the God of Israel as their helper." He heard Andee's words quoting from the psalm in his head as he thundered up the path, feeling nothing as his feet fought for footholds.

Please, God, I'm not good at this, but I want to trust You. Help me trust You!

He found the flattened Jacob's ladder flowers, indentations where Andee had dug her feet into the ground, and what looked like stuffing. He picked it up, sifting the batting through his fingers. Nina's whale.

He wanted to hit something hard. Nina had been hiding something—a transmitter for a bomb? a radio? It had been inside that toy for four days and he hadn't suspected a thing.

Like a hammer driving home the last of his suspicions, the truth finally fitted into place. He'd dreamed this scenario a billion times. With the mountains as sentries, any remote detonation signal from a safe distance would have to happen from the air. While others planted the bombs on the pipeline, probably acting as hunters or hikers, Nina had most likely planned to hijack Andee's plane to send the radio/GPS signal that would flood millions of acres of Alaskan soil with crude oil. She'd used the stuffed animal to get through customs, probably removing the voice box of the whale and replacing it with the hardware to get the job done.

But now that Andee had crashed said plane . . . what was Nina up to?

Apparently Plan B.

Mac had to alert the right people. To stop Nina and her group, whoever they worked for.

Did he go after help, save the pipeline, or . . . find Andee?

There was only one right answer.

Mac tripped, landing hard on his knees and hands. Blood warmed his palms as he shot back to his feet. Below, he saw the rapids, heard the roar of the river.

His breath sawed in his lungs, cutting, burning as he topped the cliff. And then he spotted a rope, used to traverse the river, dangling over the edge, cut from the other side.

The other side, the side on which lay the pipeline . . . and Andee.

Everything inside him wanted to explode, to shout her name. But his voice echoing across the canyon just might be enough to kill them both.

Chapter 18

"GERARD, WHAT ARE you doing here?"

They had to wrestle her father to his knees and put him in a submission hold while Andee traversed the gorge. She saw the horror on his face when she touched ground, the way his eyes fought to glaze over, to show nothing, to feel nothing.

It was a look she hadn't seen since that day on the tarmac, her sixteenth birthday, when her mother had demanded, "Choose."

As Andee stared at her father, forced to his knees, his hands tied behind him, a gun to his head, that moment returned. A flash of pain that cut so deep it felt like lightning had scored her down the middle.

Choose. The word froze her, just as it had so many years before when her world shattered. She'd listened to the impossible word echo in her ears, staring at the two people who embodied her future.

Did she choose flying with her father, the one who'd taught her to trust herself, to believe that she could overcome her fears and find the strength to reach the other side? Yet he was the one who disappeared, who chose, over and over, his job above his daughter.

Or did she choose her mother? Steady. Wise. Accomplished. Wanting only Andee's future. The one who tucked her into bed each night, who fed her, clothed her.

An impossible choice.

But as her father met her gaze now, horror in his eyes, she realized that maybe she hadn't been the one forced to choose at all. Had her mother looked at her . . . or Gerard? What if she had demanded that Gerard, not Andee, choose?

Gerard had gotten into his plane and flown off. Without a word of explanation, leaving Andee to fill in the blanks.

She wondered now if perhaps, finally, she didn't have the answers. Maybe his choice had cost him even more than it had cost her. Maybe he hadn't come after her because he *couldn't*.

Not because he didn't want to. Maybe his choice had to do with this very moment, seeing his daughter—or his wife— suffer. The thought pushed tears into her eyes.

"I told you, MacLeod, that you'd do what we wanted," the one called Constantine said.

Andee listened closely to him, noticing he spoke without an accent. The man who'd followed her across the river and cut the rope trekked out ahead of them, then turned and glared, as if impatient.

Andee felt hands on her neck, forcing her to her knees. She refused to wince at the pressure and simply clamped her jaw and allowed her hands to be taped behind her. She kept eye contact with her father, willing him to explain.

"Get up, MacLeod," Constantine said, gripping her father's jacket collar. "We have some flying to do."

"Not unless you let her go."

Andee felt the barrel of Nina's gun press against her temple. "Get up, MacLeod."

Andee thought he might break into two pieces from the way

his expression wavered, his jaw quivering with a rage she'd never before seen. "I'm sorry, Andee. I thought I could protect you from all this. I thought that keeping you away from me might—"

"Shut up!" Constantine cuffed him, and Gerard fell chin first into the dirt. He pulled Gerard up by this jacket. "Get up. Now. Or she dies." He glanced at Nina and nodded.

Realization came like a fist, clamping hard. "They want you to fly them over the pipeline," Andee said.

Gerard met her eyes, said nothing. He didn't have to. Andee remembered the device in Nina's pocket, Mac's wild theories, and she knew.

"You're going to blow the pipeline from the air," she said. "You've already set the charges, and you're going to destroy—"

Nina grabbed her hair. "If we kill him, we still have you. Shut up." She eyed Constantine. "How far to the plane?"

"A half kilometer maybe. We parked it on the Dalton."

"Let's go."

Nina forced Andee to her feet, pushed her ahead toward the brush.

Gerard met her in stride and kept his voice low. "I know I made mistakes with you, Andee. But right now I need you to be the girl I raised you to be. I can't protect you anymore, but you can protect yourself."

Andee glanced at him, frowning, ducking as a branch slapped at her from Constantine's plow through the forest ahead of her. She'd heard Nina threaten Mac on the two-way. She'd wanted to cry out, to tell him the right answer. But she already knew what he'd choose. The pipeline. That was the only choice.

"Run," Gerard whispered. "Run for the river." He snuck a look at her, his eyes holding that twinkle, the one right before they had an adventure. The one that told her he had a plan.

And leave him here alone? But Nina had her gun. And—
"I can't."

"You can. Run!"

He spun, kicked at Nina, and Andee bolted. She flew past
Nina, who barely missed her, and sped through the woods, her
footsteps sure. She heard shots, then screaming and shut
herself from them. *Run!* The hot blood in her ears filled her
veins with adrenaline. She ripped and tugged at the bonds as
she ran, feeling her hands break free.

She burst into the clearing where she'd crossed over the
gorge.

And then she was flying over the edge, her arms windmill-
ing, her body caught in the spray of river as she fell.

✦ ✦ ✦

No!

Mac froze as he watched Andee fling herself over the edge
of the cliff. She'd materialized from the woods like some forest
animal and screamed as she hit the air. His knees gave out as
she plummeted into the white water below.

A man appeared right after her, pointed a gun where she'd
been, then advanced to the edge, searching.

Mac picked up a rock and with everything he had in him
threw it across the gorge. It hit Andee's shooter in the neck.
The man fell back and shot at Mac. He dived behind a boulder.
Bullets chipped rocks around him, but it bought Andee time.
Precious time.

Except, well, if she didn't get out of that river fast, hypothermia would grab her like a bear after hibernation and pull
her under. That is, if she didn't go over the falls first.

Go, *go!* Mac willed the shooter. He peeked to see him

disappear into the woods. Good. Maybe they'd believe they shot him.

Or not. *Please let Phillips and Ishbane have reached someone!*

Mac advanced to the edge of the gorge, searching for Andee. He saw her, a black head bobbing in the water. "Andee!" Giving one last look at the hole in the forest left by the shooter, Mac flung himself over the edge.

He circled his arms, fighting to stay upright. When he hit the water, the cold stole the breath from his lungs. It sucked him under; water closed over his head. Everything in him told him to kick, and he lunged hard for the surface.

Air. He sucked it in even as he felt the current take him. It wrestled him downstream as he fought to stay afloat. "Andee!" The cold burned his limbs, fire in every pore. The water filled his nose and blurred his vision.

"Andee!" He choked, coughing. Banging a rock, he pushed off from it, righting himself. *Think, Mac.*

He backstroked, turning himself so he faced downstream. His legs forward, he let himself ride the current, pushing away from rocks, arrowing downstream.

Andee had long since disappeared.

His body felt numb as the canyon flowed by. The river roared in his ears, thunder that threatened to consume him.

Then he saw her. She was clinging to a boulder the size of a half-submerged moose, a blur of red as the white water lashed his vision. "Andee!"

She looked in his direction, and the current nearly ripped her clutch from the boulder. He watched her grit her teeth as she pulled herself up, climbing onto the rock. Then she turned around and held out her hand.

Mac had his feet on the rock, slowing him when he caught her grip. Fear flashed across her face for a second as his weight threatened to pull her back into the water. He'd let go before he let that happen. He dug his fingers into the rock, and with her pulling, he managed to get a firm grip. He hauled himself out of the water and climbed onto the rock, breathing hard and shivering.

Andee sat beside him, her hands tucked around her knees, shaking. Water coursed down her face, into her neck, her saturated red jacket and spilled from her boots.

He put his arm around her, pulled her tight against him, his heart still pounding. "Are you okay?"

She nodded, or maybe that was trembling. In any case, she leaned against him. "I can't believe you jumped in after me! Are you crazy?" she said through chattering teeth.

"Maybe." He leaned back so he could look in her eyes, her beautiful eyes. "I reacted on impulse. I just . . . I couldn't let you die, Andee. Not if I could save you. I—"

"I'm okay, Mac."

"But I'm not." His own words rocked him. No, he wasn't all right at all. When he'd seen her go over the edge, only one thought fought for control of his mind: *Andee.* Not duty or patriotism or honor, just Andee.

He took her face in his hands. "You scared me. I saw you go over, and I thought you were dead. I couldn't stop myself. All I thought of was getting to you, pulling you out of the water before you froze to death." She opened her mouth as if to protest, but his words continued in a rush. "Andee, I know perfectly well that you're capable of taking care of yourself, but deep inside, I had to make sure."

She stared up at him—big eyes, mouth parted—and all his emotions rushed through him in one roaring gulp.

He kissed her. Hard. Letting all his desperation flow into a kiss that was probably just as much about himself and his fears and everything he'd bottled up for a decade as it was about showing her he loved her.

Loved? Aye, maybe those feelings that exploded within him, those hot, needy feelings that had pushed him off a cliff could be called love. That, along with the fact that every time he was around her he longed to be the man who made her smile and feel safe, who listened to her and believed in her.

And then, wow, she kissed him back. Curled her hands into his jacket, and despite the fact that both of them were shaking, she kissed him just as desperately.

As if, perhaps, she'd been afraid and needed him too.

He pulled himself away, just enough so he could see her eyes and hopefully determine her emotions. "I . . . that's the second time I did that without asking first." He swallowed, a fruitless effort to get ahold of his breath. "You have to know that I don't normally kiss a lady without asking first."

"Or jump into a river after her? I don't suppose you do." Andee smiled, but her expression looked haunted. "I don't either, but we don't have time to talk about this right now. My dad is up there with Nina and a couple other terrorists, and they're going to kill him."

Mac saw the tears that edged her eyes. She wiped them away and bounded to her feet. "We gotta get help."

Mac trailed her as she balanced over the rocks toward shore. He grabbed her elbow in case she slipped and took another wild jump. "We can't get them in time. But we can get to camp. I left the two-way with Phillips. I'm hoping he got through to someone."

Andee nodded.

Mac felt the numbing cold advance on him as he followed Andee to shore.

Chapter 19

ANDEE HEARD MAC behind her, pushing her toward camp. Everything hurt—her skin, her feet, her arms, and especially her heart. Because her father was out there, because for the first time in her life she understood.

Her father hadn't rejected her. Not really. Not in *his* eyes. Because despite Gerard's choices, he'd still loved her. And in the end, that was what mattered.

And what's more . . . Mac had followed her into a river because he thought she needed him. Never mind that she'd pulled herself out. The fact that he'd dropped his agenda— everything he'd believed in—to come after her . . .

She really didn't know what it felt like to be on the receiving end of search and rescue. To know that someone was out there, with her on his mind. Until now.

She glanced over her shoulder at the soggy, shivering man, his curls draped behind his ears. His blue eyes held a fire she'd come to expect, probably the passion of a Scot, and she knew, now that she was safe, that her father would be next on Mac's save-the-world agenda.

"Hurry, Andee," Mac said, coming up to put his arm around her.

"I know, Mac. They're going to take off any second. Nina had a transmitter—"

"You're shivering. I'm afraid you're going into hypothermia."

She felt his arm around her waist, felt her feet barely touch the ground. "But what about the pipeline?"

Mac's face was rigid. "I'm only one man. And I can only do what I can. I'm trusting that God's abilities are greater than mine."

A smile tipped Andee's lips, but she still worried. She should probably remember that also. That maybe God had everything under control, even when she felt like it all rested on her shoulders.

In the end, perhaps the Almighty could be trusted to guide her steps if she walked them in faith.

They found the trail. Mac held her hand as they ran, keeping her from tripping, pulling her up when her feet refused to cooperate. She felt her body start to become heavy, sluggish.

She tripped, but before she hit the ground, Mac scooped her up in his arms. She didn't have a bone to resist as she laid her head against his chest. He held her tight against him. She smelled river water on him, but she pressed her lips to the base of his neck, feeling his whiskers brush her cheek.

"Don't go to sleep," he said, a low growl of warning.

She nodded, but her head bobbed, feeling as if it weighed a billion pounds.

"Andee! Don't go to sleep!"

"No." But worry loosened its hold, and her mind began to let go of the vision she had of millions of gallons of oil saturating the valley. Of her father's eyes, urging her to run. She saw Mac, leaning against the wall of the airport, looking dangerous and arrogant as he sized her up. Saw him carrying Sarah and racing down the scree hill to save her life. She heard his voice as he stared at the stars:

"As fair art thou, my bonie lass,
So deep in luve am I;
And I will luve thee still, my dear,
Till a' the seas gang dry."

She smiled into the memory of him holding her after she'd scared away the grizzly and the glow of candlelight against his handsome, whiskered, warrior face as he'd wished her happy birthday.

"I love you, Mac."

"Do ya now?"

She smiled again, her head bobbing against Mac's chest, warm now, and she thought she saw visions, crazy happy visions of friends she knew calling her name. Heard Sarah's voice singing to her.

She saw Mac, his face close to hers, touching his lips against her forehead. "Don't leave me, Emma."

✦ ✦ ✦

"Where is she?" Constantine hollered when Juan ran up behind them, out of breath.

"She jumped!" Juan bent over at the waist, gulping in breaths. "But she's in the water. She won't survive."

Yes, she will. That's my girl. Gerard glared at Constantine.

Constantine looked at him. Gerard met his gaze with a look of triumph. Constantine cuffed him, and he tasted fresh blood.

"She won't live," Constantine snarled. "That water's near freezing." Still, he stood over Gerard, shaking his head.

"Let's go," Juan said, leveling his gun at Gerard. "Get up."

Gerard turned into a rock. Unmoving. Let them beat the tar out of him—he wasn't going to participate in treason.

Juan kicked him, a warm-up to the ugly finale. "Get up!"

Nina bent beside him. "I know where she's camped. You get up, or I'll go back and shoot her. If she lived through the jump."

Gerard met Nina's gaze with cool eyes. "You're better off shooting me now, because I'm not flying you anywhere."

"Okay, I'm leaving. Here's the transmitter." Nina reached into her pocket, pulled out a small black remote, and handed it to Juan. "Good luck." She turned, walking away from them.

Gerard watched her go. She didn't look back, just kept walking.

The vision of Andee, a bullet in her head, bleeding out on the tundra grass made him cry out. "Stop! Okay. I'll . . . let's go." He'd get them in the plane and take it down. Before they blew the pipeline.

I'm sorry, Andee. But it seemed that his entire life had been leading up to this event. In the darkest places inside him, he knew there'd be no happy ending for him and his family.

He should have let go of that dream a decade ago.

Gerard climbed to his knees, his feet, suddenly feeling exhausted.

Constantine smiled as if to say, *"See, a little motivation and everyone gets along just fine."*

Gerard fought the urge to rush him, finish it. But if he failed, they could still reach Andee. He'd wait until they were at two thousand feet, then cut the motor. Listen to them scream. In the end, Mary's prediction would be half true—he alone would die in a fiery crash.

They hiked in silence, time weighing upon them like the

press of cold against his ears. He could already make out Dalton Highway and the white hull of his Cessna 185 four-seater on the road. Constantine had forced him to land here, the closest entry point to Nina's GPS signal. Constantine had been nearly crazy with demands and threats after they'd spotted their contact last night on the ridge, using a mirror against the fading light. Juan's climbing abilities took a swipe at Gerard's confidence when the man constructed the rope bridge. He half wished he hadn't taught Andee how to climb.

Constantine walked behind him and prodded Gerard with his gun. Pain spiked up his spine. "Do you think she'll remember you as a hero?"

Gerard said nothing. He wasn't sure what Andee would write on his tombstone. At the least, his death would free her from this obligation she felt to spend her summers in Alaska. Even he, as thickheaded as Mary sometimes accused him of being, saw his daughter's desperate attempts to regain everything they had lost. Everything he'd sacrificed. It pained him to know how much he looked forward to her efforts.

"You made her jump off a cliff. Some father you are." Constantine shook his head. Gerard kept his face a stone. "They say a person has about two minutes once they hit the water."

Gerard saw Constantine glance at Nina. Her dark eyes glinted with triumph, despite the dirt on her face and a bloody gash behind her ear. "Has it been two minutes already?"

"I wonder if her body will go over the falls, or if some grizzly will have her for lunch," Juan added.

That. Was. *Enough.* Gerard spun and kicked Constantine hard in the gut. The air whooshed out of him, and he fell to his knees. Another kick across his temple sent him flying.

"Shoot him!" Constantine yelled as he fell to the ground.

But Gerard wasn't stopping. Over a decade of waiting, of hiding, of praying that Constantine and his clan wouldn't hunt him down unleashed in a blurry of frustration. "You cost me my daughter!" Gerard kicked Constantine a third time in the jaw.

A crack across the back of Gerard's skull sent blinding sparks into his eyes, pain, and then the taste of blood in his mouth.

Constantine roared in triumph and launched himself at Gerard.

Gerard curled into a ball, trying to protect his chest, but by the ferocity of the attack, he doubted Constantine would leave him able to stand.

Constantine shouted. Gerard jerked his gaze up in time to see him land in the loam, thrashing under the grip of an apparition from the woods. A man wearing a dark Gore-Tex rain jacket, a black stocking cap, and mud smudged on his face pushed Constantine into the dirt and dug his fingers into his throat.

Gerard fought his way to his feet, breathing hard, brain fuzzy. He turned and saw Juan retreating into the woods.

No!

A shot zinged over their heads.

"Micah, get down!" Another man, with dirty blond hair and wearing a lethal expression, grabbed Gerard by the shirt. "Get down!"

The man pinning Constantine ducked, then hauled him up by the collar of his jacket.

Another shot sent him into the trees, dragging Constantine behind him. Constantine landed on the forest floor, Micah's knee in his back.

Gerard followed the blond man and fell hard beside them.

Constantine's eyes were wild, staring at him in terror. About time.

"Sparks, just stay low," Micah said, no emotion.

Gerard watched, his memory clicking into place with a smile. *Micah and Conner? Andee's pals?*

Commando Micah leaned close to Constantine's ear. "We're looking for our friend, Andee MacLeod. You'd better hope she's okay."

Aye, Gerard thought as the blond man cut his bonds.

✦ ✦ ✦

"Put her down!"

Mac curled Andee to his chest, ready to do battle with the man who advanced on him across their smoldering camp and sounded fresh off some cattle drive. Under his cowboy hat, the fierceness in his dark eyes matched how Mac felt. Especially with Andee unconscious in his embrace. He'd felt close to unconsciousness himself, shivering and numb, but he wasn't about to put her in the hands of one of Nina's terrorists.

"Get back," Mac growled.

"Put 'er down," the Texan returned in the same tone.

"He's FBI, Hank."

Mac heard Sarah's voice from somewhere behind him and took in how her words registered with the man dressed in a blue jacket, wool pants, and hiking boots. He looked like someone Sarah and Andee might know, someone prepared for the outdoors. "You're a friend of hers?" Mac asked him.

"Hank Billings. We've been looking for you guys for two days. Finally tracked down the GPS signal on your two-way yesterday. Couldn't wait for the weather to clear so we came in on four-wheelers."

We? Mac looked around the camp. He saw a woman with an auburn braid snaking out of her hat leaning over Sarah, who was still strapped to the backpack frame. "Who are you?"

"Lacey Micah. I'm a friend of Andee's."

Hank came to Mac and held out his arms. "Let's get her warm."

Mac hesitated, then released Andee into Hank's grip. He noticed how the man gently laid her down, tried to rouse her. Lacey rose and joined him, taking Andee's vitals.

Hank looked up at him. "You'd better get changed. What happened?"

Mac's teeth chattered, and he folded his hands under his arms. "River. She jumped in the river."

Hank nodded, like the news that Andee had jumped into a freezing river happened on a regular basis. Mac took a step toward her, stumbled, and fell.

Phillips grabbed him before he hit his head. "C'mon, pal; you need to get warm." He dragged Mac over to a bag of supplies strapped to a four-wheeler. Mac watched Hank lean over Andee as Phillips handed him a fleece pullover, a pair of long johns, and wind pants.

"They've got her dad. They're going to blow the pipeline." Mac ducked into the brush, where he worked off his wet clothes. "We gotta stop them."

"Do you know where they are?" Hank asked.

Mac shrugged on the thermal shirt. "Maybe three or four miles northeast of here. They must be parked on the Dalton. There's nowhere else to take off from here. But I think they're on foot."

Hank spoke into a radio he took from his belt. "Micah, come in."

Mac heard static, then a voice. "Roger, Hank, we're here.

We found him—and a few terrorists too." In the background, Mac could hear popping, like gunfire.

"You okay?" Hank's expression was tight.

"Getting there. MacLeod says they're headed to the Dalton."

Mac frowned at him, trying to get his bearings. Who were these guys? He pulled on the pants, then tugged on a pair of dry wool socks before shoving his feet into his wet boots.

"I need a life flight for Andee. She's hypothermic." Hank glanced at Mac, worry on his face.

"Roger that," said the voice. More gunshots followed.

Hank stared at the radio for a second before he shoved it into his pocket. He flicked his gaze to Mac. "They'll be fine. From where they're broadcasting, they have a better chance of getting through."

"Are they armed?" Mac pulled on the fleece and emerged from the woods. He tried to put a visual to the drama he'd just heard.

"No, well, aside from the fact they both spent about a decade in Special Forces." Hank knelt beside Andee. "Lacey, get her out of these wet clothes and inside a sleeping bag. See if you can warm her up."

Mac approached, studying Andee's pale face, her shallow breaths. "Is she going to be okay?"

"I don't know," Lacey said, compassion evident in her green eyes. "I'm not sure she'd want you guys around for this."

Right. Mac turned, saw Phillips on the rock, his head bent in prayer. His softly spoken words came back to Mac: *We expected to die. But as a result, we stopped relying on ourselves and learned to rely only on God, who raises the dead.*

Mac felt his knees begin to give and reached out for a boulder for support. God had given him a second chance. Not to save the world . . . but to trust Him. Mac couldn't stop Nina, and apparently he couldn't save Andee. The thought took away his breath. He had no option but to trust God.

Please, God, don't let her die. The plea filled his head, his heart, his soul. He'd always been the big-picture kind of guy. The many for the one. But when the one was Andee, that thought nearly crippled him. No. But God could do both, couldn't He?

"Joyful are those . . . whose hope is in the Lord their God. He made heaven and earth, the sea, and everything in them. He keeps every promise forever."

God was big enough to create the world *and* the people in it. *Big enough to save Andee and* the pipeline. Somehow. "God wants to come to our rescue," Phillips had said.

Mac cupped his hand over his eyes, feeling himself shake. *God, I know You got us this far. Please don't let Andee die.*

"Mac, you feel up to helping the guys?" Mac raised his eyes to Hank, who stood before him, holding out a two-way. "Micah and Conner might need you to identify your terrorist. Take the four-wheeler. I need to stay here with Sarah and Lacey, and stabilize Andee."

"I can't leave her."

Hank gave him a look, the same one Brody had given him, the one that reined in his thoughts and focused them. "I promise that we care about her as much as you do. And this part we do well."

Mac took the radio, glancing at Andee.

"We'll take care of her, I promise."

Mac stood there, feeling ripped into two ragged halves.

"Go," Phillips said.

Mac climbed on the four-wheeler and gunned it through the river and up the opposite shore. He didn't look back.

The four-wheeler roared over the rocks as he rocketed down shore, looking for a place to climb. Obviously, if the terrorists had made it in on wheels, he'd find their way out. He discovered their path through the trees and floored it, barely hanging on as the machine bounced over the taiga forest due east toward Dalton Highway. He zagged around trees, praying.

Gerard McLeod was a legend at the bureau. As Mac had carried Andee in his arms to camp, he'd run through his memories about the ex-FBI agent. From his fuzzy recollection, Mac thought Gerard had been on the Fairbanks Drug Team, flushing out dealers on the North Slope. He wondered if he'd been a part of the Rubinov bust, sending an entire family of entrepreneurs to jail. A bust that had led to the killing of two of the involved agents and their families.

It occurred to Mac that perhaps Gerard's choices had less to do with furthering his career and more to do with protecting his family. At any rate, he prayed that Gerard had given Andee her tough-as-a-grizzly demeanor out of his own resources. *Don't go down without a fight, Gerard!*

Overhead, he heard a helicopter chewing its way toward Andee and Sarah and the others. Mac could nearly see Dalton Highway through the thinning of trees. Anticipation filled his veins.

Boom!

The ground shook, and an explosion nearly rocked him off the four-wheeler.

Mac slowed, wordless, as he watched black smoke plume above the treetops.

Chapter 20

ANDEE FELT THE warmth—a haze, really, of impressions—
both of fear and of soothing voices. She fought to climb her way
to the surface, to galvanize her energies to focus on waking up.
In the distance she heard the low hum of something, like a
mosquito or perhaps a bee. She raised her hand to swat it and
found her hand trapped.

Panic seized her and she gasped. Her eyes opened; above
her she saw a familiar face, fuzzy but recognizable.

"Andee, you'll be okay. Just hang in there."

Lacey? Andee opened her mouth to form words but nothing emerged. Lacey Micah was here in Alaska? But how? She
felt so very tired, so numbingly cold, and pain crept into every
pore in her body.

Her expression must have betrayed her confusion because
Lacey smiled, her eyes warm. "I got you as warm as I could.
The chopper is on its way." She pulled the sleeping bag up
around Andee's face.

"How did you get here?" Andee looked around, saw the
blue sky, the green pine, heard the river flowing nearby. It felt
like Alaska, but Lacey lived in Kentucky.

Lacey smiled. "Your very worried friend Conner. And of

course—" she glanced beyond Andee—"Hank expected Sarah's call three days ago. When he heard your plane hadn't checked in and that searchers couldn't locate your ELT transmission, let's just say that he doesn't think anything of calling Micah at 3 a.m. Micah contacted his friends in the Alaska National Guard, and I think Conner and Micah and I were wheels up within four hours. Good thing Dani was around to watch Emily, or I would have missed all the fun." Her gaze darted to Sarah. "You'd think Hank had a thing for Sarah or something."

Andee cracked a slight grin despite the violent tremors that raked through her, followed by a wave of pain. She groaned, and the press of fatigue weighted her eyes.

Lacey wore concern on her face as Andee looked up again. "She's in pain, Hank."

Another face came into view—Hank's. He looked like a Wild West hero in his cowboy hat and cockeyed grin. As Andee stared at him, suddenly it all came rushing back—Mac, the river, her father.

"Gerard!" Andee battled the waves of exhaustion, fear pushing at her as she struggled against the confines of the sleeping bag. "They're going to bomb the pipeline!"

"Calm down, Andee." Hank pushed her back down. "He's okay. Micah and Conner found your dad, and Mac is on his way."

On his way? To where? "What about the pipeline?"

Hank didn't answer her, but he wore a stricken look.

"Nina did it." The voice came from above her, and Andee turned her head to see Ishbane holding Mac's radio. "She blew up the pipeline."

Andee followed his gaze to a plume of black smoke in the far-off horizon. No. *Oh no.* She felt light-headed, and she sank back onto the ground and closed her eyes. "Mac was right about the pipeline all along. I should have listened to him."

"You got us to safety, Andee." She opened her eyes to the gentle voice, as Phillips crouched beside her. "You can't do everything. You made the right choice, the only choice you could. You gotta believe that God has it all under control."

It seemed that she'd heard that somewhere before. Phillips's warm smile found her soul. "You're going to do great as a fisher of men," she said.

His eyes sparkled.

Andee looked at Lacey. "How's Sarah?"

The drone in the sky grew louder and drowned out Lacey's reply. The wind kicked up as a rescue helicopter flew over, then landed on the opposite side of the river. Two men jumped out, dressed in the garb of the Alaska Mountain Rescue Group.

Andee nearly leaped with joy, despite being trapped inside a sleeping bag.

She watched as they forded the river, carrying a Stokes litter. They loaded Sarah first, stabilizing her neck with a C-collar and administering an IV of desperately needed fluids. They carried her across the river, aided by Ishbane and Phillips. Then they returned with another litter for Andee. It felt eerie to be on the receiving end of search and rescue, especially with Lacey holding on to her litter, stabilizing her. It hadn't been so long ago that it had been Andee helping Lacey through her pain.

They returned last for Flint, carrying him across the river and loading him into the chopper.

Flint sat down, his eyes betraying pain. But he sought

Andee's gaze. "You did it, Andee. You brought us home." He nodded, giving her a wan smile. "Thank you."

Andee didn't know what to say. Not with Mac still out there, not with Nina and her gang victorious in their sabotage. She probably should have let Flint keep his shotgun.

Ishbane sidled next to Flint. He looked exhausted, but his dark eyes held a new hue. "I'm sorry," he told Andee. "I should have believed in you."

She shook her head, shaking. "No, you should have believed in *us*. We all did it. We believed we were dead, but God saved us, showing us that He could rescue us." In so many, many ways.

"Are you going to Prudhoe Bay?" Flint asked Ishbane.

Ishbane braced himself as the chopper fired up, and with the engine roar, Andee barely heard his words. "No, I think I'll go home. See if anyone might be waiting for me."

Lacey settled beside Andee, Hank at Sarah's head, as the helicopter lifted into the air. Andee wondered what might be waiting for her and where she might call home. Again, fatigue washed over her, dragging her deep. She fought the tug.

In the back of her thoughts she had a memory, something soft and sweet that filled her fuzzy brain and coaxed her back into slumber. *I love you, Mac.*

But what now? Would he blame her for the pipeline's destruction? Or worse, blame himself for choosing to follow her into the river instead of tracking Nina and the other terrorists?

Everything that had passed between them might not matter anymore. Mac was FBI. So maybe he, like her father, would never have much room for her in his life. Despite any feelings between them, they might be headed for *Gerard and Mary*, Act II.

As the chopper veered south, Andee looked out the port window in time to spot black smoke spiraling into the sky.

✚ ✚ ✚

Mac motored toward the pipeline and the fireball. Another explosion made him stop the four-wheeler and dive into the bush for cover. Smoke billowed into the sky—black, acrid, the oil fueling the inferno. The blaze seemed alive, growling as it ate its victim.

He couldn't believe he'd failed. Or rather that God had failed them both. Especially after he'd made the agonizing decision to trust. What if he hadn't gone after Andee?

He didn't search for an answer because he couldn't bear a glimpse at the what-ifs. *Please, God, save Andee!*

He climbed back onto the four-wheeler, wondering where Andee's friends were. As if in answer to his thoughts he heard gunshots popping through the blaze. He angled toward the flames that topped the trees, cutting through the forest. Responsibility gnawed at him and dissected his options. Did he help Micah and Conner, or did he gun it for the nearest shut-off station?

What if this was only the first of many explosions?

Please, please let pipeline security notice the smoke from the line.

He debated for a moment before the sound of more gunshots galvanized him. Whoever was shooting—and he had a good guess that it was the terrorists because Hank had said that Micah and Conner didn't have weapons—knew just how many bombs had been planted and where.

Mac slowed the four-wheeler, hopped off, and crept toward the Dalton. Hiding behind a bushy pine, he parted its branches and stared out onto the road.

Sitting in the middle of the gravel road was an old Cessna 185. The plane burned, flames shooting skyward, as if it had been loaded with gas or oil. The smell bit at his nose, but he nearly crumpled with relief as he looked beyond the plane to the pipeline.

The pristine, still-intact pipeline.

Intact for now.

More gunshots snapped Mac to attention. He scanned the forest for the shooters. He guessed one was Nina. She wouldn't be hard to find in her red, fleece-lined jacket and cap. The others, well, he'd caught a glimpse of one across the river. Dark hair, green army jacket, bunny boots.

He dropped to the ground, listened, and headed toward the sounds. He wished he had a weapon, but his hands and feet had enough fury to power a small nuclear station, and they seemed sufficient artillery.

He crept through the forest like a fox, ducking under trees. They couldn't be far. Especially if they had fired the plane without remote detonation.

Another shot.

And then Mac spotted them.

Or at least what he thought was movement. He trained his gaze on the shadow he'd seen, and sure enough, moments later the person jumped to his feet from behind a downed pine and fired off another round.

Mac stole close, his heartbeat in his ears. He could see the man easily now, his black cap, a line of sweat dripping down his tanned face. He recognized him from their brief encounter at the river. How Mac wished he'd actually left a welt when he'd fired that rock. River Man stood again and Mac sprang.

In his peripheral vision, Mac saw more movement, but he concentrated on tackling the shooter. He connected, and the man went down hard, just as a shot winged over Mac's head. Mac subdued River Man before he had a chance to breathe, crushing his face into the loam, grabbing his hands, and twisting them back into a submission hold. The man thrashed against Mac's grip.

"Welcome to Alaska," Mac growled.

Screaming behind him made him turn. His mouth half opened at the sight of Nina similarly pinned, the knee of her assailant dug into her spine. The man—or rather *commando*—looked up. Mac recognized Special Forces when he saw it. The soldier/camper had greased his face with dirt, and he wore a black turtleneck, a wool stocking cap, and jeans.

"Hi," the man said, his eyes pinned to Mac's.

Mac met his gaze. "I really hope you're on our side."

Nina struggled, and the man tightened his hold on her. "I hate to do this to a lady," he said.

"She's no lady," Mac snapped.

The man gave the barest of frowns, then looked past him. "We're clear, Iceman!"

Iceman? Mac heard the snapping of brush, and another man appeared.

Dressed in black, with a stocking cap and an expression that made Mac bristle slightly, he held a 9 mm pistol in his gloved grip. The man stopped. "Micah," he finally said to Mac, "and that's Conner. We're looking for Andee MacLeod."

Weren't they all in a way? But still, *these* guys were Andee's friends?

Mac nodded, fighting his last image of her—pasty white, weak, hypothermic. *Please, God, let her be all right.* "She jumped into the river to escape. She's with your other friends now." Mac brushed off the fear that reached up to strangle him. Focus. "I need to get some backup in here." He took out the radio.

"And call for a helicopter while you're at it," Micah said. "I have Andee's dad, and he's in bad shape."

Mac turned to the pipeline frequency and contacted the pipeline security. Their terse tones confirmed that yes, they'd spotted the smoke, and they were already headed toward their position to assure the pipeline's integrity.

Mac watched with grim satisfaction as Conner and Micah bound Nina and her cohort with their shoelaces. He'd used that trick before. Then they dragged the pair over to Micah's gully of cover. Another man, wearing a grimy black parka, lay incapacitated, bound, glaring at the other two. And next to him, watching him with a death look and white-fisting a thick club, sat a man who looked like he'd gone one too many wrestling rounds. Mac recognized Scottish features—black hair and blue eyes—somewhere in that mass of cuts and bruises.

"Gerard MacLeod?" Mac asked as he knelt beside the injured man.

"Is Andee okay?" the man answered, confirming Mac's question.

Mac didn't know how to answer. He swallowed, dredging up a reply. Maybe? As if speaking for him, a helicopter droned far overhead. "She's hypothermic. But hopefully headed to Fairbanks." He noticed the catch in his voice.

Gerard leaned back against the tree, closing his eyes, as if giving in to pain for the first time. "My Andee is a fighter," he said softly, but Mac saw the worry on his battered face.

"Okay," Micah said. "I know this might sound a bit shoot-first-and-ask-later, but really, what is going on here? When Gerard told us to blow up his plane, it seemed prudent to obey. Sorry about your ride, though, Gerard."

Gerard looked at him and shook his head. "If they had gotten into the air, it would have been all over."

"They're terrorists," Mac elaborated. "Pipeline saboteurs." He glanced at Nina. "This one was on the plane with us, and she kidnapped Andee with big plans to meet her partners in crime." He saw Nina's eyes narrow and fought back the urge to unload just exactly how he felt about her betrayal.

Please, Lord, let Andee be okay. He turned away. "I love you, Mac," Andee had said as she'd slipped in and out of consciousness in his arms. *Oh, Andee, I love you too.* Only he hadn't said that.

Yet.

"Who are they working for?" Micah asked, standing beside one of Nina's accomplices.

"I don't know." Mac had his guesses, however, starting with Al-Hasid's cell. He fixed his gaze on the man at Gerard's feet. It seemed he looked . . . familiar. In fact— "Is that Constantine Rubinov?" Drug lord, murderer, now terrorist? And Al-Hasid contact?

Gerard said nothing but let escape the smallest of smiles.

In the distance, Mac heard the hum of four-wheelers. For the first time in days, he, too, let a smile crease his lips.

Chapter 21

ANDEE FELT WARM, so very warm, the smell of cotton around her like a cloud. Her mouth, however, seemed to stick shut. She heard laughter, so close that if she just reached out, maybe she could grab it, let it draw her out of the darkness.

"Andee?"

The male voice sounded familiar, like a hymn long buried in childhood or the smell of flapjacks cooking on a woodstove. "Andee, wake up now."

Her eyes opened. Shadow filled the room. She tried to unscramble the smells, the voices.

Then she saw him. Jim Micah, his short dark hair, his gray eyes solemn as they searched hers. "Hey, Andee."

She must be dreaming, because Conner stood behind him, his blond hair longer than she remembered, tousled in wind-blown waves. There was a nasty scrape along his jawbone, yet he grinned at her. "Hi."

"Where am I?" she rasped.

"Here you go." Lacey, Micah's pretty wife, leaned over the bed opposite him, offering Andee a drink of water.

Andee drank through the straw, the water hitting her

parched throat and burning a little. "Where am I?" she asked
again.

"Fairbanks Hospital." The voice that answered her came
from behind Lacey, and Andee turned her head. She smiled
when she saw him leaning against the wall, his hands tucked
under his arms, wearing loose-fitting jeans and a light blue thermal shirt that did devastating things to his blue eyes. Those
blue eyes that she'd seen locked on her as he'd held her in his
arms.

Mac. He smiled back, looking relieved.

"Hi," she said. "Are you okay?"

He chuckled and shook his head. "Of course you'd ask
that. Aye, my bonnie lass, I'm okay. Now that you're awake."

Memory rushed in. Sarah. Her father. The pipeline.

Mac must have read her thoughts because he stepped next
to Lacey and took Andee's hand. "Sarah's in the bed next to
you."

"How is she?" She turned, looking past Micah.

Sarah sat up in the bed, her hand on Hank's head. He was
sleeping with his head on the bed propped on top of his folded
arms. "I'm okay," she said, facing Andee, "but my head is
pounding."

Andee winced, seeing that they'd shaved Sarah's blonde
hair. A bandage swathed her scalp.

"Twenty-two stitches and a concussion."

"I'm sorry," Andee said.

Sarah shook her head. "Not your fault."

Andee closed her eyes, accepting Sarah's words. Then,
"What about the pipeline?" She searched Mac's face.

Mac smiled, a slow liquid grin that she felt in her veins.
"I think your pals Conner and Micah should tell you how they
saved the world."

"We have your father to thank, Andee," Micah said. "When we heard your plane was missing, Conner and Hank and I headed north. Conner had the emergency info you gave him, and we figured we'd get in touch with your father because the search teams hadn't found you. When we got to his cabin, he was gone and we could tell there'd been trouble. Thankfully, he'd turned on the ELT in his plane, and we found it sitting empty on the Dalton Highway a few miles north, along with a trail that might as well have been outfitted with neon lights, thanks to your dad. We tracked him down only to find him in the hands of three armed terrorists. We decided to step in—" he shook his head—"but he probably didn't need our help. In the end, he put up a good fight and even told us to destroy his airplane."

"Ouch. That had to hurt."

"It would have hurt more if he'd been in it. And if we hadn't caught Juan and his girlfriend." Conner looked over Micah's shoulder. "Believe me when I say that Gerard's counting his blessings." He winked at Mac.

Andee narrowed her eyes. "What's going on here?"

Mac squeezed her hand. "A happy ending." He gazed at her with such warmth in his eyes that she felt a blush edge up her face.

"So I take it you met Team Hope?" Andee asked.

Mac nodded. "Nice friends you have. The first time I met Conner and Micah, they were in hand-to-hand combat with a couple of terrorists from Venezuela, while trying to dodge bullets."

"Thanks, by the way," Micah said, smiling at Mac. "Her aim was improving."

Mac looked good with a blush, and Andee had to wonder exactly what he'd done. "Where are they?" she asked him.

"FBI interrogation. They'll be there for a while. I'll go in later and see if I can fill in some of the blanks Nina left out. But the short of it is that Nina had intended to hijack you in Prudhoe Bay and make you fly to Disaster and get your father and her two buddies, and then the happy party would fly over the pipeline and detonate all three explosives. With all the mountain peaks, it was most likely the only way the signal would reach all the explosives simultaneously. Then they probably hoped to escape to some Micronesian island in the Pacific."

"That's why they took my dad? To force him to fly?"

"Or force *you* to fly, with a gun to Gerard's head."

How close she'd come to losing Gerard. Again. "But who were they working for? Some Al-Qaeda group?"

Mac shook his head. "Nina is Venezuelan DISIP, as is Juan. The FBI identified them when we brought them in."

Andee frowned at him, puzzled.

"Venezuela secret police. Or at least they were. We're not sure if they're still working for Chavez or not. The fact that we found them with Constantine Rubinov tells me they may have been connected with a terrorist group we've been tracking for some time. These days, it's not uncommon to see a number of terrorist groups working together for the same agenda. At any rate, we caught them before they could do serious damage."

Andee quirked a smile at Mac, remembering her skepticism at his wild scenarios. "Venezuela, huh?"

He shrugged, but she saw a look of triumph in his sweet blue eyes.

"Are you still going to retire from the FBI?" The question rushed out of her and for some reason tightened a noose around her throat.

Mac's smile dimmed. "I don't know yet. I guess it depends." His gaze held hers.

Micah cleared his throat. "I'm hungry. Anyone else hungry?"

"I'm starved." Conner squeezed Andee's arm.

"I could eat a moose," Lacey said. "Want anything, Andee?"

She wasn't sure how to answer that. A warm bath? A pizza? Maybe Mac's arms around her? She shrugged and Lacey nodded.

Andee had a feeling Lacey might know exactly how she felt.

As they left, Mac pulled the curtain between Andee's and Sarah's beds. Andee heard Hank start to stir, but all thoughts of Hank and Sarah vanished as Mac sat on her bed. He'd cleaned up since she last saw him. Although reddish whiskers still covered his chin, his hair was slightly wet and curly and tucked behind his ears, and he smelled clean and spicy, the essence of male.

She could hardly believe she'd once thought of him as arrogant. Charming, devastatingly handsome, ruthlessly loyal and passionate, but not arrogant.

In fact, maybe just human, like her. Struggling one day at a time to be the guy God wanted him to be and trusting Him enough not to look back.

"You really scared me," he said. "Jumping off a cliff. Nearly freezing to death. My little human ice cube." He ran his hand down her cheek.

She leaned into his hand. "We need to talk about this FBI thing."

His smile fell. He pulled his hand away, not meeting her eyes.

"I think you should stay in the FBI. I know that I accused you of having to save the world, but you're just that kind of guy, and that's okay. And I'm sure that Brody would have been proud of you, Mac. Don't quit the FBI. They need you."

He raised his eyes, and she saw his confusion.

"But I need you too," she said. "Think you can deal with that?"

"What are you saying, Andee?"

She was pretty sure the next words would be locked inside forever if she didn't force them out now. "I'm saying that I'm willing to give us a chance. To stick around for the winter with my dad, maybe get him to move to Disaster."

Mac smiled slightly.

"Mac, I can't take another man letting me down, but . . . you didn't do that. You jumped in after me."

"I didn't save you. You saved yourself."

"But you *wanted* to. That matters. And next time I might just let you."

He twined his fingers through her curly hair. "That's because you matter, Andee. To me. I'd jump off a thousand more cliffs into icy water just to be with you."

She wrinkled her nose at him. "You're such a romantic, Mac." She sighed, however. "I know that whatever is inside you that makes you want to save the world is here to stay. You can't shrug it off or break free of it because it's part of you, Mac. But in the end, I know you chose me. Which means when you can't choose me, I'll trust that you want to."

He leaned close. "Listen, I understood when you said that you couldn't take someone letting you down."

She stilled, not quite sure what he might be saying.

"The thing is, before I met you I felt numb inside. But I was really slowly disintegrating. I've always been sure I could never let someone in my life, that somehow she'd get hurt. Like Brody. Sort of how your dad felt, I think. When I met you, for the first time I felt alive. I realized that knowing you, being with you, was worth trying to figure it out. As soon as Nina grabbed you, all I could think about was getting to you, finding you, and protecting you. And it scared me, because I've never ever really felt that way before. But after we got out of the river, I understood that maybe that was how love is supposed to be— I couldn't feel the joy without the fear and probably a little pain. I'm going to try not to let you down, Andee. You can trust me. Because I can't *not* choose you."

Andee could hardly breathe, caught in his gaze, the lilt of his smile. "Then you don't regret—?"

"You're in my heart, Andee. Like a breath or a song—"

"Or a poem?"

He smiled. "Like a poem from the Highlands." She saw a new twinkle in his eye.

> *"And fare-thee-weel, my only Luve!*
> *And fare-thee-weel, a while!*
> *And I will come again, my Luve,*
> *Tho' 'twere ten thousand mile!"*

"Is that poetry I hear over there?" Andee heard Sarah's voice lift, with a giggle.

"Can I use that, Mac?" Hank's drawl morphed Mac's accent into his own Texan. "My only luve, will you marry me?"

Andee's eyes widened, and Mac's gaze froze on her. Then he got off the bed and pulled back the curtain.

Sarah and Hank looked up from their kiss. Hank leaned away from Sarah, who smiled at Andee, a tear running down her cheek.

Oh, boy.

"Close the curtain, Mac," Hank said in a quiet tone.

Mac closed the curtain and stood above Andee. "We gotta get out of here." He scooped her up in his arms, blankets and all. Andee grabbed her IV stand, rolling it behind as Mac opened the door with his foot and carried her into the hall.

"Where are we going?"

Mac smiled. "To the happy ending I promised you."

She turned in his arms, surrendering to the place she wanted to be, right here next to him, letting herself be protected, just enough, by this man who'd charged into her life and believed in her, trusted her, came after her.

Loved her?

She drank in the taste of those words.

This seemed happy enough. Hank and Sarah engaged. She, in Mac's incredibly strong arms. Nina and the other terrorists captured. God had been with them, through her fears, her mistakes. Not only that—He'd reminded her through a formerly arrogant Scot that the Almighty might even know her deepest desires. He might even give her everything she'd always dreamed of. Perhaps Sarah was right. It was time to live without regrets, facing into tomorrow, into the sunrise of each day.

"How's Ishbane?"

"Headed home. I think Flint is down the hall, and last I checked, Phillips was sacked out in the next bed."

"And . . . how's my dad?"

"I think you two might have some talking to do." Mac stopped before an open door and turned her slightly. "Look at that," he whispered.

Andee lifted her head and her heart swelled. Her mother sat in a chair beside her father's hospital bed, holding his hand. Gerard wore a smile Andee had seen so many times before. He looked at her, caught her eye, and winked.

Andee just stared at them. "I don't understand."

Mac backed them away from the door. "Your mother flew up this morning. Got here about an hour ago. And after seeing you were okay, she went right in to him. Maybe things will turn out differently this time."

Andee wanted to wiggle out of his arms, to demand answers, but the sight of her father running his hand through her mother's hair, the look on his face, well, she couldn't interrupt. Not now.

"There's something you should know about your father, Andee. Gerard McLeod is a legend at the bureau. Once upon a time, he ran the Fairbanks Drug Team. He took down a particularly notorious and well-connected group of drug runners with particularly vengeful relatives. I did the math, and I have to wonder if your father didn't send you away right at the time the Rubinovs' extended relatives were tracking down the families of those agents on the team."

Moisture brushed Andee's eyes.

Mac reached up and thumbed away an escaping tear. "Just thought that might be food for thought."

She nodded, glancing back at her parents. Together.

Mac carried her down the hall to an atrium that faced north toward the Brooks Range, barely outlined by the sinking sun. He held her tight, making no move to put her down as they stared at the view, the mountains turning purple, the sky streaked with red.

"We never made it to Disaster," Andee said quietly.

Mac chuckled. "Oh, I think we did. And we survived it."

Andee looked up at him, ran her fingers through his stubbly beard, losing herself in his eyes. "I'm falling in love with you, you know."

"Aye," he said and bent his head and kissed her gently, perfectly. Hinting at her future or *their* future. He tasted of sweet coffee and of all the magical stories she'd tucked away of heroes and lords and knights in shining armor.

She hated it when he pulled away.

He rested his forehead on hers and sighed. "I did it again. Kissed you without asking."

She smiled. "I wouldn't have it any other way."

He closed his eyes, pulled her close, and whispered in her ear:

"Till a' the seas gang dry, my dear,
And the rocks melt wi' the sun;
And I will luve thee still, my dear,
While the sands o' life shall run."

"FBI, you're such a poet," Andee said in a lazy, teasing voice.

He smiled, letting her see everything in his heart. "Only for you, my bonnie lass. Only for you."

A Note from the Author

"MOMMY, IF YOU could live your life over, would you make the same choices?"

When my son asked me this question the other night, it made me ponder. Would I? Yes, for the most part. There are probably a few I wouldn't make again. Like that perm gone wild or the boyfriend with the bad breath. But really, our choices make us the people we are, and without one choice pushing me to the next, I probably wouldn't be where I am today.

Not that life has been easy. Or that I've always made the right decisions. Over the last two years, we've had big changes—in career, in lifestyle, in location. And we haven't always made the best decisions. (Case in point—the day I decided to clean out my basement and ended up accidentally burning down the garage!) But through this journey, I've discovered that in every event, every disappointment, every joy, every struggle, God is there. And that is a treasure I wouldn't have found if every decision had been wise or easy or right.

I often hear people say, when confronted with a crisis, "God doesn't give me more than I can bear." I couldn't disagree more. I've been in a number of I-can't-bear-this! situations, and over and over I see that it's when I'm swamped and going down fast, I have no choice but to turn to God. He parts the waves, reaches down, and snatches me from death.

Sorta like what Paul says in 2 Corinthians 1:9-10: "In fact, we expected to die. But as a result, we stopped relying on ourselves and learned to rely only on God, who raises the dead. And he did rescue us from mortal danger, and he will rescue us again. We have placed our confidence in him, and he will continue to rescue us."

Many times Paul must have thought, *This is it. I'm done for*. And yet he trusted in God, and God saved him.

As I journey through this life, making decisions, trusting God for guidance, I have two choices. I can look behind me and say, "*Why* did I do that?" Or I can look forward, toward heaven and God's smile, and say, "I trust You for this step and that You'll catch me if I fall."

Thank you for reading Mac and Andee's story. I pray that their journey encouraged your own and that God uses it to remind you that blessed is the person whose hope is in the Lord their God.

In His grace,

Susan May Warren

About the Author

Susan May Warren recently returned home after serving for eight years with her husband and four children as missionaries in Khabarovsk, Far East Russia. Now writing full-time as her husband runs a hotel on Lake Superior in northern Minnesota, she and her family enjoy hiking and canoeing and being involved in their local church.

Susan holds a BA in mass communications from the University of Minnesota and is a multipublished author of novellas and novels with Tyndale, including *Happily Ever After*, the American Christian Romance Writers' 2003 Book of the Year and a 2003 Christy Award finalist. Other books in that series include *Tying the Knot* and *The Perfect Match*, the 2004 American Christian Fiction Writers' Book of the Year. *Expect the Sunrise* is the sequel to *Flee the Night* and *Escape to Morning* and her third book in this romantic adventure search-and-rescue series with Tyndale.

Susan invites you to visit her Web site at www.susanmaywarren.com. She also welcomes letters by e-mail at susan@susanmaywarren.com.

Looking for a little romance?

Check out Susan May Warren's Deep Haven series:

Happily Ever After

Tying the Knot

The Perfect Match

Turn the page for a sneak peek
of *Happily Ever After*. . . .

WELCOME TO HEARTQUEST

HEART
QUEST.

Visit

www.heartquest.com

and get the inside scoop.

You'll find first chapters,

newsletters, contests,

author interviews, and more!

Prologue

He barely escaped with his shirt.

"I am *never* signing another book as long as I live." Reese Clark's voice echoed like a gunshot through the five-story Mall of America parking garage. He swept off his black Stetson and dragged a hand through his unruly, shoulder-scraping brown hair. He grimaced at the layer of sweat that came off in his hand.

The book signing had disintegrated into chaos, just as he'd expected. After two hours of orderly lines, with women breathing in his face and fawning over him as if he were a teenage movie idol, the peace had evaporated. Normal, law-abiding women began to push and argue.

He'd climbed on his chair, waved to the back, and assured the crowd he would sign every copy of *Siberian Runaway*. Yet they still fought for space in the line that curved past Macy's, snaked down West Market, and probably ended around the far corner of Nordstrom, another block farther. Despite ample bookstore security and two well-muscled mall uniforms barking orders, the crowd erupted. The noise and confusion resurrected enough ugly memories to send him looking for escape in the concrete parking labyrinth.

"Reese, come back here!" Jacqueline Saint marched up behind him, her spike heels echoing in monstrous volumes against the cement floor. "If you want to sell books, you'll wipe that pout off your face and march back inside."

He scowled at his publicist. "Back off, Jacqueline. You saw them in there." He made a show of shuddering. "I'm done. I'm not doing this anymore. One more fanatic reader and I'm going over the edge." Reese drew a deep breath. The smell of motor oil, cement, and dusty ceilings twisted his empty stomach. "I need some air."

Jacqueline dug her ruby red manicured fingernails into his arm. "You've got to loosen up, Reese. This isn't Chicago. No one is lurking in the men's room. I've made sure security is on you like glue. You're fine."

He stiffened. "Maybe I just have a better memory than you do."

He heard her clucking, a habit that could shred his nerves to rags. "The price one pays for fame," she said, not gently.

He tried not to rise to that. She was the closest thing he had to a real friend right now, and that thought turned like a knife.

"Listen, you're almost done," she soothed in false tones. "One more week on the morning-news circuit, then you can disappear and cultivate that 'mystery man of the mountains' image you love." Her voice hardened. "Until then, baby, you sign books."

Reese jerked out of her grip. "Give me five minutes . . . at least."

Jacqueline raised a thin eyebrow and ran her cool gray eyes over him as if evaluating prey. Checking the time on her gold watch, she nodded crisply. "Five minutes. Clock starts now."

Reese tightened his jaw and stalked away. Jacqueline might be the best publicist his editor had to offer, but after three months of her nonstop company, he was ready to topple her off those lizard-skin spikes.

He exhaled a hot, uneven breath. One week left. Then he would have nine peaceful months before the release of his next book. Soon he'd be off to the mountains—good riddance civilization. Not that he itched to shoulder a pack or climb inside his worn, polar sleeping bag again, but a multihued mountain sky, the threat of a storm, and even mosquitoes the size of his fist seemed a more welcoming atmosphere than a crowded mall bookstore. More welcoming—and safer. He'd take a face-to-face encounter with a grizzly over a lovesick fan any day, month, or year. He'd seen enough of crazed women up close and personal to make his blood turn cold.

The book tour served its purpose, however—funds to explore the planet. His books sold millions. Why, he still didn't understand. He wrote them because they called to be written, but women hungered after them, buying them in hardback, hot off the presses. Jacqueline reasoned it was because his hero never found the woman he sought, and his readers all fantasized they could be the one.

Reese wandered between a Lexus and a grimy blue Chevette and leaned on the edge of the railing to peer down onto the highway, a spiraling mess of noise and exhaust. Beyond the concrete, the red-and-orange autumn foliage shimmered in the trees lining the Mississippi River. An errant breeze drifted toward him, carrying the tinge of drying leaves and the crisp anticipation of fall. They beckoned to him, and he never felt more trapped. Yes, he loved the writing, the traveling . . . it was the invasion of his privacy that pushed him to his last nerve. He was already plotting his escape. As traffic hummed below, Reese sunk his head in his arms.

The car behind him coughed and sputtered. It wasn't the Lexus. Reese whirled, intending to scuttle between the two vehicles. He made it as far as the front driver's door. It swung open, crashed into his knees, and swiped dirt across his tailored suit pants. As the driver barreled out of the Chevette, he jumped back, frowning, and dusted off his knees. "Watch it!" he growled.

He heard an offended gasp and immediately regretted his tone. Rudeness wasn't his standard.

"You watch it. My car can't move; you can!" The spitfire comeback didn't match the petite blonde steaming before him. Shoulder height and dressed in a black skirt and a white cashmere sweater, she didn't look the type to drive such a clunker or to meet her problems head-on. He blinked at her.

She clamped her hands on her hips, her eyes blazing. "What are you doing next to my car, anyway?"

He raised his brows. "Well, I certainly wasn't going to steal it."

Her mouth flew open a second before she harrumphed and shook her head. With one swift move she reached down beside the seat and popped the hood. When she stepped back and slammed the door, the sound clamored along the low-hanging ceiling.

Silence passed between them as she stared at him. "Well, are you going to move, or are you paid to block traffic?"

"Sorry," he mumbled as he raised his hands in surrender. He scooted back to the railing.

The woman brushed past him, widely avoiding the scum on her car. She slid two fingers under the hood and heaved it open. As she propped it up, she shot Reese a sidelong look. Her eyes seemed to soften. "Sorry," she muttered. "I'm having a rotten day. First I lock myself out of the house, then I rip my skirt climbing through the window, then Macy's computer eats my layaway. And now, old Noah here won't start."

He bit his lip to stifle an unexpected grin. "Noah?"

She tucked a chunk of golden hair behind her ear. "Don't ask."

Still warring with a smirk, he stuck his hands into his pockets and leaned back against the cement wall, intrigued by a woman in fancy duds jiggling cables, adjusting the oil cap, and fingering the connections to her car battery. Remarkably, she had only a light coating of grease on her fingers when she turned back to him.

She chewed her delicate lip for a moment. Her forlorn gaze shifted past him, as if the answer lay in the bronzed hills. Then abruptly, she pinned him with a tentative look. "Know anything about cars?"

Reese rubbed his chin. He wasn't interested in getting dirty. Especially since he had to return to a crowd of cheering women in the bookstore. . . . "Yep, I know a few things." He stepped up to the car and leaned over the engine compartment.

Beside him, she peered into the blackness. "What do you see?" Her hair fell over her face, and she flipped it back.

Reese glanced at her and stifled another snigger. She had wiped a dash of oil across her cheek, like a football player. She *was* having a bad day.

Pinching his lips together, Reese examined the black hole of her car. Rusty wires merged with fraying cables, and sticky muck layered the corroded battery. After a moment of perusal, during which the odor of oil seeped over him like a fog, he reached in and tweaked the spark-plug wires. "Give her a try," he said, slapping his hands together.

"Really? That's all?" Her mouth opened in amazement when he nodded.

"Loose spark-plug wires will stop you cold every time."

Her green eyes glowed with sudden delight, and for the first time he noticed they were the color of finely cut emeralds, with magical golden flecks. They reached out and held him until he blew out a breath and broke away. "Give her a try," he repeated hoarsely and looked for a place to wipe his blackened fingers.

"Righto!" She sprang toward the driver's door.

Reese fished around in his back pocket and found a handkerchief. So much for his starched appearance. He worked the grease off his fingers.

The motor roared to life, and with it, inner snapshots of Reese's high school days. The hum of a Chevy could never be forgotten, especially the sweet melody of his Corvette, shined and stored on blocks in a place he was trying to forget.

With a sheepish grin, the blonde climbed out of her car. "It looks like you saved me." Her face brightened into a genuine smile. "Thank you so much." She reached over the open door. "Mona Reynolds."

Reese took her grip. "Clark."

Her eyes shone, and didn't she have the most beautiful smattering of freckles dotting her high cheekbones when she grinned?

"I suppose I should buy you a cup of coffee, huh?"

He handed her the handkerchief. "Nah, I happened to be in the right place at the right time." She frowned at the handkerchief, confused. He pointed to her face. "You've got a dab of war paint there."

She wrinkled her nose and ducked into the car, adjusting her rearview mirror.

Reese snared the moment to gather his senses. Coffee suddenly sounded nice. An escape with a pretty, sincere woman who didn't fawn over him might be just the breath of air he needed.

She turned around, a line of red where the oil had been. "Thanks." She handed the handkerchief back to him.

"About coffee . . . ," he began.

"Oh, I would really love to treat you. Give me your card, and I'll call you."

His hope deflated. "Uh, well, I don't have one on me."

"Oh." She appeared stymied, her lips puckering into an intriguing pout. "Well, maybe you could give me your number or your e-mail address?"

Reese pulled off his hat and rubbed a hand along the brim. His vision of a quiet coffee date with him safely disguised as an out-of-town business executive named Clark disintegrated under the glare of reality. This was getting too complicated, especially with a crowd of fans waiting inside. It would only take running into the media and things would turn ugly. He shook his head. "Actually, I'm just passing through town."

She looked crestfallen, and he nearly changed his mind. After a silent moment, she sighed. "Well, thanks again. You were my hero today."

He smiled at that. Playing the part, he snuggled the Stetson back on his head and pulled the brim like a courteous cowboy.

She shut the car door, waved once as she backed out, then disappeared in a fog of exhaust.

Reese scowled against the acrid smell, and disapointment pinched his heart. For a second there, he thought Mona might have turned out to be more than just a fan. He'd never find a woman who would be able to see beneath the Reese Clark veneer. It was painfully clear he and women just weren't meant to be.

"Reese!"

He and Jacqueline weren't meant to be either. Reese trudged back to the skyway and his book tour.

Applebee's parking lot seemed fairly crowded for the predinner hour. Enormously late, Mona found a spot in the back and hustled to the entrance.

Stopping at the hostess booth, she craned her neck and spotted Liza Beaumont waving crazily at a high table in the middle section. "Excuse me, my party is here," she said to the annoyed hostess and hurried toward Liza before her roommate made a scene and started hollering her name.

"Well, look how she's grown!"

Mona skidded to a stop, cringing as Edith Draper rose from her seat at Liza's table. The older woman headed toward Mona, her wide manicured hands reaching for Mona's face. Her mother's best friend thought she was still twelve years old.

"Hello, Mrs. Draper," Mona said weakly.

"I just wish your mother were here to see you take this big step. Imagine, owning your own business. I couldn't be prouder of you if you were my own child!" Edith's eyes glistened.

Mona surrendered to a hug. "Thanks, Mrs. Draper."

She drew back and waggled a finger in Mona's face. "Oh no. I'm Edith now. I'm going to be your neighbor."

Mona smiled warmly. She couldn't help but be drawn in by Edith's enthusiasm. "Okay . . . Edith."

"I ordered you a coffee," Liza announced as Mona slid onto a high stool and hooked her heels on the bottom bar.

"You look harried, dear." Edith put a wrinkled hand onto Mona's arm.

"I've had a horrible day," Mona replied. "I don't want to talk about it." She scanned the restaurant before returning her gaze to Edith. "Where's Chuck?"

The older woman waved her hand and shrugged. "You know how men are—have to use the bathroom wherever they go."

Mona smirked and spied Chuck Parson emerging from the men's room. Hitching his black jeans around his basketball stomach, he looked uncomfortable in his own skin. Poor guy. He was out of his element.

"Mona!" he called out from halfway across the room. Mona saw a waitress glare at him. Sliding off her stool, Mona met him two steps from the table. He wrapped her in a bear hug. "You're looking better than ever."

She sighed. She had them all fooled. Her insides were in knots, and her knees wanted to give out. If this thing really happened, her dreams were just a skip away. She kept pinching herself, waiting to wake up. God was so good to her to give her this miracle. She planned to grab on tightly to this chance and never let go. Now— to remain calm and focused. She had her heavenly favor, and God expected her best effort to make it happen. One shouldn't look lightly on the Lord's grace. Besides, God helped those who helped themselves.

She untangled herself from Chuck's embrace, and they climbed onto the stools. A waitress approached, balancing sodas and a steamy coffee. Mona didn't bother to look at the menu. "Chinese chicken salad and a side of plain toast."

Liza also ordered her regular—double-bacon cheeseburger and curly fries. Mona shook her head. It wasn't fair. Liza had legs that reached to her chin. The woman didn't know what it was like to just look at a Twinkie and see it appear on your thighs. Mona monitored her every bite with precision. She couldn't afford to buy new clothes. But she and Liza had been roommates for nearly a decade, and Mona had learned to live with the envy.

"I brought the layout and some pictures." Chuck hauled up a vinyl briefcase dated from the seventies. "Now don't get discouraged. It has potential. You just need eyes to see it." He dealt the photos on the table like playing cards. "The porch might need a little hiking up here and there, but the foundation is good. There's a cozy apartment above the garage and an outbuilding, just like you wanted." He paused and scanned Mona's face with unmasked anticipation.

She picked up a photograph. It was perfect. The two-story Victorian answered both her prayers and her wildest dreams. "I'll take it."

Edith clutched her arm. "Dear, are you sure?"

Mona nodded and glanced at Liza. Liza's black eyes sparkled as she grinned wildly. Mona read the look. "Yep. I know what I've been waiting for, and this is it."

Edith leaned back, a smile of satisfaction on her face. "I can't wait to tell your mother."

Mona fought the urge to roll her eyes. The last thing she needed was Edith Draper giving her mother in Arizona a chapter-by-chapter chronicle of her life.

Liza leaned close, her exotic perfume running over Mona like a wave. "This is it, Mone. The place where dreams come true."

Mona felt fear ripen in her stomach. *Please let Liza be right.*

"Oh!" Edith cried, clapping her hands together. "You have to see what I picked up today at the Mall of America."

Mona crossed her arms over her cashmere-clad chest and sighted a smudge of oil still staining her fingers. She grimaced. "I have to wash my hands."

"No, wait." Edith snared a bag at her feet. "I caught a book signing today."

"Who was it?" Mona grabbed a napkin and attempted recovery.

"I forget his name. He's that really famous writer . . ." Edith snapped her fingers as if she were a genie, waiting for the answer to poof.

"John Grisham?" Mona offered.

"Tom Clancy?" Chuck suggested.

"No, he's that one that was attacked a couple of years ago . . . in Chicago, I think. I read about it in *USA Today*. Some article about dangers to celebrities. Reminded me of something out of a Stephen King novel. A fan cornered him in the men's room and robbed him . . . stole his boots or his hat. . . . I think he even ended up in the hospital." Edith dug into her bag and pulled out a hardcover. She cocked her head as she examined the cover. "Not a bad-looking fella, either, the author. Even if he does need a good haircut." She plunked the book on the table, front cover down. "Reese Clark!"

Strikingly handsome in a forest green, plaid flannel shirt, a smiling man in a black Stetson stared back at her from the back cover. His brown curly hair dragged on his shoulders, and his blue eyes spoke of some hidden mystique. Reese Clark, Mona's favorite author. *Authors aren't supposed to be that good-looking,* Mona thought as she squinted at it. She wasn't great at remembering faces, but it seemed she had seen that one before.

Suddenly the memory hit her, and she cried out in shock.

"What is it?" Edith went ashen and put a hand to her throat.

Mona pinched the bridge of her nose and squeezed her eyes shut. "I'm a complete idiot."

Liza leaned forward. "Well, besides the fact you just painted your nose black, why?"

Mona looked at her fingers and grimaced. "My car broke down at the mall. The guy who put it back together was Reese Clark."

She could have buried herself inside any one of the three astonished gapes.

"And you didn't get his autograph?" Edith looked at her as if she had sinned.

Mona shrugged. "I didn't recognize him."

Liza stifled hysterics. "Mona, you wouldn't know your own dog if it came up and bit you."

She made a face at Liza. But her roommate couldn't have said it better. Despite Mona's infatuation with his ongoing hero, Jonah, Reese Clark could have popped her a fairy-tale kiss and she wouldn't have known it was him. She groaned. "I actually invited him out for coffee. He probably thought I was some goggle-eyed fan trying to invade his privacy." After Edith's story, it was no wonder he had backed away from her at the speed of light.

"Oh, well," Mona murmured, heading for the ladies' room, "some things just aren't meant to be."